Simon sat where he was, assaulted by emotions he refused to name

His gaze rose to Jayda's once more. She looked at him with what appeared to be warm approval mixed with a measure of sympathy. He felt understood, in a way he hadn't experienced before.

They were crawling into his heart–he could feel it. Jayda and Tiffany were invading his life. He *had* to resist. He'd worked hard to encourage the impression that he would do whatever it took to advance his career.

Becoming partner had been his goal for so long, he'd forgotten that there could be anything more important.

He wouldn't let normal, ord[illegible]yda or the kid with the hugs get in t[illegible]t now.

Dear Reader,

I had the privilege of raising a child who is not biologically mine–a child of my heart. He and I have a unique bond, even now that he's grown into a man. He's given me my first grandchild, whom I adore. To my glee, this little boy is turning out to be a bundle of energy, just like his dad.

I wanted to share some of the joys of that kind of relationship through this story of attorney Simon Montgomery and social worker Jayda Kavanagh and the child they become determined to adopt. Many things are stacked against them, but love prevails, as it often does. It is my fervent hope that this story will give you a sense of how fulfilling adoption can be, let you glimpse the special joy it can bring into a person's life, and perhaps encourage some to give a home to a child craving love and stability.

Please let me know your thoughts or feelings about Jayda and Simon's story. I'd love to hear from you through my Web page at www.elizabethashtree.com.

Elizabeth Ashtree

THE CHILD COMES FIRST

Elizabeth Ashtree

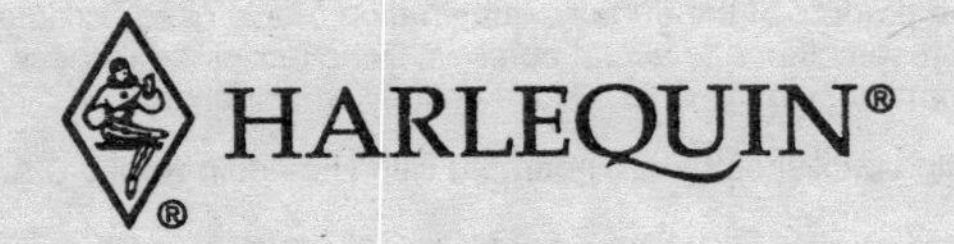

TORONTO • NEW YORK • LONDON
AMSTERDAM • PARIS • SYDNEY • HAMBURG
STOCKHOLM • ATHENS • TOKYO • MILAN • MADRID
PRAGUE • WARSAW • BUDAPEST • AUCKLAND

ISBN-13: 978-0-373-71503-9
ISBN-10: 0-373-71503-X

THE CHILD COMES FIRST

This edition published by arrangement with Harlequin Books S.A.

www.eHarlequin.com

Printed in U.S.A.

ABOUT THE AUTHOR

Elizabeth Ashtree has been telling stories since she was a child, and as an adult finally found a way to put her imagination to good use by writing novels. She holds a B.A. in anthropology and a J.D. from the College of William and Mary. She served as an officer in the U.S. Army Judge Advocate General's Corps and is currently an attorney for the Department of Defense.

Books by Elizabeth Ashtree

HARLEQUIN SUPERROMANCE

828–AN OFFICER AND A HERO
1036–THE COLONEL AND THE KID
1089–A CAPTAIN'S HONOR
1216–A MARRIAGE OF MAJORS
1264–INTO THIN AIR

To Jordan, my grandson, who has reminded me
just how much fun little boys can be.
And to his grandfather, my husband,
who has been unfailing in his love and support.

CHAPTER ONE

"BRIBERY'S NOT MY FAVORITE kind of case." Simon Montgomery had just shown Craig Dremmel to the door. Now he stood beside his secretary's desk to give her an update on his meeting.

"But you'll take the case, anyway," Denise said with certainty.

"For the money Dremmel's willing to pay, of course I'll defend him." A wealthy land developer such as Dremmel was just the kind of client he was expected to bring in. Simon had been assured that he commanded the respect of his colleagues, the trepidation of his opponents and the admiration of women, but he still hadn't made partner. Taking on a notorious public figure would greatly improve his chances of becoming the youngest attorney to reach that elevated level in the hundred-year history of Boyden and Whitby, LLC.

"Does he really stand a chance of getting off?" Denise asked the lawyer.

"Hard to say, given what I know so far. It won't be easy." Which meant there would be more billable hours to put in the case. That would make the partners happy, regardless of the outcome. But Simon liked to win. "I'll need to finish up some other cases first, so I can hit the ground running the minute his retainer arrives." He turned to head into his office, where piles of paperwork awaited.

"Hold on," she said, getting to her feet. "I know you have a full day, but you need to meet with Ms. Kavanagh. She's been waiting an hour."

He'd noticed a woman sitting in the reception area. Pretty in a simple, natural way, but lacking the finely polished appearance or the aura of ambition he'd become used to from the women he liked to spend time with—women who would help him advance his career. He looked at the folder Denise held out. "An hour? Why didn't she make an appointment?"

"She was supposed to see Mr. Canter, but he got called away on business with an important client," she said, as if reciting from a script.

"Yeah, Canter left for an emergency golf trip to the Cayman Islands this morning," he remarked. He and Canter didn't get along all that well, but the man was a partner. They were not on an equal footing—yet. A few more successes in the courtroom would help. And bringing in clients such as the powerful commercial real-estate developer Craig Dremmel.

"Mr. Canter specifically asked for this case to be handed over to you."

"Why me, specifically?" He took the file from her, knowing he had little choice but to take it.

Denise looked down at her desk, clearly searching for the right thing to say. "Maybe because it's a pro bono case?" she ventured.

Simon sighed. He'd been the one to pressure his mentor, senior partner Glen Boyden, to establish a pro bono program that called on every attorney in the firm—not just the junior associates—to take on at least two indigent cases per year free of charge. Though Simon's motivation had been to get the firm to give back something to the community, Glen had agreed to the idea primarily as a public relations ploy. Regardless, Simon had gotten his way. Some of his colleagues had been pleased they'd be given time during the year to take on such cases. Most of them, however, had seen the new initiative as an impingement on their billable hours.

Simon nodded. "I'd say that's probably the reason. So much for my scheduled desk time," he said. Turning again for his office, he wondered how he'd manage to take on this new case while still doing his best on all the others.

"Do you want me to send her in now?" Denise asked.

"Sure," he said, resigned to the inevitable. As he approached his desk, he flipped open the folder and scanned the first page. Then he stopped in his tracks and went into the hallway.

"Denise," he called. She'd made it halfway to the reception area, but she turned around and came back. When she was once again standing in front of him, he glared at her accusingly. "Did you see the age of this client? It's a kid, a little girl. I don't know the first thing about juvenile cases—or juvenile offenders, or juveniles in general." Or at least he knew nothing about kids except what he'd gleaned from his own childhood. Dated material, at best. And colored by the traumas of those earlier difficult years. He had no business taking on a juvenile case.

Denise had worked for him long enough to get away with rolling her eyes, but wisely she didn't say a thing. So Simon asked, "What does the woman in the waiting room have to do with this child?"

"She's your client's social worker, Jayda Kavanagh. She's also been made the guardian ad litem. And you don't have to worry about this being a juvenile case. The girl is being tried as an adult."

"That makes no sense. A child who needs a guardian ad litem is being tried as an adult? And from what I'm reading in this file, I'm coming into the case late," he said. "This is not going to be good," he muttered as he trudged back to his office. "Send Ms. Kavanagh in, please."

While he sat at his desk, he read more from the folder. Eleven-year-old Tiffany Thompson was accused of willfully killing three-year-old Derek Baldridge. Because of the gravity of the crime and Tiffany's history of violence, she would be tried as an adult in Baltimore's Third Circuit. Simon would have liked the chance to argue that decision—he could have made certain the case stayed in juvenile court. But a public defender had already let the issue slip by. To Simon's chagrin, it looked as if he'd be joining the case too late to do much good on some important preliminary matters.

Denise led in the social worker and indicated a chair, asked if she could get them anything, nodded when they said they were fine and closed the door when she left. Simon stood as Jayda Kavanagh approached his desk, holding out his hand in greeting. With her golden-brown hair dipping to her shoulders in a casual cut and her natural peaches-and-cream complexion, she was in many ways the opposite of the highly polished professional women he was used to. Nothing particularly special about her, but he would have had to say she had pleasant features, in a down-home sort of way. And he liked her handshake, firm and sure. Clearly, she wasn't intimidated by his expensive suit or his fancy office.

With introductions over, she got right down to business. "Tiffany needs your help, Mr. Montgomery. I hope you'll take her case."

"It seems Renauld Canter agreed the firm would represent Ms. Thompson, so that's already been decided." He kept his expression neutral.

Intelligent eyes stared back into his. "I take it you didn't choose Tiffany as one of your pro bono cases. But once you get to know her, I'm certain you'll want to help her."

Simon glanced down at the file, open now to a page containing Tiffany's history. "Do you have reason to believe she's innocent?" he asked. Almost every client claimed he hadn't done it. But most of them had. Simon doubted this one would be any different. And yet he was surprised that a social worker would take the time to defend such a kid. The folder said the girl had been in foster care since she'd been a toddler. She wasn't likely ever to find a permanent home. People familiar with the system referred to such foster kids as "lifers."

Simon ought to know. He'd been a lifer himself. Yet somehow, he'd made it. His foster mother had seen to that when she'd officially adopted him. Maybe Tiffany would be another one-in-a-million case. Who was he kidding? She was far more likely to be a psychological mess with a well-honed survival instinct that helped her manipulate softhearted people such as Jayda Kavanagh.

The social worker looked at him intently. "I *know* she's innocent. Tiffany could not have hurt that little boy. When you meet her, you'll see. But I don't have any evidence, if that's what you mean. That's why we need your help."

Simon sat back and considered the woman for a moment. She was nothing like the overworked and underpaid social workers he remembered from his own childhood. She still had a passion in her for the children she served. Or at least for this particular child. That meant she had to be new to the job, not worn down by the failures of the system and the delinquents who were almost always beyond help. Yet she appeared to be in her mid-thirties, not fresh out of college.

"How long have you been doing this kind of work?" he asked.

Her eye widened, as if surprised by this. "Almost fifteen years," she said. "Why do you ask?"

"Because you seem so undefeated," he said, wondering if she'd understand. "I figured you must be new to the job."

"You mean I haven't been discouraged until I'm beyond caring."

He nodded. "I know that's a stereotype, but it's one I've found to be true."

"Some cases are hard to be passionate about, but not Tiffany's. She's one of those rare kids, you know? You'll have to meet her to see that for yourself. But she's still locked up in the juvenile detention center. I'm hoping you'll help me get her out."

He flipped a page in the file. "She isn't out on bail?"

"No. She's been incarcerated for more than a month now. The public defender assigned to her case didn't do much to help her. Will you?"

Simon looked at her steadily for a few seconds before answering. He didn't want this case. He had too many pending actions already. He'd done four pro bono trials this year and had only found enough time to handle them by putting in ridiculously long hours. And with this client's history, any trial would be a certain loser. But for reasons he didn't understand at the moment, he couldn't keep himself from wanting to do something for a kid whose public defender had completely let her down. And for the undefeated social worker who seemed so determined to help her.

"I'll do my best," he said. But he knew there was little he could do.

JAYDA BELIEVED SIMON Montgomery. He had a sincerity that she never would have expected to find in the ruthless man she'd read about on the Internet. He wore an expensive, perfectly tailored suit, and his hair was cut to exhibit just the right mixture of boyish charm and urban sophistication. His nails were manicured and buffed. Everything about him expressed his confidence, his desire to win. References to the firm on the Internet almost always led to a story involving Simon Montgomery. The man was a legend, though he appeared far too young to have made a name for himself already.

What Jayda remembered most about him was that five years ago, fresh out of clerking for a state supreme court justice, Montgomery had landed a high-profile case. A prominent and wealthy citizen had decided he would not pay for a crack defense team when his son had been accused of vehicular manslaughter. Daddy had washed his hands of his drunkard offspring, and the young man had been forced to settle for an unknown Simon Montgomery as his attorney. Against all odds, Simon had won an acquittal. And he'd lost very few cases since then.

"Do you defend people more vigorously when you believe they're innocent?" she asked. She'd had enough experience with lawyers through her job to know that the answer to this question frequently revealed interesting details.

"Every client deserves a fair trial. A vigorous defense

for anyone accused of a crime is what keeps the judicial system vital and impartial."

Jayda would have laughed at such a pat answer, except that Mr. Montgomery seemed to believe his words. "But it must be easier to give a case your best effort when you know the suspect has been unjustly accused," she prodded.

He shook his head. "I give every case the same attention. Tiffany's will be no different," he countered. "We should discuss the possibility of a plea."

"No." She didn't hesitate. Tiffany hadn't killed Derek, and she shouldn't have to say she'd done it just to secure a reduced sentence that would put her behind bars for some length of time, anyway.

Montgomery looked startled by her quick answer. His expression made him appear almost boyish, and she realized that his chocolate-colored eyes and black hair—with no hint of gray—added to his youthful appearance. Most women would find him attractive, she realized. Jayda knew that beneath the facade there likely rested so much single-minded ambition and such an intense sense of entitlement that he would not take no for an answer. That would be good for Tiffany. But such driven men scared the hell out of Jayda. Just sitting opposite him made her palms sweat. But she wouldn't let him see any part of her fear. That was not the way to deal with such men.

"You should at least consider..." he began, but she held up her hand to stop him.

"Tiffany will want a trial," she said. Unlike so many of the other children Jayda had worked with, Tiffany really was innocent. She deserved to be exonerated, and the only way to achieve that was through a trial.

"Tiffany is eleven years old," Montgomery said. "I don't know much about kids, but my guess is that she's not really mature enough to make an informed decision on such an important matter. You've been declared her guardian ad litem. It's up to you to guide her in this."

"I'd tell her not to accept a plea bargain."

His lips thinned and he almost glared at her. She lifted her chin defiantly, mostly as a show of courage. "She's not a perfect kid. She couldn't be, with all she's been through. But she's so smart and she has such a big heart, even if she tries to hide it sometimes. You have to meet her, and then you'll understand."

"You keep saying that, about meeting her. And yet she's not here because the public defender couldn't even make a case for bail. What are you not telling me?" His gaze seemed to bore into her, and she had to resist the urge to race for the door leading out of this chilly, glass-enclosed space. That was no surprise, given her own history. Lawyers routinely brought on a desire to flee, even though she knew from many sessions with therapists that this was not entirely rational. Not all lawyers were like her uncle, she reminded herself.

This one waited now for an explanation. She had to admit the truth—he'd find out soon enough from Tiffany's file. "No bail was set because we couldn't find a place for Tiffany to go. No one will foster her, and she has no family. Not a single relative."

Jayda could see sympathy softening the hard edges of his gaze. She hadn't expected that. Social Services, inability to find any foster parent willing to take Tiffany in would tend to confirm her status as a problem child. Yet, it appeared Montgomery hadn't leaped to that conclusion.

"I'd take her myself," Jayda added, "but my supervisor won't allow me to get that involved with any of the kids assigned to me." Marla Wrightman had been firm on that point. The woman understood Jayda's desperation to get

Tiffany out of the detention center, but she couldn't support a social worker becoming so deeply involved on a personal level.

"Tiffany is alone in the world," Jayda said, hoping to build upon the unexpected sympathy she'd glimpsed in this man. "And that's not her fault."

He remained silent a moment, then seemed to collect himself. He glanced down at the folder on his desk. "She has a history of acting out. And she's accused of murder. Not negligent homicide or involuntary manslaughter, but second-degree murder. What sane people would feel they could take such a child into their home?"

Jayda leaned forward, holding his gaze. "We have to get her out of the detention center. Surely you can guess how bad such places can be. And she didn't kill Derek Baldridge."

"What about the other incidents of fighting and such?"

"She was barely walking and talking when the first one was recorded, and the others were self-defense. Sometimes she has a temper, but she's had a tough life. Come with me to the juvenile facility and talk to her right now—ask her to explain. I hope you'll see that she's worth saving. Please."

A few frozen moments passed before she knew he'd do as she'd asked. With a rueful half smile, he eased back against his chair. "I'll need a few minutes with my secretary to rearrange my schedule," he said. "And I'll drive us there. On the way, we can talk more about Tiffany and this crime she's accused of. I can bring you back to your own car when we're finished."

"Okay," she said. But she didn't like the idea of being alone in a car with this man she didn't know. Trapped. She'd likely have nightmares about it later. They'd merge with the ones she'd had since childhood, ever since her uncle had come into her life and made it a living hell with his groping hands and lurid games. And yet she'd agreed to ride in the car with Montgomery, anyway—for Tiffany's sake.

SIMON DIDN'T KNOW WHY he'd wanted Jayda to ride with him. He'd always been so careful to be seen only with women who dressed and carried themselves in just the right way, women who could enhance his prestige in his chosen profession. He wouldn't let anything tear down all he'd achieved so far. Certainly not a prim social worker with an overabundance of concern for a child accused of murder. Yet, he'd asked her to ride with him in the car he'd refurbished with such loving care....

He loved his restored Mustang almost as much as he loved winning in the courtroom, and he wondered what Ms. Kavanagh would think of it. Most of the women he knew couldn't understand the deeper beauty of this hot little vehicle, but they almost always appreciated the vintage Mustang for its ever-increasing monetary value. He figured he'd be treated to outright disdain from the social worker because he drove something so impractical.

"Here we are," he said as he approached the low, sleek car with its gleaming hunter-green finish. Resisting the urge to polish an isolated smudge with the microfiber swatch he always kept in the pocket of his Armani suit, he led her to the passenger side and eased the key into the lock—no remote entry for a car such as this. When he opened the door for her to slide into the seat, he had the inexplicable feeling that he was inviting her to slide into his life. Why that would flit through his mind when she was so utterly wrong for him, he couldn't imagine.

She didn't immediately get into the car, but stood back a few paces. Her eyes glowed as she took in the lines of the vehicle, focusing on one detail after another. She nodded to herself, seeming to be lost in her observations, then she smiled.

"Is this a Shelby GT?" she asked. "A 500, right?"

His jaw dropped. He'd never met a woman who could identify the car. Most could tell it was a Mustang, but that was about it. "Yeah," he said. "Fully restored."

"I can see that," she said as she moved to the back end to examine the taillights. "A '67, if my guess is right." Then she bent down to check out the exhaust system. "Original?"

"I wish," he said. "Unfortunately, it's a replacement." Simon had to remind himself to breathe. Not only did she recognize the car, but she'd checked out the undercarriage. And when she'd leaned forward to see beneath the car she'd unintentionally given him a great view of her shapely backside as her demure skirt tightened around her. The unexpected spark of physical interest shocked him nearly as much as her appreciation of his car.

He had to look away before she caught him gaping. "Yup. It's a 1967 Shelby Mustang GT500," he recited inanely. "Not many women know much about cars."

She straightened and nodded knowingly. He took a surreptitious half step backward at the sight of perfect white teeth and a barely noticeable dimple on one cheek. Not my type, he reminded himself firmly. No matter how much she appreciated his Mustang.

"My cousin's husband is a big car buff. He collects model cars and he has this very vehicle in one-eighteenth scale. He'll be thrilled when I tell him I saw a real one, up close and personal."

"You can tell him you got to ride in one, too," he said, returning to the passenger door and sweeping his hand toward the interior. He stood there while she got in—an interesting process to observe, given the low bucket seats and that skirt of hers. Women didn't wear skirts much these days, he realized. Jayda did her best to keep the whole thing modest, but Simon found himself watching her do it, anyway. He closed her door, then took his time rounding the car to the driver's side, hoping to calm his pulse. He'd known her for less than an hour, and she'd already managed to challenge his beliefs about what he wanted.

CHAPTER TWO

THE RIDE TO BALTIMORE'S GAY Street—ironically enough, the road on which the juvenile detention center sat—didn't take long. Jayda kept her mind on Tiffany's case and on giving Simon Montgomery the girl's history. Otherwise, she might have found herself dwelling on how close their shoulders were in the constricted interior of the restored vehicle. They weren't touching, but only inches separated them. She could smell the faintest hint of after-shave, a pleasant-enough scent. To her satisfaction, she managed to control the urge to lean as far away from him as possible. Her therapy must be working. When the sun came through the car window, she found herself noticing his hair wasn't quite black, after all. It was actually a deep brown, to match his eyes. A pleasant surprise, to be able to consider him as a person rather than as a threat.

Too often in the past, she'd judged powerful professional men through the caustic memories she had of the uncle who had groped and fondled her during her teens. Her mother's brother had been an ambitious, successful attorney, too, and as a result Jayda had always been attracted to men with the opposite characteristics—easy-going guys with little interest in dominating a relationship. The last one had been Brian—a happy-go-lucky waiter at a nice chain restaurant. He, like her other boyfriends, had worked out at first, but none of them had lasted more than a year. Either she'd become bored or they'd become insecure. Her most recent therapist told her she probably needed to find someone more her equal intellectually. But strong, smart men still overwhelmed her. She decided to take her reaction to Simon Montgomery as a good sign. Maybe she was beginning to escape the iron hold her earlier memories had over her. She could hope.

"We both know that as guardian ad litem, you need to look out for Tiffany's interests during the legal proceedings," Montgomery said as he downshifted and pulled into a parking space. "And I'll need you to tell me whatever you think I should know that she might not want to talk about. What you hear and add to my interviews with her will still be protected as attorney-client communication, so don't hesitate to talk as we go along."

Jayda nodded. "Tiffany's smart. Sometimes a smart aleck," she added with a rueful smile. "But she often understands the proceedings better than I do—mostly, I hope to be an emotional support to her."

As they got out of the car, he said, "I've never been here before, so it would be great if you'd lead the way."

Jayda had been to the Gay Street facility far too many times. "The people who run it probably mean well, but it's still not a good place for any kid to end up. I hate that Tiffany's spent so much time within these walls. Every day she's here there's a chance she'll be beaten or abused by a fellow inmate."

He didn't say anything to this, but Jayda saw his mouth tighten with tension. Did he appreciate the importance of winning his client's release? She couldn't tell. Without speaking, he opened the entrance door for her and she walked in first.

"I called ahead while you were rearranging your schedule with your secretary, so we shouldn't have to wait long to see her," she said. "I've never found anything specifically wrong on her previous visits, but things can change quickly, and for the worse, in a place like this. I hope to get her out while she still has some little girl left in her."

SIMON HAD BEEN INSIDE many prisons. He'd visited clients in mental institutions. But the juvenile justice center into which he walked with Ms. Kavanagh really gave him the creeps. He supposed his reaction could be attributed partly to his own experiences in similar places, even though he'd been too young and his time in those facilities had been too brief to have left him with any lasting memories. Unlike the places he'd been kept in right after his parents' deaths, this was a fairly new building, opened in 2003. It should have been the best of the best. It wasn't.

He did his utmost to shrug off his sense of discomfort as he waited for the red tape to be sorted out so that he could meet Tiffany. As he waited, he began to identify sounds that made the hair stand up on the back of his neck. "Can you hear that?" he asked the social worker.

"Yeah, I can hear it. It's always like this."

Faraway shouts, the dull clang of heavy metal doors, the unmistakable sense that children were weeping. That was how he heard it, though none of the noises was actually identifiable. "How long has she been here?"

Her gaze swung around to collide with his. Anger flared behind her gray eyes. "Too long, wouldn't you agree? Haven't all the kids been here too long?" She looked away and seemed to collect herself. Her tone was softer when she said, "A little over a month."

They waited together in silence for Tiffany to be

brought to an interview room. At last, a matron in a dark uniform asked them to follow her. They were led to a gray door with a meshed window inset at an adult's eye level. Through it, Simon got his first look at Tiffany Thompson.

He'd expected to find a big-for-her-age, tough-as-nails, hard-looking preteen—someone who actually appeared capable of committing the heinous murder of a three-year-old boy. But instead, he saw a small girl with pigtails and doe eyes sitting at a gray metal table in a chair far too large for her. She had on a tan T-shirt and ill-fitting elastic-waist pants; her feet, in a pair of slip-on sneakers, didn't touch the floor, but her ankles were crossed and she swung her legs back and forth idly as she waited. She nibbled anxiously on her fingers.

The social worker opened the door and walked in first, and a huge smile lit the girl's face.

"Jayda!" She launched herself from the seat and flew into the woman's wide-open arms. Hearing the name spoken aloud in the child's voice made it real for Simon, and he ceased thinking of her as Ms. Kavanagh and began to think of her as Jayda.

"I missed you," Jayda said after she'd set the girl back on her feet. "How are you? Have you been okay?"

"Yes, I'm fine," Tiffany said, but her eyes shifted away. "I can take care of myself. I'm small, but I bite." She gave a mock smile, showing her teeth and flashing a defiant glare.

Jayda winced. "No biting," she warned. "We're going to do everything we can to get you out of here." She turned toward Simon, drawing the girl's attention to him. "This is the new attorney I found for you."

Simon put on his best lawyer face. Not quite certain how to approach an introduction to a child client, he resorted to habit and offered his hand to shake. "I'm Simon Montgomery," he said.

Solemnly, Tiffany put her small hand in his. "Tiffany Thompson," she returned. Tiffany studied him carefully with a penetrating gaze. For the first time in years, Simon felt his expensive suit was an ineffective disguise that did little to hide the in-over-his-head guy he sometimes felt himself to be. "Are you going to do any actual lawyering, or will you be another slacker who lets me be victimized by the system?"

"Tiffany," Jayda warned. "Best behavior, please."

Simon found such forthrightness refreshing. So many of his clients bowed and scraped with him, but not this kid. "I am not a slacker," he assured her. "Let's sit down and talk about everything, okay?"

"Okay." Tiffany climbed back into her chair and clasped her hands on top of the table.

He saw that her nails were bitten down, and he couldn't blame her. She was definitely in a nail-biting situation. But she held herself still and gave him the impression of a poker player attempting to keep tells to a minimum. Tiffany was apparently savvy enough to know that body language could give away information she might not want people to know.

Jayda slid her chair closer to the table and turned to the girl. "Mr. Montgomery is a much better attorney than the last one, and he's promised to help you."

"Why?" Tiffany asked pointedly.

Simon wasn't sure how to respond. No one had ever asked him that before, not even his other pro bono clients. Once again, falling back on the familiar, he gave her one of his practiced smiles, the one intended to instill confidence in worried clients. "Because everyone has the right to a fair trial," he said.

She nodded, staring at him with unblinking saucer-size eyes that declared innocence, just as Jayda had promised. But Simon knew from experience that even the sweetest face could mask a black heart. Glancing at Jayda, he saw the caring in her eyes and hoped the child wouldn't disappoint her.

"So, Tiffany," he said, holding her gaze once more, "I need to ask what happened between you and Derek that day. Can you tell me about it?"

She nodded again and began to speak. "Miss Hester had to go out and I had to look after Derek. I didn't like it—I'm not supposed to be a babysitter," Tiffany said. "But I didn't have a choice. So we just watched TV for a while."

There was sincerity in her voice. Guilty or not, Simon knew she'd make a great witness if he decided to put her on the stand. "Then what happened?" he asked.

"Derek started banging a toy truck around, making noise and poking me with it." She looked down at her hands, the first sign of discomfort. "I yelled at him to stop. But he kept doing it and hitting me with the truck. I don't remember touching him or anything. I might have pushed him away, though. He just started whining—like this." She made a keening sound, high and loud. As she imitated the boy she rocked back and forth, and Simon assumed this was what Derek had done.

"Then he sat down hard on his butt. His eyes looked funny. He just sat there. After a minute, he fell over and he didn't get up. His eyes were open but he wouldn't say anything, even when I tugged on his arm and leg. I was freaked out."

She'd had good reason to be, Simon thought. Tiffany was now charged with Derek's murder. If she was telling the truth, she hadn't done it. If she was lying… It didn't really matter one way or the other, because guilty or not Simon always made certain his clients got every last ounce of fairness.

"Had you done anything else to him? Touched Derek in any way so that he fell over?" he asked.

She looked up into his eyes. Hers were glistening, her expression hurt, frightened. Or she gave a very good imitation of those emotions. "No, I didn't make him fall over."

Simon could detect no hint of a lie, but Tiffany also hadn't answered his question about whether she'd done anything to him.

Jayda shot him a reproachful glare, then turned her focus back to Tiffany. "What did you do when Derek wouldn't respond?" she prodded.

"I could tell he wasn't breathing right. So I got on the floor next to him and tried to sit him up. Miss Hester came home when I was holding him from behind." She bowed her arms outward, as if she still held the other child by his armpits. "I might have been crying because I knew something bad was happening. And I figured I'd get the blame. Miss Hester yelled at me to leave him alone, so I dropped him and jumped away." She winced and ducked her head, as she added, "He fell back onto the floor, all limp—I could hear his head hit. I was crying," she repeated. And she was crying now, Simon realized. Huge tears welled in her brown eyes and then rolled down her cheeks.

Sitting with Tiffany Thompson in this dingy room, Simon found himself wishing he could trade in a bunch of his past acquittals won on obscure legal technicalities for the verdict this young girl seemed to deserve. But then he reminded himself that Tiffany could just be an accomplished actress. He'd seen it before, though not in anyone quite so young. Holding back his judgment about her would be best. He didn't want to be surprised to find out she'd been lying all along.

Jayda offered a tissue from her purse, but Tiffany slapped away her hand, preferring to swipe at the dampness with a sleeve. Jayda's eyes closed momentarily, as if searching inside for patience. "I know you're upset, Tiffany, but you shouldn't take it out on people who want to help you." The social worker's expression was a study in compassion.

"No one's helped me so far," the girl whispered bitterly.

Uncomfortable, Simon looked down at his client's folder. Tiffany's reaction to kindness reminded him pointedly of his first weeks in his foster parents' home. It had been so hard to accept the fact that he was safe and that his security was more than fleeting. Tiffany's rudeness to her guardian reminded Simon of those difficult times, triggering recollections he hadn't thought about in many years and would have preferred to leave buried.

"Let's go over some basic things," he suggested, hoping to quell Tiffany's anger, Jayda's frustration and his own memories. "The man who works for the government—he's called the prosecutor. He's going to try to convince a group of people called the jury that you killed Derek on purpose."

Jayda spoke up. "Tiffany's young, but she's extremely smart. You don't have to talk to her as if she's a toddler. She's a big fan of *L.A. Law* reruns on TV. Just try not to speak in that legalese her previous lawyer used and we'll both be able to understand you."

"I know all about the people in the courtroom," Tiffany said, sitting up a little straighter. "Besides the people you mentioned, and the judge, there's also defense counsel, a bailiff and a stenographer and..."

Jayda reached out and patted Tiffany's hand, putting an end to the list.

"I get the picture," Simon said. Tiffany seemed to be an exceptionally intelligent child. And it made sense to him that she was happiest when she was talking about academic things she knew about. There'd been times when he hadn't wanted to stay focused on the real world, either. But she had to know what was coming, no matter how frightening it might seem. "Okay, I'm going to give it to you straight."

He paused and looked hard at the girl. She held his gaze, waiting, probably resigned to a fate no eleven-year-old should have to imagine. "The prosecutor is going for second-degree murder. A guilty verdict could mean thirty years in prison." Tiffany took this in without a quiver. Simon didn't dare let his gaze drift toward Jayda. They both knew that a prison for adults—where she'd go if convicted as an adult—would make the juvenile detention center seem like Disneyland. He just went forward with the information. "If we go all the way to trial, I'll make sure the judge gives the jury the option of manslaughter, too. If you were found guilty of that, it would mean two to ten years. Worst-case scenario would be about five years served." Tiffany stared at him, wide-eyed and pale. Surely she'd heard this before, but maybe he'd been too blunt.

This time, he couldn't keep himself from glancing at Jayda. She wore almost the exact same stunned expression as Tiffany, even though this couldn't have been the first time she'd thought about the girl serving time in prison. He gave them a few moments to process the information.

"What do you mean, *if* we go to trial? Do I have a choice?" Tiffany asked.

He remembered Jayda had been adamant that the girl should not cop a plea. But he wanted to hear what Tiffany would say. "The prosecutor will probably offer you a plea bargain, to save the government the expense of a lengthy trial. It would likely be a good deal, too, because no one wants this case reported in the newspapers any more than it has been already. The victim was very young and you're pretty young yourself. He'll decide it's better not to drag this case through a trial, if he can avoid it."

She thought about this. Then she asked, "Would I have to agree that I killed Derek?"

Simon exchanged a glance with Jayda. "Yes. You'd have to admit guilt."

She squinted her eyes at him and he glimpsed the stubborn, hardened side of her that was otherwise hidden by her sweet outward appearance. "But I didn't do anything wrong," she insisted. "I don't know why he died."

"Well, there's no evidence that anyone else could have hurt Derek, so the prosecutor may be able to convince the jury you did it on purpose, even if you say you didn't."

She scowled at him. "I'm not just *saying* it. I really didn't do anything to Derek that should have killed him. He fell over by himself. It's not fair that my two choices are to go to prison or to pretend that I killed a little boy." She began to nibble on the fingernail of her left pinkie. The action made her appear smaller, younger, more vulnerable.

Jayda sat forward then. "There are more choices than that, Tif. That's why we brought Mr. Montgomery in on this case. He's famous for getting acquittals on hard cases."

"That's good," Tiffany said, looking at Simon with additional respect. She put her hands together on the table once more. "Can you get an acquittal for me, too?"

Simon felt the weight of responsibility fall on his shoulders. He found himself hoping he wouldn't let her down. But the case would be a complicated one. "If you go for the bargain, you'd plead to a lesser offense than murder. Maybe involuntary manslaughter, which would be like saying you did it by accident."

Tiffany shook her head negatively. Jayda mirrored the gesture.

Simon stifled a sigh and turned a page in the file. "You have some other experiences of bad behavior in your record, Tiffany," he said gently. "You're going to have to explain what appears to be a history of violence."

"I can do that. All those times, I was just protecting myself. I'm not a bad person—I don't want to be mean. But if someone is messing with me, I have to be tough. If you don't protect yourself, you'll just keep getting hurt."

"And each time you were violent, someone was hurting you?" he asked.

Tiffany evaded his direct gaze, but Jayda came to her defense. "The record may be exaggerated, too," she interjected. "I know what's in her file and I already know what Tiffany says happened. She was very young when two of the incidents were reported. She can hardly be held accountable for what she did in a childish moment. She didn't even get to say what happened at the time. It's wrong to hold those isolated incidents against her."

He could use that argument, if the incidents came out in court. "What about when you threw an ashtray at your foster mother last year?" he asked.

"I wasn't throwing it at *her.* I was throwing it at her boyfriend, who was chasing me around so he could beat me with his belt." Tiffany wore a mutinous expression now, and righteous anger lit a fire in her eyes. "I ate the last

Twinkie, which Miss Consuela had packed for my school lunch, and he wanted to smack me around for it. Maybe I shouldn't have thrown the ashtray, but I had to defend myself somehow."

"Is there any way to prove that's what happened or to show your actions were in self-defense?" he asked. "Maybe Consuela would vouch for you?"

Tiffany couldn't hold his gaze. "No. She's the one who put the story into my record. She wanted an excuse to exchange me for a different foster kid. But there's no way to prove her version of the story, either."

She had him there.

"It's outrageous that she's being treated this way," Jayda nearly shouted. Her fist came down on the table, and she added, "Tiffany has been a victim more times than I can count, and now the court is victimizing her one more time by trying her as an adult. Does she look like an adult to you?" She smacked the surface a second time, making Tiffany cringe and blink—a common reaction in kids who were used to being hit.

Operating on instinct, Simon reached across the table and placed his hand over Jayda's balled fist. He looked into her furious eyes and did his best to soothe her without words. Outbursts of anger would do Tiffany no good, and might even do her harm if the girl picked up on the helplessness felt by the adults who were charged with protecting her.

At once Jayda's tension eased and she slipped her hand out from beneath his larger one. Simon was sorry the moment hadn't lasted longer. Her hand had fit perfectly into his, and he'd liked the warmth and energy she exuded. Perhaps it had been his imagination, but he thought that there had been a connection between them when their hands had touched. As soon as that thought struck him he was glad the moment was over, because he didn't want there to be a connection between them.

"Maybe something happened to Derek *before* Tiffany began watching him that day," Jayda suggested. "That's the only possible explanation."

She'd taken the thought right out of his head. If Tiffany hadn't killed Derek Baldridge, then he'd been in the process of dying before she'd been given her babysitting chore—something she shouldn't have been asked to do by her foster mother in the first place. He looked at Jayda and gave her the slightest nod. He didn't want to say anything in front of Tiffany, but any number of things could have been done to Derek that would have caused him to die later. He could have been shaken, beaten…thrown.

"The public defender never ordered another examination of Derek or the coroner's report to look for proof," she said.

"Well, we'll get a new reading of the report—or a new autopsy, if necessary." He used the word "autopsy" with reluctance in Tiffany's presence, but he knew she'd hear worse before this was all over.

"An autopsy tells the medical examiner, who's sometimes called a coroner, what caused the person to die. The examiner looks at blood and internal organs and does reports like toxicology," she said, as if reciting from the Discovery Channel.

"She's a fan of *CSI,* too," Jayda explained.

Simon had to hold back a chuckle. The kid was as smart as Jayda had promised. And as focused on legal procedure as he'd been on sports when he'd been her age. Sports had helped him to connect with his foster father. His interest in law had come much later.

"I read, too," Tiffany said. "I've been getting books on criminal forensics. The library here is better than in other places I've been. I need to know as much as I can about stuff that relates to my case. Because knowledge is power," Tiffany said in her lilting voice. Spoken by anyone else, that last line would have sounded sassy. But coming from this child, it sounded like the truth.

This time, Simon couldn't keep himself from smiling. She was bright, articulate, and she hid a remarkable strength beneath the sweetest facade. A perfect client. He knew he shouldn't make any decisions about her yet, and he cautioned himself not to get caught up in the persona the girl presented. But he admitted to himself that he was already making plans for how he would get Tiffany out of the detention facility quickly and into a safe foster home. He leaned back in his chair, easing away from this girl who had the power to draw him in. His policy of never becoming involved in his clients' personal lives suddenly appeared to be at risk. And with Jayda, as well. Once again, he had the frightening sensation that these females were somehow sliding into his life.

He caught and held Tiffany's gaze, trying to see into her soul. "I want to be sure you understand that everything you say to me is protected and no one else can find out about it," he said. "I'm your attorney, so no one can make me tell them what you say to me. The same goes for Jayda, when she's with me."

She nodded to show that she understood him. "Attorney-client privilege," she said.

"That's right. So, I want you to be sure to tell me the truth at all times. And tell me all of the truth, not just parts of it. Do you understand?"

"Yes."

He looked into her eyes. "Did you have anything to do with Derek's death?" He'd already asked her, but she hadn't answered him directly, even if she'd persuaded Jayda of her innocence.

She hesitated for a fraction of a second, and Simon's heart sank even as his doubting mind was vindicated. She'd lied. Her hesitation made that clear.

But then her eyes lifted to meet his, honesty shining from them. "I don't think so. I might have pushed him and his truck away from me. He was a pretty big kid for his age, and we'd wrestle sometimes. Kids hit and push one another sometimes, right? But we'd been getting along okay for a while—at least a week. But I dropped him when Ms. Hester yelled at me." Her troubled gaze collided with his. "I shouldn't have been able to kill him that way. Should I?"

The last two words were said in a small, worried voice and Simon found himself believing in her again. She appeared to be doing her best to honestly answer his questions. As a result, her doubts about her own behavior came shining through. More than anything else, this helped Simon to feel the first hint of real certainty about Tiffany.

"No, Tif. You didn't do anything that could have killed Derek," Jayda said with conviction. She focused her gaze on Simon, as if challenging him to refute her statement in front of the child. He wouldn't do that.

He just hoped Tiffany was as genuine as she seemed. Because he could tell Jayda wanted her out of the facility, out of harm's way, out of trouble with the law—acquitted. And Simon knew he'd have to use every last trick he knew to give Jayda what she wanted.

CHAPTER THREE

JAYDA COULD HARDLY BEAR to say goodbye to Tiffany. She knew her attachment to the girl had to do with her own history, but she couldn't help her feelings. Though she was a lot tougher, Tiffany seemed so much like the kid Jayda had been, helpless and alone. An almost overwhelming need to protect her from further harm seemed to settle in Jayda's heart.

As she hugged Tiffany, Jayda had a hard time letting go. Tears threatened and her throat went tight. But Jayda regained her composure by force of will and promised she'd see her again soon. Finally, she made herself let go. Tiffany stood back with a stoic expression on her young face.

"C'mon," said the uniformed matron gently. "Let's head back to your room." As Jayda stood watching, she saw the guard put a large hand lightly on Tiffany's shoulder, as if comforting her. A rare kind gesture in a place like this.

"We have to get her out of here," Jayda blurted as she turned and followed the lawyer toward the parking lot. "God only knows what's happening to her inside. I can't get any reassurance she'll keep her assigned cell to herself, and a roommate could take advantage of her. You can see she's small for her age—anything could happen to her."

Simon stopped to look at Jayda as she vented. When

she realized she'd sounded off with a good deal of vehemence, Jayda calmed herself down. "I'm sorry," she said. "It's just that she's so small and helpless."

"First, I don't think she's helpless at all. She's smart, and she seems capable of forcing the system to work for her. I can see that just from spending this brief time with her. She's extremely savvy and sharp, even though she's young. It won't help any of us to worry over the fact she has to stay here for now."

"You know how it is. The other kids will look for ways to prey upon someone like her. It's the natural order of things, for the bigger, stronger kids to hurt the weaker ones."

"I do know how it is. But she's not weak, either," he said.

Jayda looked at Simon and wondered what power he thought Tiffany would have against the brutality she might encounter. "Please, Mr. Montgomery. Get her out on bail."

He considered this for a moment. Then he said, "We're going to be working together for a long time. You can't keep calling me by my last name—please call me Simon."

Jayda nodded, even though she wasn't sure how she felt about using his given name. It seemed far too intimate, somehow.

"May I call you Jayda?"

She shrugged as if she didn't care. "Sure," she said. But she worried that allowing him to be so familiar would lead to something—feelings, perhaps—that she wasn't prepared to handle. Already she was noticing his good qualities more than she wanted to. But it wouldn't be practical or normal to keep calling each other by their last names.

Besides, Simon seemed to be a nice man. He'd been

kind to Tiffany, and that said a lot about him. And Jayda had appreciated his gentle support when he'd put his hand over hers during the interview, after she'd gotten herself worked up. Against all expectations, his warm fingers had comforted her, soothed her, calmed her. If she were honest with herself, she'd admit she'd been unaccountably tempted to turn her hand over to hold his for a moment, palm to palm. Or maybe she'd just wished that she had a man with whom she could share such intimacies. At present, her social life was nonexistent.

Simon opened the car door for her again, a bit of chivalry she'd thought long dead. As she slid into the passenger seat, her cynical side wondered if the gesture was made solely to keep her from touching the custom paint job of his precious car. Yet, when he got in beside her, he was still focused on Tiffany.

"I have some things I need to work on overnight, if we want to try to free her. It won't be easy, but maybe I can get a new bail hearing. First, however, we'll have to find a foster parent she can live with. Are there any possibilities you haven't tried on your end?" He started the engine and they headed off toward his office building.

"We looked all over Baltimore, both in the city and across the county. We even asked the child services of the surrounding counties. No luck. But I can try again."

He nodded. "Do that, and let me see what I can do on my end. If you'll meet me for breakfast tomorrow at seven, we can go over our strategy."

"Breakfast?" she inquired. "I usually like to get to know a guy before I do breakfast with him." Even as this came out of her mouth, she realized she was making a mildly suggestive joke. Was she flirting with Simon Montgomery?

He chuckled, apparently taking her comment with the

humor she'd intended. Then he said, "It's the only time I have open. I have three other big cases going on and we just got another one today. But Tiffany needs immediate attention. Breakfast is an open hour for me. Take it or leave it," he said bluntly.

"I'll take it." And she'd have to be more careful with the comments that popped out of her mouth from now on. Her supervisor, Marla, would certainly frown on a lack of professionalism. "And thank you. For taking Tiffany's case. For finding time in your busy day to focus on her."

He smiled as he downshifted, turning onto the street that would lead them back to his building. "All in a day's work, ma'am. We attorneys may not seem much like knights in shining armor, but every now and then we get the opportunity to save a damsel in distress."

She smiled again, fascinated to realize how easy it was to be with him, how comfortable it felt to banter with this intelligent and powerful male. "Well, Tiffany *will* be a grateful damsel, if you can get her out of that place and into a decent home."

"And what about you?" he asked with a playful grin. "Will you be a grateful damsel, too?"

She had to force herself not to stiffen up. He hadn't meant anything by his question, she told herself. He was just flirting back—responding to something she'd started. She had no business getting huffy. Surely he didn't mean to imply that she owed him anything for helping Tiffany. Simon was not like her uncle, who *would* have intended such a comment to mean she'd owe him fondling privileges—and other sexual favors he'd never managed to actually collect from her.

The playful light in his eyes faded away. "Sorry. I was just trying to be funny," he said. Perceptive guy, noticing that she'd suddenly gone quiet.

She needed to get the conversation back onto a lighter footing. Composing herself, she said, "Tiffany's a good kid in a horrible situation. Anything you can do to help her will be appreciated by both of us. And I know you'll do your best for her—I could see you were as taken by her as I am."

"I just hope we're not both being taken in by a clever young actress. She seems sincere and I like her a lot. She's smart and articulate. But I also know that kids can sometimes be manipulative. When she slapped away your tissue, that may have been her most honest moment."

"I've been in this line of work a long time. I know how some kids can be, and Tiffany is different. Even more important, she didn't kill Derek."

"Why are you so sure?" he asked her, as he pulled up next to her car in the garage. "The evidence points to her being the only one who had the opportunity. By Tiffany's own admission, the foster mother hadn't shaken him or done anything else harmful to Derek."

"I can't prove it, if that's what you mean. I just...know."

"You mean, like believing in God? Or knowing you're in love?"

She turned to look at him and was struck again by how close they were to each other. If they had been on a date, it would have been so easy to lean toward each other to kiss. But this wasn't a date and he wasn't leaning over the gearshift. He just gazed into her eyes with an intensity that made her worry he would be able to see all her secrets.

"Something like that. Where am I to meet you in the morning?"

"Jimmy's, 801 South Broadway. Seven o'clock."

Jayda nodded and got out of the Mustang. "I'll be there," she said, bending down so she could see him as she stood beside the vehicle. He grinned at her and she closed the door. As he drove away, she remained there by her car, thinking idly about the intensity of his smile. Then she shook herself back to reality and headed to her own office, where other cases awaited her attention. Juan Lopez needed arrangements made for attention-deficit testing, she had to review the foster-home situation for Carrie Peebles, and fourteen-year-old Malachai Dermley had been arrested again and Jayda would have to meet with his public defender. And there could be any number of additional cases that she didn't know about waiting for her on her desk. Tiffany's case was not her sole concern, no matter how much she'd like it to be.

"YOU'RE STILL HERE," MARLA said from the doorway. She crossed her arms and leaned against the jamb as she looked at Jayda, her beautiful African features inscrutable.

"So are you," Jayda said. "And you have a four-year-old you're supposed to go home to. You have to give up these late nights at work."

Marla scowled slightly. "Bad habits are hard to break. So my advice to you is not to start any. Go home yourself."

"Can't. I've finally got Tiffany some real legal help and now I need to do my part."

Marla straightened up, staring at Jayda intently. "Tiffany. Again. If you get any more involved in her case, I may have to reassign her to someone else."

Jayda stared back. "Please don't," she said, firmly meeting Marla's gaze. Marla had warned her not to become too attached to any of the kids assigned to her, but Tiffany had worked her way into Jayda's heart. Jayda couldn't say any of that to Marla, so instead she protested, "You'd potentially hurt her court case the instant the prosecutor found out she'd been reassigned. Even such a small thing could cause her to spend years in prison, whether she's guilty or not."

Marla shifted from one foot to the other. "I'm not 'causing' anything, Jayda. I'm simply looking out for my staff, making sure they stay objective and balanced. You're the one jeopardizing Tiffany's case by getting too close to her."

"I'm not," Jayda insisted. "I admit it might seem that way. But I promise you I still have the proper level of detachment. And you'll be relieved to know her new attorney, Simon Montgomery, is exceptionally skeptical about her and keeps warning me she could be manipulating us. He's not ready yet to believe she could be genuine. So I have him to help me stay neutral."

"Okay," Marla said. "I'll accept that for now. You lucked out getting such a high-profile lawyer for her—and one who seems to have some common sense. But if I see you slipping, I'm going to pull you. What are you trying to get done for her at this hour of night, anyway?"

"Simon Montgomery thinks he can get her another bail hearing, if I can find a foster home for her to go to."

"Didn't you tap every possibility the first time?"

Jayda nodded wearily. "I just want to make sure I didn't miss anyone. Or maybe something has shifted in the interim. Someone might have gone back to their parents, leaving a new opening in a foster home somewhere."

"Good luck getting anyone to agree to take her. She's a handful."

"Mostly, she's a good kid. When she acts out, she's venting frustrations with a system that hasn't served her very well. So, that's why I'm still here." Jayda offered a small smile. "But you don't have to be. Go home and hug your boy. And give your baby-sitter a break."

Marla scowled again. Jayda accepted that she wasn't the easiest boss to have, but usually she was fair. And she worked hard for her clients. Five years ago she'd nearly lost her job after she'd fallen for a schoolteacher who'd been accused of molesting one of his students. Even though he'd been acquitted, their secret relationship eventually had soured—and then become not-so-secret when Marla decided to keep the resulting baby. Jayda wasn't even sure the guy knew Marla had given birth to his son, months after he'd moved to Chicago. Marla's cautions to Jayda were, at least to some extent, an effort to help another staff member avoid the same kind of difficult emotional upheaval.

Marla turned to go, then stopped and took a step backward, looking down at her feet as if contemplating something significant. "One thing more," she said. "Don't let your feelings for 'Simon' get away from you, Jayda. He's Tiffany's attorney and you need to maintain a professional distance between the two of you."

"I don't have any feelings for—"

"Cut the crap," she interjected. "From what I've heard, Montgomery's smart, he's handsome, and now he's taken on Tiffany's case with zeal. You probably have a crush on him already."

"No!" Jayda shouted. "That's not..."

"Don't forget. I've been there and done that. I know all the signs. But you can fight it. Do us all a favor and resist, because after me, I don't think this office could stand another scandal." She walked out before Jayda could put together a coherent protest.

Once Marla left, Jayda let her head drop to her folded arms and weariness swept over her. And as she sprawled atop the foster-care documents, she wondered if there could be any truth to Marla's accusation.

No, definitely not, she decided. Simon Montgomery was exactly the sort of man she'd always avoided. Besides which, he scared her half to death.

"YOU MADE IT," HE SAID AS she approached his table at Jimmy's the next morning. "I kept the menu for you. Sorry, I already ordered." He tapped his watch, indicating time was short, then handed the menu to her.

"Thanks," she said as she slid onto the red vinyl seat. "What's good?"

"Everything." A waitress rushed by with several heavily laden plates for a table down the aisle. The heady scent of bacon and fresh pancakes seemed to prove Simon's assertion.

Jayda contemplated the choices and also made note of the folder of papers Simon had been reviewing. Tiffany's file, with some unfamiliar documents mixed in. She sighed. "I wasn't able to find a foster home for her." Confessed like the sin it seemed to be. She'd tried so hard, but had been defeated.

He looked up at her through the steam of his coffee. "You called everyone? You've used up all the favors owed to you?"

"I'm going to make some more calls today. I don't have access to the lists of foster parents from other counties, and none of the other Social Services offices in the area returned my calls before closing time last night. I don't have much hope, though."

Something shattered in the kitchen, making Jayda jump. But she squared her shoulders and added, "So, I'm going to approve myself as her foster mother. She can stay with me." Inside, her stomach tightened at the thought of trying to sneak this decision past Marla. The woman would surely find out at some point. And then anything could happen, including Jayda losing her job.

"That's not going to work," Simon said. "You have rules against that, right? I think you already mentioned that. And I'm not going to jeopardize Tiffany's case because you can't bear to leave her at the juvenile facility. So, forget it."

Their waitress came and Jayda ordered coffee and an English muffin. Simon scoffed at her choice and informed her that breakfast was the most important meal of the day. She didn't want to tell him she might not be able to eat anything at all if her stomach didn't settle down. She'd spent a sleepless night, tossing and turning and thinking about Tiffany's situation and then mulling over all that Marla had said.

"The good news," Simon said, "is that we have a new bail hearing set for two days from now."

"What good will that do us?" she asked. "I seriously doubt I'll find a place for her by then. In fact, we could go weeks without any success."

He shifted uneasily. "Are you sure Tiffany won't cause any trouble if she's put into someone's home?"

"Define 'cause trouble,'" she hedged. "She's a kid. Kids don't always behave well."

"Especially kids who've spent time in detention centers. I know. And I'm not asking for perfection—just reasonably good behavior."

Jayda looked at him, watched him take a bite of his eggs and wondered what he was getting at. "Yes, I think you can count on her behavior. But no one will take her." Jayda said the last part with exaggerated enunciation, as if he must not have registered this important fact when she'd said it earlier.

"How can you be so certain she won't be more than an ordinary household could handle?"

She didn't hesitate. "Because I know her. She might occasionally be a brat or throw a pre-teen tantrum, but that's just normal." He studied her, assessing her, as Jayda added softly, "Because she deserves to have someone believe in her at least once in her life."

Looking deeply into her eyes, Simon seemed to be searching for something. Jayda feared he would see too much and she dropped her gaze to her coffee cup. Then something compelled her to be completely open with the attorney. "She reminds me of myself at that age," she explained. "And I know that I can trust her."

"Sometime soon, you'll have to tell me your story," he said gently. "But right now, I should tell you a piece of mine."

That got her attention.

"The quick version. My parents died when I was four, and relatives fought over who should be burdened with me. I alternated between those people and various foster homes. Finally, I found a permanent place for myself with a couple I've thought of as my parents for many years. My dad's dead now and my mom hasn't taken in any more foster kids in years, but I believe she's maintained herself on the list. 'Just in case,' she always says."

"If your mother was a suitable foster parent, I would have found her already," Jayda said.

"She lives in Howard County. Social Services there might have deemed her too old to be a foster parent at seventy, or they may have believed she'd be unwilling to take on a juvie murder suspect with Tiffany's record of acting out. And I certainly won't saddle her with Tiffany if there's any chance that she could be serious trouble."

Jayda sighed. "She's eleven. There's always a chance she'll be trouble. She's smart and she likes to get her way.

But she won't set the house on fire." Her coffee arrived just as she said that and she offered a polite thank you to the waitress.

Simon's expression went a bit sheepish. "My mother doesn't expect perfection either. If she did, I'd have been booted out of her house more times than I could count. Hold on a minute," he said, smiling, as he took his cell phone out of his jacket pocket.

He hit one button and put the unit to his ear. Obviously, Mom was on speed dial. But almost as soon as he said, "Hello, Mom, I need to ask you for a favor," things went downhill and Simon's smile faded to a scowl. Even though she heard only one side of the conversation, Jayda could appreciate the story behind it.

"I do *not* only call you when I want something," he protested. His eyes had gone wide with indignation, but then something different came into his expression. Jayda knew Simon was feeling guilty.

"Okay, you're right. I've been too busy with work." He listened for a few seconds and added, "Yes, I know. I need to slow down, remember what's important…find a woman." At this remark, his gaze lifted to Jayda's and she was startled by the effect this had on her. That strange fluttering renewed and her pulse quickened. Her body understood that the extremely handsome Simon Montgomery was an available male, even if her mind rejected him as a personal prospect.

"Yes, grandchildren. Before you die. I know. It's my duty as your only child." He winked across the table at Jayda, letting her know he was amused by all this. But in another moment, he dropped his forehead into his palm, elbow propped on the table between them and listened some more.

"Why didn't you tell me the roof was leaking?" he asked. "I could have called someone to come fix it." He listened and then said, "That's why I work hard. So I can make lots of money and take care of you." His free hand reached for his coffee cup, but he didn't take a drink. He just turned it around and around as he listened.

As the turning sped up, Jayda worried that Simon was on the verge of doing something stupid—like hanging up on his mother, who was the last hope for Tiffany's freedom. He needed to get a grip. Impulsively, she reached over and placed her fingers on his hand, stopping the cup and—she hoped—easing his tension just as he'd done for her at the detention center. Immediately his hand relaxed, then turned to clasp hers, as if they'd comforted each other this way many times before. When Jayda glanced at his face, she saw the strain was gone. A grateful smile replaced the tight line his mouth had been.

The instant she realized what she'd done, initiating such an intimacy, she wanted to slip her hand away. But he held on—gently, but firmly. She tried to relax into the warmth and strength she felt from his fingers holding hers, easing back against her seat as his tone with his mother lightened.

"Mom, I admit I've been completely self-indulgent and I promise I'll do better. But right now, there's a little girl in deep trouble. She needs your help." His features softened and the light came back into his eyes as he listened to his mother's response. He'd managed to say the right words.

As he explained the situation to the woman who'd raised him, Jayda watched Simon's mouth and found herself wondering what it would be like to kiss him. She tipped her head slightly to the right and imagined leaning in and touching her lips to his. He had beautifully chiseled lips—mobile, expressive. He'd be a wonderful kisser, she decided, and her skin tightened in response to the thought. Would she ever have the chance to find out for sure? Did she want to?

No. She withdrew her hand from his abruptly, which turned out to be less awkward than it might have been, because at the exact same moment he closed his phone and had to use both hands—one to open his jacket and the other to slide the cell back into its pocket. Still, Jayda couldn't help feeling shaken by the notions that had been drifting through her mind. What had she been thinking? Simon Montgomery was way out of her league. And her boss had just about ordered her to keep things professional.

"She said she'll do it," Simon announced. "But as is her nature, she exacted some promises. Mainly, I have to drive the two of them to court and to meetings or wherever they need to be. And I'll have to show up in the evenings to take care of Tiffany myself." He held Jayda's gaze as he added, "But I'm not going it alone with this kid. I'll expect help."

"You can get someone to…"

"Not 'someone,' Jayda. *You.*"

"Me?" Reluctantly, she nodded. Thoughts of Marla's warnings danced through her head, but at least this would be a better, wiser arrangement than having Tiffany live with her in her apartment.

Simon's grin made her wonder what she was being dragged into. Her foreboding doubled when he said, almost teasingly, "We'll be spending a great deal of time together, you and I. I'm looking forward to that."

CHAPTER FOUR

"I'LL NEED TO MEET YOUR mother and do a home survey, then fill out some paperwork with her," Jayda said, but her eyes were already full of optimism. Simon couldn't help feeling good about putting that glow into her expression. He also couldn't keep from noticing how the morning light streaming through the window of the diner turned her hair to gold.

"I'll take you out there this afternoon," he said, wondering even as he spoke the words if Denise would think he'd lost his mind, given the disaster this would make of his already overloaded schedule. She might even threaten to quit, and Simon *needed* his secretary. Her organizational skills, her connections, her research capabilities enabled him to win his cases. He'd be lost without her. "I have to appear in court this morning, then file some motions. I should be able to free up some time around three-thirty."

She sipped her coffee. "Thanks, but that's not necessary. I can go there by myself. I've been doing home surveys for years without any help."

"But not at my mother's home. I'll come. There'd be hell to pay if I didn't go with you." Anyway, it would be a nice drive out to Ellicott City on this unseasonably cool June day. He'd look at his mom's leaking roof, check the place to see what else needed doing, spend a few hours making his mother happy. When was the last time he'd done that? When was the last time he'd done anything that didn't advance his career as a lawyer?

In the past twelve hours, he'd done a number of selfless things that the partners would not consider career-enhancing. He'd worked the phones and called in some favors to get Tiffany another bail hearing, praying all the while that Jayda would be able to find someone to foster the girl. Briefly, Simon had considered becoming Tiffany's guardian himself, but even if he could get himself into the foster parent registry, such closeness with his client could have a negative effect on the case. His objectivity as her attorney could be questioned. Worse than that, his apartment hadn't been designed with a child in mind. Neither had his lifestyle. So he'd decided he'd ask his mother to take Tiffany in, if Jayda found no one else.

There would be a price to pay for asking this favor of his mom. She'd hold him to his promises regarding Tiffany with the strength of titanium. He had no idea how he'd keep up his end of the bargain and still stay abreast of all his cases. The lifestyle he'd worked so hard to create would undoubtedly have to be rethought. The only benefit he could see in all this was that he'd get to spend some time with Jayda. It was a thought that confused the hell out of him. Jayda didn't strike him as a woman with whom he could have a casual fling, and she couldn't become a lasting part of his life. He needed to get things back on a strictly professional footing with her, despite their earlier flirting.

"Besides," he said to her, "I'm not about to give my mother the opportunity to tell you all her stories about my youthful indiscretions. At least not unless I'm there to defend myself." He smiled as he said this, but mentally he berated himself. Why did he care what stories Jayda heard? What did it matter? How could her opinion of him make any difference in the long run?

"I look forward to the stories and to hearing you defend yourself. Should I meet you at your office?" She took out her wallet.

"I'll get the bill. You're a client, after all, and I have an expense account." He winked at her and she chuckled. "Meeting at my office would be perfect."

She slid out of the booth and stood. Average height, slim figure, brown hair and eyes, functional clothing. Nothing special. And yet…

"I'll be there," she said.

"NICE AFTERNOON FOR A DRIVE," Jayda said when they were once again side by side in his Mustang. The seats were just as close together as they had seemed the first time, but she found herself a little more relaxed today. Progress.

She watched Simon put his key into the ignition, but then he hesitated a moment before turning it. "I haven't gone out to Ellicott City in months." He sounded almost wistful. "It's pretty out there, and I should go more often. For my mom. And for me." The engine roared to life. "You know how, when you go back to where you grew up, you can regroup, recharge… Restore?"

Jayda nodded, telling herself that most people would understand the sentiments he expressed. But she didn't feel anything positive about the house in which she'd grown up. In fact, she'd vowed never to go back, and she'd kept that promise to herself. Some time ago, her mother had sold it and moved into an apartment. Jayda wondered if she could ever make herself visit her only living parent again. Doing so would likely help her to put the past into perspective and ease her toward forgiveness.

"Where did you grow up?" Simon asked, driving a little too fast out of the parking garage. But he was a good driver, completely in control of the vehicle.

"Arbutus," she said, wondering how she could turn the conversation. She didn't really want to think about Arbutus—or her uncle—at this particular moment. Not that there was *ever* a good moment.

"We're practically neighbors, then. We could have been to the same football games in high school."

"Uh-huh," she murmured. She'd never been to a high school football game. "So, I brought along the paperwork your mother needs to fill out to apply to foster Tiffany. I had to persuade Howard County Social Services to agree to the plan. They gave in eventually, but they were too busy to help much. Maybe you could give me information while we drive and I can fill in some of the sections before we arrive."

"Sure," he said, and for a while they focused on mundane information regarding the house and neighborhood, his mom's age and health, references and criminal history—or lack thereof, in the case of Barbara Johanson, who'd raised Simon since he was six.

"There's something I should probably warn you about before we arrive," he said as he made the turn off Route 40 onto 29.

Jayda waited, hoping he wasn't about to share anything that might compromise Mrs. Johanson's ability to take Tiffany into her home.

"She's a bit of a matchmaker. At least where I'm concerned."

Jayda let out her breath surreptitiously. "And?"

"Well." He paused and appeared uncomfortable. "You're an attractive unmarried woman about my age and..."

A thrill ran through her, because he'd said she was attractive. When had anyone ever said that about her before? Previous boyfriends told her she was pretty, but hearing it from this dynamic man was different, somehow.

"And...?" she prodded again, finding the exchange, and Simon's discomfort, entertaining.

"And she doesn't much like the women I date—ambitious, professional career women." His phone rang. He pulled it from his jacket pocket and glanced at the caller ID. "Speaking of which," he said under his breath as he answered the call.

Jayda's fun hissed away like air from a balloon. Simon apparently didn't put her in the same category with professional career women, and that stung. It wasn't very entertaining listening to him talk to one of his professional career women on the phone, either, even though he didn't say much.

"I have to go, Megan," he said after listening for a moment. "I'll call you."

Jayda watched him hang up and then thumb the cell off. No more calls from Megan for a while, at least.

"Anyway," Simon continued, as if his love life had not just intruded on the conversation, "Mom will see you're down-to-earth, sweet, nurturing. Normal. She might encourage us to get together socially."

Okay, those were all nice things. Jayda felt particularly pleased at being deemed "normal"—if he only knew. She was glad she could fake it so well.

"We just have to make it clear to her that things must remain professional between us. I'm sure we can manage that," she said as Simon pulled to a stop along the curb of a lovely suburban street dotted with well-tended, middle-class homes.

"You don't know my mother," he commented grimly as he got out.

Jayda followed him to the two-story house. They went around to the side door instead of the front one and Simon let them in without knocking. Even so, they were greeted by a blinding flash of light.

"There we go!" said a woman whom Jayda could just barely make out through her temporary state of light blindness. "Your first picture together. It can also go into Tiffany's memory book—the beginning of her new life with us."

"Oh, yeah, and she's an amateur photographer, too," Simon muttered.

"Who's an amateur? I'm preprofessional. Come in, come in. Don't stand by the door."

Jayda went forward despite the lingering spots caused by the flash, once again following the broad expanse of Simon's back. He introduced the two women as they headed into the house. Not once in all of her years as a social worker had she experienced such an exuberant first meeting with a potential foster parent. Under other circumstances Juvenile Services might have made a snap judgment that this woman was a little too eccentric for the foster program, but she was Tiffany's only hope. And if Simon was any indication, Mrs. Johanson must be a wonderful parent.

They went through a modest, sparkling clean kitchen into a family room. "I know you need to see the whole house and yard," said Mrs. Johanson. "Would you like the tour right away?"

"Yes, that would be fine." This woman knew the drill

and she showed Jayda each room, focusing on the one that would belong to Tiffany—a nicely appointed bedroom ready for a girl to make her own. As they moved from room to room, Jayda noted that Simon's mom, though already seventy, still got around easily and was full of life.

"This is Simon's room," said Mrs. Johanson, and she opened another door on the second floor with a flourish. "I've kept all his things here."

Sure enough, the room was decorated for a boy in blue-and-red plaid, with blue and red trucks on the wall border near the ceiling. Jayda thought she heard a sigh from the man who had once called this room his own, and it was all she could do not to smile. Undoubtedly, viewing his childhood bedroom gave her a lot more information than most people would ever have regarding the mighty Simon Montgomery.

"What are the trophies for?" she asked, seeing them along a shelf above the desk.

"Oh, our Simon was very into karate and jujitsu. He got all the way to his black belt," his mom volunteered.

"I was a kid. It was a child's black belt. Nothing special," he said from behind the two of them.

"Oh, but we were so proud," declared Mrs. Johanson. "Carl and I went to all his matches, right up until Carl's heart attack."

Jayda looked at Simon to see his expression. When she saw the pain barely hidden in the depths of his eyes, she understood he wouldn't like talking about the loss of his adoptive father. A hint of vulnerability might peek out, and a man in Simon's tough profession couldn't allow that.

He looked directly at Jayda and said, "I was thirteen. It was hard on both of us." And he slung an arm across his mother's shoulders and gave her a quick squeeze. "But we got through it. I got that black belt for him, more than anything. He loved the idea of me earning it. So I did, even though he had died."

"Carl knew. He watched from beyond and he knew," said Mrs. Johanson.

Jayda felt a bit like an intruder as the moment of remembering stretched on. But she stayed where she was, waiting for mother and son to collect themselves. They did so, and led the way back out into the hallway.

"You can see the whole backyard from here," said the older woman, pointing to a window at the end of the hall. "It's a good place for kids to play. It'd be a good place for grandchildren, someday."

Jayda peered out, noticing the fenced area, and nodded. "Perfect," she agreed. But when she looked back at Simon, he was scowling. "You're still on the list for foster care, so there's just a bit of paperwork to do. Let's get that over with, okay?"

"Yes, why don't you do that," said Simon. "I'll check out the damage from the leaking roof and be back down in a minute."

Jayda went downstairs with Mrs. Johanson and they got the documents out of the way. She assured the older woman there was little chance of a problem and advised her that Tiffany would be placed with her if the judge would set bail at her hearing.

When Simon reappeared, he had taken off his suit jacket and loosened his tie over the undone top button on his crisp white shirt. Jayda had never seen him in anything other than his expensive suits to match his perfectly groomed nails and hair. But now, a few locks had fallen onto his brow and his fingertips were smudged.

"I had to go up into the attic," he said as he brushed his

hair back with his fingers. He looked boyish, yet so damn sexy that Jayda could hardly breathe. Fortunately, he and his mother began to chat for a while, giving Jayda a chance to renew her vow that she would think of Simon Montgomery only as Tiffany's lawyer.

Simon agreed to pick up his mother before the hearing, so she could be there for support. She'd meet Tiffany for the first time at the courthouse prior to the proceedings.

"And I'll have someone out to fix the roof and the ceiling in your bedroom as soon as possible," he assured her.

"I know you will, Simon. But you need a woman by your side. Don't overlook any of the ones you might come across."

To Jayda's amusement, Mrs. Johanson patted her strapping son on the cheek. The scene was downright adorable. As they headed back to the car, Jayda realized she'd witnessed something very personal. It made Simon seem more human, and far less frightening.

WHEN THE UNIFORMED MATRON brought Tiffany into the holding room at the courthouse for her bail hearing, Jayda wanted to cry. The little girl came forward with her wrists bound together by a nylon handcuff strip.

"Why is she restrained?" Simon demanded, enunciating the words with fierce control. "The written procedures clearly state that you consider safety and flight risk before binding kids. What were you thinking?"

"She was already cuffed when I came along to escort her here," retorted the guard, unintimidated by Simon's anger and unmoved by the age or diminutive size of the girl in her care.

"Take them off her this instant," he said in a low, simmering tone.

Jayda slid her gaze over to Mrs. Johanson. The woman looked steadily at Tiffany, her eyes full of emotion. As the cuffs were cut from the child's wrists, Simon's mom turned away and put one hand to her mouth as if trying to regain control. When she turned back, she had a warm smile in place and exuded that positive attitude that had made Jayda's first meeting with her so pleasant. Even though she might be faking it, Jayda admired the effort.

Mrs. Johanson wasted no time getting to introductions. "Tiffany, I'm Barbara Johanson. I'm hoping to be your new foster mother." She held out her hand to shake—a daring move, given that most foster kids would be angry, resentful or terrified at a first meeting.

But Tiffany rose to the occasion, as Jayda had hoped she would. She solemnly accepted the woman's friendly hand. "Thank you," she said. They were such simple words, but they expressed so much. Most important, they revealed the kind of person Tiffany was inside, despite the occasional tantrum or sulk.

"You're very welcome," said Mrs. Johanson. Her straightforward acceptance of Tiffany's gratitude was the perfect reaction. The two stood for a few seconds, hands clasped together, taking each other in and creating a silent bond. Jayda had worked hard to make connections with all the children with whom she worked, but Simon's mom seemed able to succeed without any effort at all.

"You can call me Barbara. I think you're old enough for that, don't you?"

"I'm eleven and a half." Tiffany offered this information as if to say her maturity most certainly could not be in question.

Barbara glanced up at Jayda and her eyes seemed to indicate, "So young!" Then she turned her attention back to the girl. “We brought you some of your own clothes to wear during the hearing. Would you like to change?”

Jayda watched them dig into the gym bag containing a pink sweater and denim skirt she’d picked out for this occasion.

“I don’t like this outfit,” Tiffany said. “I’ll look like a baby,” she insisted.

“It’s all we have,” Barbara said calmly.

In one swift movement, Tiffany swept the gym bag onto the floor so that it hit the wall and the contents spilled out.

“Tiffany,” Jayda cried. It wasn’t the first time the girl’s anger had gotten the best of her, and it wouldn’t be the last. But why now, Jayda bemoaned silently. Why couldn’t she hold it in just a little longer, so Barbara could have a good impression of her—at least until after the bail hearing.

“Those clothes are worse than these prison scrubs!” she yelled. Barbara stood there, stunned, as Tiffany kicked the bag a few feet to one side.

“Stop it at once,” Jayda began, as she reached to restrain her. But Simon stepped in.

“Let me talk to her,” he said. Without waiting for an answer, he turned back to Tiffany and gestured for her to join him in a corner of the room, apart from the two women. He hunkered down so he could look into Tiffany’s eyes as he spoke, his expensive suit hugging his thighs as he did so. Jayda couldn’t hear what he said, but Tiffany seemed appeased, and she picked up the gym bag and went into the restroom with it.

“She’ll change into what you brought for her,” he explained.

“What did you say to her?”

“I told her that it might be in her interest to look

younger in front of the judge. She's nothing if not logical. Give her a good reason for something and she'll go along with it."

"Funny, I know someone else who's just the same way," said Barbara, eyeing her son with amusement.

He nodded. "If she didn't show some anger now and then or act out a little, I'd be worried about her holding in too much." He put his hand on his mother's shoulder. "I'm confident you'll work her past those difficult moments, just as you did with me."

Barbara nodded. "I'm a lot older now than I was, Simon. I'll need your help, just as you promised."

"I'll help. And so will Jayda."

Jayda caught Simon's gaze. His inclusion of her in his immediate future made her want to back away before he captivated her completely. He was a handsome, powerful, passionate man. Being near him made her quiver with fear—unless it was some other emotion entirely.

"THERE'S A LOT OF TIME TO reflect in a courtroom," Simon whispered to Tiffany as they waited their turn before the judge. "It can get pretty boring. And then suddenly you're on and you have to give your words a lot of energy. It's kind of a crazy way to make a living." They'd been sitting for an hour, listening to the drone of other hearings. The schedule had long since been abandoned, as frequently happened, even though they'd been required to be in the courtroom at the appointed time. "At least you get out of juvie for a while, and have something different to do." He nudged Tiffany with his elbow as he said this and she smiled up from the seat beside his. "Maybe we can arrange it so you don't have to go back."

"I hope so," she agreed. She seemed relaxed, confident.

He knew she expected him to make good things happen for her. He only hoped that he could.

"Be careful you don't raise her expectations too high," Jayda said from his other side.

He could feel her tension and wondered, did she always expect to have her hopes dashed or did she simply lack confidence in him as an attorney? He wasn't sure which answer he preferred. Simon supposed he didn't need Jayda's confidence. He had enough of that on his own. And he'd hate to find out her desires were unmet so frequently that she dared not harbor any. Jayda Kavanagh ought to have her dreams fulfilled, just to balance out all the good she did for the kids she worked with.

"In re Tiffany Thompson," called the clerk of the court.

"Here," said Simon in return, approaching the judge's bench beyond the railing. Tiffany and Jayda followed him, as they'd been instructed to do. "Your honor, Simon Montgomery, representing. Jayda Kavanagh, guardian ad litem," he added.

"Bail has already been denied, counselor. Why are we rehashing this?" asked the judge.

"Bail was not seriously pursued by previous counsel because the child had no foster home to go to at that time. A suitable foster home has now been found, approved by Juvenile Services." Simon did his best to hold the gaze of the judge, hoping to force the man to focus on this particular case among a long line of cases. "It's in the best interest of the child and the public that she be released into the care of a qualified adult. It would also help relieve overcrowding at the juvenile facility."

The judge nodded and turned his disinterested gaze to the other table. "Does the State have a position?" the judge asked the representative from the Maryland prosecutor's office.

"The State objects, Your Honor. The defendant is on trial for second-degree murder. She has a history of violence and may commit additional felonies if not under the supervision and control of Juvenile Services at all times. She's also a flight risk."

Simon looked at the youthful attorney making these excessive statements, and had to work hard to keep the shock out of his expression. He'd been calling the prosecutor's office ever since he'd scheduled this hearing. But he hadn't been able to get through to anyone familiar with the case. Earlier today, when he'd attempted to come to an agreement with this green lawyer, he'd gotten nothing but a grunt in return.

The judge looked toward him again, expectantly. "Your Honor," he said. "The defendant is eleven years old and has nowhere to go. She is not a flight risk. Moreover, no history of violence has ever been proven in court, nor is there any indication of felonies, past, present or future, committed by this child." He indicated Tiffany by looking down at her, standing demurely at his side. She looked as small and helpless as he'd hoped she would. The judge looked at her, too, just as Simon knew he would. "She'll be safe and well-cared-for in the foster home, and the foster parent is fully capable of keeping her under control." He knew firsthand how resourceful the woman in question could be at keeping a spirited child under control.

The judge dropped his gaze to the folder in front of him. He scanned a computer screen. "Is Mrs. Johanson present today?"

"Yes, Your Honor." Simon turned and gestured for his mother to stand up. She did so, looking proud and confident and holding her chin at a determined angle.

"Mrs. Johanson, you're aware of the charges against the defendant?"

"I am," she said.

"And you're willing to take the defendant into your home?"

Simon rejoiced at the skillful way his mother pretended she didn't know him at all, just as he'd coached her. And he couldn't have been happier at the way she looked toward Tiffany with effusive fondness. "I'd be glad to do so," she said.

The judge nodded. "Because of the seriousness of the case, bail is set at two hundred fifty thousand."

While this would seem impossible for a youthful defendant without any family, Simon had already decided to front the ten percent required to make bail for her. He'd get it back when she appeared in court, anyway, and it wouldn't be missed from his sizable bank account.

"And the defendant will wear an electronic monitor at all times," concluded the judge.

Simon's heart sank. Electronic ankle monitors were extremely inconvenient. His mother couldn't and wouldn't leave Tiffany home alone, and now she'd need permission every time they wanted to go anywhere together. And the monitoring agent wouldn't give them permission, except for court-related trips and for health purposes. It would mean he'd have to play an even greater role in Tiffany's care than he'd expected. Otherwise, his mother might begin to feel like a prisoner, too.

"Your Honor, I ask that you reconsider the monitor. This child is not a flight risk and—"

"I've made my decision, counselor. We're done here," the judge said, banging his gavel down conclusively.

As he sat down to put all their documents back into a

folder, Simon glanced toward Jayda and saw that she understood the negative implications of this ruling. That was a good thing, because now he'd really need her help. His career and lifestyle could not be put completely on hold in order to babysit Tiffany Thompson. Jayda had talked him into taking on this case, so she'd have to step up to the plate and do her part, too. Yet even as he thought about foisting a large portion of the responsibility for Tiffany off on the social worker, a surprising thing happened.

Tiffany spontaneously stood and put her arms around his neck, giving him a big, warm hug. Simon didn't know what he should do, and he found himself awkwardly patting the girl on the shoulder, noticing that she smelled like Ivory soap, which reminded him of his own childhood. He hoped she'd step back quickly. Instead, she whispered, "Thank you for getting me out of juvie, Mr. Montgomery." Then she let go and turned toward her new foster mother.

Simon sat there, assaulted by emotions he refused to name. His gaze lifted to Jayda's eyes once more. She stood by, looking down at him with what appeared to be wholehearted approval mixed with a measure of sympathy. He felt understood, in a way he hadn't experienced before. And this was so disturbing that he got to his feet too fast, nearly toppling his chair.

They were crawling into his heart, he could feel it—Jayda and Tiffany were invading his life. He *had* to resist. His mentor and senior partner Glen Boyden had all but told Simon he should marry Glen's niece, or someone just like her. Someone like Megan, perhaps. Simon had worked hard to encourage the impression that he would do whatever it took to advance his career—even marry the right woman in order to enhance his image. Becoming partner had been his goal for so long, he'd forgotten there could be anything more important, despite his mother's repeated efforts to correct his thinking. He wouldn't let normal, ordinary Jayda or the kid with the hugs get in the way of that now.

CHAPTER FIVE

"AND HE WAS ALWAYS GOOD at sports," Barbara Johanson told Tiffany. "Carl and I encouraged him. We figured if he was busy, he wouldn't get into trouble."

Simon stayed with the females as Tiffany waded through the long process for the monitoring device and Barbara entertained her with stories from Simon's childhood. There had been the garden snake he'd brought home as a pet, claiming it would grow into a boa constrictor. And he'd taken his bicycle apart entirely one day, to see how it worked, but then had been unable to put it back together without hours of help from his father.

"Okay, enough with the stories about little Simon," he said as he passed out Quizno's sandwiches that he'd had to pick up for them. They weren't going to be allowed to stop for dinner on the way to Ellicott City, and they'd already missed lunch.

He'd canceled his afternoon appointments again to take care of these three women. If he kept this up, Tiffany would be his only remaining client after all the others had departed for more attentive counsel. But Jayda had cleared her calendar for the child defendant and Simon could do no less. Besides, he felt responsible for Tiffany ending up with the ankle monitor. If he'd tried harder to reach someone at the state attorney's office, perhaps he could have avoided this ordeal.

At last, an officer came to put the ankle bracelet on Tiffany. "It's tight," she whispered, and there was an edge to her voice.

"You won't even notice it after a while," Simon assured her.

"It's tight so you can't wiggle out of it." The officer's name was Curtis, and he said it casually, but the comment rankled Simon. He could feel his anger rising again, just as it had when he'd seen Tiffany come into the courthouse in cuffs.

Jayda caught his eye and gave him silent encouragement, then turned to Tiffany. "Hey, I bet you can't guess what the nickname for this ankle bracelet is," she said. "It's like one of the Muppets."

Simon knew the answer, saw that Curtis did, as well, and gave the guy a warning glare to keep quiet. It was good of Jayda to banter like this with Tiffany while they waited for the monitoring people upstairs to do their tests and connect the new bracelet to the system.

"Um, Snuffelupagus," Tiffany said right away. The gleam in her eyes told Simon she was teasing.

Poor Curtis looked perplexed for a moment, then grinned.

"Close," Jayda said without missing a beat. "You want another try?"

Tiffany smiled and thought. "Cookie Monster," she tried, clearly aware that this couldn't be right, either.

Jayda made a show of mock exasperation, then looked at Barbara. "You want to guess?"

"Oscar," Simon's other tried. When Jayda and Simon shook their heads, she shrugged. "We give up. What's it called?"

"ELMO," Curtis announced triumphantly. "Short for electronic monitoring device."

"But, no one ever guesses that," Jayda admitted. "I have to say I've never had anyone guess Snuffelupagus before, so that's a first for me." She grinned at Tiffany. Simon was happy to see the child smile back, despite her obvious weariness.

"It's kind of a good name," Jayda added. "Elmo is cute and sweet and looks out for others. So just think of this bracelet as your Elmo. It'll keep watch over you, so you can go home with Barbara."

"Just don't go more than twenty feet outside of the house without permission first," Officer Curtis warned.

"What about going to the store or out to the backyard?" Barbara asked. "Surely she can do those things?"

Curtis looked at her. "We'll set up a schedule that allows for visits to take care of court matters, but other than that she has to stay within about twenty feet of the house. Sorry. On the good side, if things go well, maybe you can get it taken off during the trial. Sometimes that happens, because by the time the trial starts it's usually obvious the offender won't run off."

Tiffany's eyes had shadows beneath them, and her face had gradually paled as the day had worn on. Simon wanted to get the child home, even if the circumstances weren't ideal. "Let's get going. Jayda and I will follow you in my car and the monitoring people will follow us in their van."

But all the way there, he worried that he was already feeling far too protective of his youngest client, now riding with his mother in the car just in front of him. He knew he should not think of Tiffany as innocent, and yet he did. He shouldn't perceive any of the things that were happening to her as unjust, but they felt that way to him.

And he couldn't seem to shake the nagging sense that he'd let her down.

"Your mother is going to need help with Tiffany now that she can't take her out to stores and such," Jayda said. "School isn't in session, so she won't get any break from taking care of her. And she can't leave Tiffany home alone."

"I know that," Simon nearly barked. Frustration closed in around him, prickly and cold. But he shouldn't take it out on Jayda. "Sorry, I just don't know how I'll get out to Ellicott City as often as Mom's going to want me to."

"We could draw up a schedule. I'll take half the days, and you take the other half," she offered.

"Thank you," he said. But then he smacked the heel of his hand on the steering wheel, venting some pent-up emotions. "I should have known they'd go for the monitor and prevented it, somehow," he said. He shifted in his seat under the weight of his failure.

He felt her palm skim over his right shoulder, lightly, briefly, comforting, consoling. Then it was gone. She said, "You couldn't have known. There was nothing you could have done. So now we just make the best of the situation we're in."

Simon saw that her hand had returned to her lap, but he wished she'd touch him again. He'd taken off his suit jacket for the drive out to the suburbs, and the sensation of her touch—or maybe that subtle energy that belonged only to her—had felt good through the thin layer of his shirt.

With his peripheral vision he could see her straight, silky hair blowing in the breeze from the windows they'd elected to keep open. No scarf to keep her hair perfectly coifed, no complaint that the wind might spoil her makeup or dry out contact lenses worn solely to change the color of her eyes. She didn't wear cosmetics. If she wore contacts, they'd be to correct her vision, not to turn her irises a formidable shade of turquoise. Jayda was a natural woman, and at least among females his own age, that was completely new to him.

He pulled to the curb in front of his childhood home. They got out and went to the Honda in the driveway. Tiffany had fallen asleep in the backseat. Simon's mother looked as if she could use a nap, too.

Jayda opened the rear door next to Tiffany. "C'mon, sleepyhead. I'll show you straight to your bedroom. You can explore your new home tomorrow." She led the girl inside.

Simon walked with his mother and tried to hide his irritation as the probation officer pulled a van up behind his Mustang. They were going to disrupt the entire household with their monitoring system.

"You're not usually so easily annoyed, Simon," his mother said as they walked toward the side door.

He had to smile. "So I'm not doing a very good job hiding it this time—is that what you're saying?"

"Tiffany will be fine. And I'll be fine, too. You'll see. Don't worry about us. The house-arrest part is just a minor concern."

He glanced back toward the men, who were taking equipment out of the van. That's when he realized that a couple of his mother's neighbors were looking out their windows to see what was going on. They'd certainly never seen this kind of thing on their street before. And electronic monitoring was more than a minor inconvenience. His mom was about to find that out the hard way. "The system uses your phone line to monitor Tiffany, so you won't be allowed to have any cordless phones. They're going to take them all. You'll get one land line and it can't be a mobile unit, just the plug-in kind."

She frowned. "I'm not sure I have one of those," she admitted.

"I'll get you one before I leave for home tonight. But there's more. You won't be allowed to use your phone for more than ten minutes at a time. You'll have to cancel caller ID and call waiting. Tiffany won't be able to be in the same room with you if you're on the phone, because her monitor will send a false alarm. She won't be able to go anywhere except to prearranged court-related things. No taking her to the grocery store, or out to Wal-Mart, or to the parks in Columbia. It's going to be annoying as hell."

She patted his arm, then preceded him into the kitchen. "I'm sure we'll manage. We always do. And you have that nice woman, Jayda, to help this time. You could certainly do worse."

That's true, was his first thought. But then he remembered that Jayda Kavanagh would in no way advance his career with his firm.

IT WAS LATE BY THE TIME Jayda left Ellicott City with Simon. He'd had to buy an acceptable phone from Wal-Mart and she'd stayed with Mrs. Johanson and Tiffany to make sure the monitoring team wasn't as surly as usual. Finally, they headed out in the Mustang, car windows rolled up against the evening drizzle.

"Tiffany really likes you," she said.

"I like her, too."

"Your mother is nice and she's great with kids."

"Uh-huh," he replied, sounding distracted.

Deciding Simon must be as tired as she felt, Jayda lapsed into an awkward silence. She thought about everything she had to do tomorrow to make up for the time she'd spent with Tiffany. In case Marla asked, Jayda considered how she'd explain herself. She'd had to reschedule four appointments and she was going to need an excuse for doing that. Then, as they approached her apartment building, she thought about what she might eat so close to bedtime. That take-out sandwich had burned off hours ago. Her stomach growled just as Simon pulled alongside the curb.

He laughed. "Maybe I should take you to dinner before we call it a night."

"No, that's okay. Thanks anyway. I have some leftovers I can reheat."

His expression became wistful for a moment, and then blanked. Jayda wondered if a man like Simon Montgomery ever cooked at home—there weren't likely to be leftovers in his refrigerator. And then her heart began to race, and she'd spoken even before she thought about what she was going to say.

"Would you like to come up and eat with me before you head home? Nothing special, just some pasta and salad. But there's enough for both of us."

The instant the words were out of her mouth, she regretted them. If he came up to her apartment for food, what else would he expect? Men like Montgomery always got what they wanted, no matter what, and he might misunderstand her invitation. So how would she get rid of him without an argument—what if he became insistent? What if he turned out to be like her uncle, after all? Oh, God, this could lead to all sorts of terrible consequences, for herself and for Tiffany.

"Aren't you too tired to entertain a guest at this hour?" he asked, giving her a chance to back out gracefully.

But the look in his eyes told her he'd appreciate the company, even though it was late. "Well, just come in and eat, and then you can go. How long could that take?" There. She'd established boundaries. That was good. That was healthy. Even so, with her palms beginning to sweat, she wondered why she hadn't just taken the excuse he'd given her to rescind the invitation. How confusing to commit herself to doing something, when it also terrified her.

Maybe because Simon seemed like a good person, and because this gave her a perfect opportunity to face a few of her demons.

"Okay. Any suggestions on parking?"

They were lucky, and it only took a minute to find a spot. Then they headed on foot to Jayda's building. It felt odd walking together without speaking, heading into her home. But Jayda couldn't make idle conversation. She was consumed with worry…and determined. Before she could sort things out, they were entering her apartment on the third floor.

"This is really nice," he said as he looked around. "Homey."

Jayda had never entertained a man here before, preferring to go to her partner's place when she'd had boyfriends in the past. Simon's bulk made the space seem to shrink, and claustrophobia took hold of her for a moment as she led him through the narrow foyer. In the living room, she suggested he make himself comfortable while she got supper started in the kitchen. He asked if he could help, but she could tell that cooking wasn't his thing. The instant she declined the offer, he sat down on the overstuffed sofa with his arms stretched out on either side along the back.

"Holler if you change your mind. I follow directions well." He smiled at her, a man at his ease.

She tried to emulate the casual mood, but her insides went skittish on her. In the kitchen, she dropped a metal salad bowl in the sink. The resounding clatter brought the man rushing into the narrow confines of the galley area.

"Are you okay?" he asked.

"Yup, everything's fine," she lied. "The bowl slipped. Wet fingers. Silly, really. It happens all the time. With this bowl, I mean. Slippery when wet." Stop talking, she told herself. Not another word about the stupid bowl. Focus on putting the washed lettuce into the colander to drain. Now think about cutting up some celery and carrots.

"Hey, I can do that," he said. As he reached around her to take the knife from her fingers. His shoulder brushed hers. It could have been accidental, but it felt like something else. Anxiety flooded through her. But at the same time she wanted to lean back into him, to see what might happen next. Simon completely rattled her. And yet he also attracted her more than any man had in quite some time.

SIMON COULDN'T QUITE understand the feelings that were racing through him. All during dinner, he was filled with contentment. And yet he wanted something else, and the urge to figure out what that "something" might be kept him on edge. He talked more, revealed more than he had in a long while. By the time they'd finished the pasta and sipped the last drops of wine, he'd become completely, uncharacteristically mellow. And yet a subtle buzz vibrated inside him.

"Let me help you with the dishes," he said.

"You don't have to do that. I'll just put everything in the dishwasher."

"Then I'll help load the dishwasher. Because if my mother finds out I didn't help, I'm in big trouble." He picked up some dishes and headed for the sink.

Jayda rinsed them off under the faucet and Simon took a place beside her fitting items into slots in the machine—plates, flatware, glasses, serving dishes all arranged neatly. But then she leaned back a bit to look around him and inspect his work. Disapproval sprang to her eyes. He looked down at his loading and could see nothing wrong with the arrangement of dirty dishes. When she casually began to shift things around, he captured her hand.

"There's nothing wrong with how I put them in there," he protested.

She had the grace to look sheepish. "I know, but I just like things a certain way," she admitted. She tried to slip her hand from his and he let her escape, but he also moved himself in front of her so that she couldn't reposition anything else.

"C'mon," he urged. "Live on the wild side and leave it the way I did it. Find out if they don't all end up just as clean."

She attempted to slip around him, laughing a little, but he nudged her away with a shoulder. "I won't be able to sleep if they aren't in there properly," she declared.

"You're kidding," he said, but he could see she believed it. All the same, he slid the lower dish tray into the cavity of the machine before she could fuss with anything else. "Oh, wow, you're not kidding. That's worrisome. Maybe you just need practice at caring less about the small stuff. It's for your own good." He attempted to close the door.

Playfully, she reached around his waist to stop the

upward swing of the dishwasher door, practically wrapping her arms around him. That subtle buzz he'd been feeling before hummed loudly as she nearly hugged him from behind.

"Sorry," she said. "My house. My rules. I get to load the dishwasher the way I want." She pulled out the tray again.

"Your house, your rules," he agreed, and he turned his back to the edge of the counter and let her redo his work. He was powerfully aware of her lithe body and its proximity to his. As if a switch had been flipped in his brain, he was suddenly aware of how pretty she was. Sexy. Desirable. Necessary.

When she straightened, she looked pleased and a little flushed. A shiny lock of her hair had fallen in front of one of her eyes and he reached to tuck it back behind an ear. The current coursing through him went hot as he looked at her mouth, and thought of kissing her.

Her expression grew wary when she returned his gaze, but she didn't step back. If she'd retreated he'd have been able to stop himself, as he knew he should. But she stayed frozen to the spot, and so he let his hand slip to the nape of her neck. And as he slowly urged her toward him, he also eased himself forward. The next thing he knew, his mouth was touching hers. In another instant, his tongue slipped delicately over her lips. And after that he was lost in the all-consuming experience of kissing Jayda.

CHAPTER SIX

KISSING IN THE kitchen. It felt so very good to Jayda. She could have gone on doing it for a long, long time. But there was a glimmer of concern inside her head that wouldn't go away. She knew that they shouldn't be doing this. And once that thought had surfaced, she couldn't ignore it. Even though she wanted desperately to relax in Simon's arms, reality forced her to ease back. Damn.

He didn't try to keep her close, and she found that extremely comforting. If he'd tried to hold on, there was no telling what suppressed nightmares might have been unleashed. Nothing like having a close relative force you to submit to frequent molestations—even if he never actually managed to rape you—to make you terrified of being held too tightly.

Jayda found herself able to remain where she was and Simon kept his hands upon her, lightly stroking her upper arms.

"That shouldn't have happened," he murmured. He didn't sound regretful, only bewildered.

"Let's agree it didn't happen," she suggested, sounding more in control than she felt. Inside, she thought she'd never be able to forget the moment. Kissing him might have been a professional mistake, but for Jayda it had been a personal triumph. She'd enjoyed it unreservedly, and there hadn't been a single moment of fear or panic.

"Yes," he said, nodding. But he still didn't stop slowly sliding his warm hands up and down her arms. "It never happened," he agreed again, as his gaze returned to her mouth.

Reluctantly, she moved away and walked to the chair on which he'd neatly slung his suit jacket. She forced herself to smile and handed the jacket to him. His expression was pensive, unreadable. She'd noticed he did this whenever something weighed on his mind. Was he wondering if they would be able to go forward from here without awkwardness? She certainly was.

"Thank you for dinner," he said evenly. He paused, saying nothing more, then he leaned forward and kissed her on the cheek. In another moment, he was gone.

After locking the door, Jayda rested her forehead on it and waited for the riot of emotions to subside. When they did, all that remained was a dull longing. She wanted Simon back. She wished she could have him in her arms again.

But he didn't knock on her door, and eventually she gave up her vigil in the foyer and began the methodical process of getting ready for bed. After slipping between the covers, she replayed the evening minute by minute. By the time she got to their passionate kiss, she was drifting between wakefulness and sleep. And when her dreams overtook her, they featured Simon's warm flesh, deft hands and talented mouth.

"SIMON WILL MAKE SURE I get a good jury," Tiffany whispered to Jayda. They sat side by side at the defense table. Simon stood before a potential juror, asking questions that would help him determine if the woman could be fair.

"Shh," Jayda said softly. "And you shouldn't be calling him by his first name."

"He told me to," she whispered back.

Barbara Johanson leaned forward and reached across the railing that separated the spectators' area from the lawyers' tables. She tapped Tiffany on the shoulder and gestured to her to hush. Tiffany smiled and nodded, unoffended. She'd taken to life with Simon's mother extremely well, despite the constraints of the ELMO. Jayda had been able to focus on some of her other kids once she'd grown comfortable that things would work out in Tiffany's new home. As an added bonus, she'd managed to avoid seeing Simon again. According to Tiffany, Simon had spent every evening with her and Barbara, sticking to his promise to be actively involved in the girl's care. But Jayda had scheduled her visits so they coincided with Simon's court appearances on other cases or when she knew he'd be busy filing or arguing motions for Tiffany. Until today, their paths hadn't crossed.

Her cowardice—and she had to admit that this was the appropriate word for her behavior—had been forced to take a backseat today. There was no way she could avoid seeing Simon on this opening day of voir dire, when prospective jurors would be interviewed until both the prosecution and defense were satisfied they had a jury that would fairly weigh the evidence. For Tiffany's sake, Jayda had set aside her reluctance to be near the man who was haunting her thoughts.

She looked at him now, freely gazing upon him while he was too busy to take notice. He stole her breath away. From his perfectly groomed hair to his dazzling smile, and from his precisely tailored Perry Ellis suit to his fine Italian shoes, Simon Montgomery captured the attention of everyone around him. Particularly the women. He used this extraordinary presence to his advantage as he interviewed juror candidates. Jayda observed his pattern—the boyishly disarming smile, the respectful address using “ma’am” or “sir,” the pointed questions politely phrased but intended to reveal prejudices, and then the sorrowful dismissal if the person revealed any bias. And on to the next one.

At last, the court recessed for lunch.

“I need to prepare for this afternoon,” Simon claimed. “You three go on without me and I’ll see you back here in an hour and a half.” His expression remained neutral as he made the suggestion, but Jayda sensed that he was intentionally avoiding her. Odd that she would feel hurt by that, given that she’d been assiduously avoiding him for more than a week.

“We had a good morning,” Tiffany declared. “Thank you, Simon, for making sure I get a fair trial.” She got up from her chair and hugged the seated attorney around his neck.

Once again, he looked completely flummoxed by the show of affection from his young client. Awkwardly, he patted her on the shoulder a few times, as if he hoped that would be enough to make her let go. And she did let go, only to beam at him with that full-hearted smile that was unique to Tiffany. The fact that she hadn’t had that smile beaten out of her during her time in the Social Services system seemed nothing short of a miracle to Jayda.

“Should we bring you something from the restaurant, Simon?” asked his mother.

“No, that’s okay. But don’t be late coming back. The monitoring people might send someone here to check that you’re sticking to the schedule we worked out with them for the day.”

"Go ahead, I'll catch up with you," Jayda said as she decided on the spot to confront Simon. It was time to end the standoff. Barbara put her arm around the girl's shoulders and led her away, whispering something to her that made Tiffany chuckle.

Jayda turned to Simon. "Are you avoiding me?" she asked him, shocking herself with such directness.

He looked at her with that cool lack of expression he seemed to adopt when he was guarding his intentions. "Yes," he admitted.

She sat back in her chair, stunned by his honesty. "Because of…" She trailed off, remembering their agreement not to speak of that momentary indiscretion.

He couldn't seem to help himself and gave her a half smile. "Yeah. That." His gaze dipped for a split second to her mouth, then quickly darted away. He focused on some papers lying on the table in front of him.

"This is ridiculous. For Tiffany's sake, we need to put that behind us and behave like adults."

"Easier said than done. Even for you," he said carefully. "You only come to the house when I'm at work. The truly ironic thing about that is you have to call my secretary to find out my schedule. Denise thinks we're having an affair."

Jayda could feel the heat rising to her face and knew a blush suffused her cheeks. "Not even in your dreams," she bit out, regretting the flippant remark as soon as it escaped her lips.

"Oh, *that's* certainly not true. My dreams are jam-packed with you." Simon had the decency to wince at the forwardness of his comment. "I shouldn't have said that," he admitted, but Jayda had already gotten to her feet. "Damn," he said under his breath, and now color rose in *his* cheeks.

The only reasonable thing she could do was walk away. So she did. But as she left the courtroom, she couldn't help but acknowledge that her dreams, too, had been frequented by Simon. A part of her was highly gratified that Simon was similarly tormented.

BY THE END OF THE DAY, tension had settled into Simon's neck, and no amount of rubbing the afflicted muscles seemed to help. It had been grueling to have Jayda watching him while he worked, her presence threatening his concentration every second. But he couldn't very well ask the guardian ad litem to leave the courtroom. She needed to be there, and he had to learn to control his reactions to her nearness. If only he could keep the images of her that slithered through his dreams from drifting into his mind, he would be able to cope.

As he packed up his notes at the end of voir dire, he wondered how this could be happening to him. Jayda Kavanagh was nothing special, he told himself. Just an ordinary woman. He'd been pursued by lots of extraordinary females over the years, and had slept with some of them without exerting himself all that much to get into their beds. So there was no reason whatsoever for his head to be spinning over this one woman.

Fortunately, she'd headed out the instant court had recessed for the day. Now only his mother and Tiffany remained beside him.

"Thank you, Simon," Tiffany said. She launched herself at him once more, but this time he half expected the hug and so he endured the affection more stoically than before. "I know you have to go to Massachusetts for one of your other cases in the morning. Will we see you at home for dinner?" she asked.

He opened his mouth to agree, resenting the situation they were in, but determined to stick by the agreement he'd made with his mother. But his mom spoke first.

"I think we should give Simon some time off and just have a girls' night for once. That would be kind of fun, wouldn't it? And Simon can catch up with his friends and water his plants at home or do whatever he would ordinarily be doing on a Thursday evening."

Relief washed over him. He felt exactly the way he used to on snow days when school would be closed. He was free for a whole evening.

"That would be great," he admitted. "I can get a cab to take you guys home and then pick you up for court when I get back from Boston." He'd been driving them in his mother's Honda—unlike his restored vehicle, it had full seatbelts. Barbara had held him to his promise of driving them around. But he really missed his Mustang, parked in his condo's garage.

"I can drive us home tonight and then back out when the trial starts again in a few days," his mother offered. "You just take some time for yourself." She gave him a motherly pat on the arm. "But don't get used to it." She accepted the keys to the Honda when he fished them from his pocket.

It took him another fifteen minutes or so to get them on their way to the suburbs. Standing on the sidewalk in the mid-Atlantic humidity under the hazy sun, Simon felt a little giddy at the prospect of a free night. It would be a relief to be alone in his condo, watching a sports channel in his underwear while downing a beer and potato chips for dinner. But he knew the fun would fade as soon as thoughts of Jayda entered his mind. Then he'd pace the floor of his spacious place, trying to figure out why she claimed his thoughts so relentlessly.

What he needed, what would most certainly cure him of this Jayda malaise, was to get laid. And it had been just long enough since he'd last hooked up with Megan Barstow that he should be able to call her again without raising expectations. While the two shared ambition and a mutual regard, they'd so far kept their relationship reasonably shallow. Simon had liked it well enough that way, and Megan seemed to feel the same. If she was free they'd enjoy a nice dinner, a drink or two and then a few hours in her bed, where he'd erase Jayda from his thoughts.

As soon as he arrived by taxi at home, he called Megan. Inexplicable misgivings passed over him in waves but he ignored them. Megan willingly canceled her plans and they went to dinner at the Polo Grill. Over drinks, they gossiped about the follies of people they both knew. This was what he and his friends did when they were together—they talked about the mistakes of others and this made them feel better about themselves. But tonight, the chatter seemed mean-spirited. Simon tried not to think about that too hard, because the banter was familiar and expected. And he'd always been good at it, getting big laughs, sounding witty and sure of himself. Or so he'd thought. Now he felt vaguely ashamed.

"And Greg screwed up in court last week," Megan said gleefully. "He was supposed to ask his forensic witness some specifics about the fibers found at the scene. Completely forgot." She sipped her drink delicately and the ice clattered against the glass for a moment. "That might have been forgiven, but then he showed up late for a meeting with Matt Collins, of all people." She glanced off and raised her little finger to the waiter when she caught his eye, indicating he could bring her another drink. "He was such a star for so long, I can't help but get a charge out of seeing him fall on his face."

Normally, he would have nodded, smiled and agreed that Greg was an arrogant prick. Tonight, he wondered how Jayda would see things. He found himself saying, "Maybe something else was on his mind."

"Yeah," she said, making it a multisyllable word, to imply he'd just said something entirely obvious. "His wife left him."

He gaped at her. "But they just had a baby. The kid can't be more than a few months old."

"Uh-huh. So. Maybe she found something better. Or maybe *he* did." She shrugged and went back to swirling her ice around and around.

He shifted back from the table, flummoxed. "Maybe she was sick of him focusing on his career to the exclusion of his family," he suggested quietly.

She laughed out loud, exposing her perfectly aligned, sparkling white teeth. "Like you've ever focused on anything but your career. Like you ever *would.* Greg's wife knew he was goal-oriented when she married him." Megan leaned toward him, exuding sexuality. "Just like I know that same fact about you."

Was she telling him she'd put up with it, accept it, if he were to nudge their relationship toward marriage? Suddenly he realized she had every reason to expect him to take things in that direction. He'd always known she'd be an ideal mate for someone with his ambitions—beautiful, educated, enterprising, ruthless. Married to her, Simon knew he'd attain the highest echelons of his chosen profession. Megan would accept nothing less.

He could have her. Tonight, or for a life together. She'd made that clear in many subtle ways that he'd barely noticed until just now. So many men wanted her. He would be the envy of them all. Capturing Megan would be a social and professional coup. And Glen would approve, might even reward him by making him a partner.

"Let's get out of here," he said, suddenly impatient to get to his mission for the evening. He didn't want to think about the future, only the next few hours.

She smiled knowingly, sure of herself. "Let's," she agreed. "Your place or mine?"

"Yours," he said, just as he always had. "I'll follow you home." And they left the restaurant together.

As he drove his Mustang behind her Audi TT, he had to try not to notice the pretty chalk drawing sitting on the passenger seat. Tiffany had an artistic talent beyond her years and she'd made this picture just for him. He hadn't yet decided what he should do with it. She'd said it was a picture of her happy place. And it was clearly a depiction of the home where he'd grown up. The drawing reminded Simon of where he'd come from. Whenever he looked at it, he was overcome by an inexplicable yearning to go back in time so he could live contentedly in that home once more. Yet, he was certain he didn't actually want that lifestyle again. Too prosaic, too middle-class, too ordinary. He'd always craved success and wealth and the finer things the world had to offer. He'd pursued them tenaciously.

He parked his car at the curb, glanced down at Tiffany's picture and scowled. What would Megan think of Tiffany? Worse still, what would Tiffany think of Megan?

That Megan was pompous and vain and mean-spirited, no doubt.

Suddenly, he had no interest in going inside. Not even for mindless sex.

He got out of the car and made his way to where Megan stood on the sidewalk. "I can't go in with you," he admitted, trying his best to inflect disappointment into his voice. "I just don't feel right. Maybe something I ate, maybe the flu. I don't want to take the chance of making you sick."

She pouted and cajoled and promised she would make him feel better. This just made his stomach hurt for real. What was he doing? he asked himself. Why not just go up, get laid and leave in a few hours? But his stomach knotted and he left a disappointed Megan watching from her fashionable stoop as he slipped back into the welcoming embrace of his classic car.

Halfway to his mother's home, he realized he didn't want to go there, either. They were having a girls' night and he was too restless to join them. So he drove home instead, and once there, he roamed the rooms of his apartment. He admired the antiques and looked at the paintings his art dealer had persuaded him to buy. Despite the expensive furniture and abundant trappings of blossoming wealth, the place seemed antiseptic. Sterile.

He missed Tiffany's laughter and her chatter and the detritus of youth that pervaded the home in Ellicott City, where his mom and Tiffany were having their girl time.

Worse than that, he missed Jayda's scent, the softness of her voice, the honest sensuality of her kiss. As he thought of what he should do about his attraction to her, he went through the routine of hooking his cell phone to the power cord on the kitchen counter. Then he realized he'd had it on silent during dinner and now there was a new voice-mail message. He pressed the keys to play back the call.

And there she was. "Hi, Simon. This is Jayda. Call me."

CHAPTER SEVEN

IT HAD TAKEN A LOT OUT of Jayda to simply pick up the phone and make the call. She'd wanted to make things right after the way they'd parted earlier that day. What a letdown when Simon hadn't answered, especially given that he'd be gone for a few days. His secretary had reminded her he'd be flying to Boston in the morning. By the time his voice-mail message at home had run its course, she'd had only enough steam left to leave a six-word message. She'd hung up before she remembered she hadn't given a number at which she could be reached.

She was still at work, of course. Where else would she be? Would he know that or would he expect her to be home—or hanging out with friends or maybe on a date? She laughed ruefully at the idea of a date. That was likely where Simon was, but she was working despite the late hour.

"Why are you still here?" asked Marla. She stood framed in the doorway of Jayda's tiny office, her purse slung over her shoulder and some files held close to her chest.

"I had this kid I needed to deal with. Trouble doesn't always wait for normal working hours. Didn't you already go home once?"

"Yeah," Marla said. "But I left some case notes behind

that I need for the morning." She indicated the folder in her arms. "I just dashed in to get them, so I wouldn't have to rush out of the house so early tomorrow."

"Well, I'm heading out, too." Jayda powered down her computer and picked up her purse. "I'll walk out with you."

"Which one of your kids has you worried now?" Marla asked.

"Thomas George Redman III. Funny how being named after his father and grandfather didn't help him with self-esteem. He's still behaving like a thug and trying to prove himself to the wrong crowd."

"That's what some of them do," Marla agreed. "How's Tiffany?"

Jayda instantly became wary, though she tried not to show it as she locked the office door behind her. She had avoided talking about Tiffany to Marla on purpose, in the hope the woman wouldn't realize how much time she was spending on her case. "She's fine, I guess."

"You got her out of the detention center. How'd you find a foster home for her?"

"Perseverance," Jayda said with a nonchalant shrug. As the two of them walked down the corridor, she heard the phone ringing on the desk she'd just abandoned and wished she could go back to find out if it was Simon returning her call.

"Well, you seem to have her situation in perspective," Marla said. "How's that attorney you got for her? Is he as pompous as he always seemed when he was winning all those criminal cases?"

Jayda hid her surprise. Simon wasn't pompous—far from it. He was nice. A guy who loved his mother and cared about his clients. Maybe a little arrogant, but no more than you'd expect from any trial lawyer. "He's not that bad," she said casually. "He's taking Tiffany's case seriously and that's all I really need from him."

"Well, that's good." Marla paused as they were about to leave the building. "Do not fall for that guy."

Jayda froze. "What makes you say that?" she asked.

Marla shrugged. "Because I can't help noticing how long it's been since you've gone out with someone. We've noted before that Montgomery is a handsome guy. You're human, and it's clearly been awhile since you got yourself some good… Well, you know what I mean. You might be vulnerable to his wiles."

Jayda laughed. "His wiles?"

Marla laughed, as well. As they got to the parking lot, she shook her index finger at Jayda playfully. "You know what I mean. And if you don't right now, you will soon enough. Simon Montgomery has a reputation. Be careful." With that warning, Marla walked off toward her car.

Too late.

HE'D CALLED HER AT HOME and he'd called her at work. Twice each. He'd wanted to reach her before he left for the airport. Glen Boyden had asked Simon to take personal charge of the interviews for Craig Dremmel's upcoming trial. He hated to stall Tiffany's case to make the time for this trip, but there'd been no real choice. Dremmel was a paying customer.

Jayda hadn't answered her phone or returned his messages. He logged on and sent her an e-mail, explaining where he'd be staying in Boston and telling her that he'd call her again when he got back to Baltimore. In frustration and annoyance, he packed for the trip. Then he went out for a walk around the block, even though it was the middle of the night. On his way back inside, he stopped at his car and retrieved Tiffany's picture. He brought it into his impersonal condo, dug through a desk drawer until he found a roll of tape and positioned the drawing on his stainless-steel sub-zero refrigerator. It was a little crooked and that made him smile. Maybe now he'd be able to sleep.

The bed looked lonely and he had the oddest yearning for the room he'd been sleeping in at his mother's house, the one he'd grown up in with the narrow single bed. Not once since he'd left Ellicott City for college had he felt a single pang of homesickness. Until now. What the hell was wrong with him? He thought about taking his temperature—maybe he really *did* have the flu. But he didn't own a thermometer.

Hot tea. That's what his mom had always given him to stave off insomnia during his teenage years. Celestial Seasoning's Sleepytime. He wondered if he had any of the stuff in those $20,000 custom cabinets his interior designer had talked him into because "they were the only ones worthy of such an amazing kitchen."

When he looked, he found a small, dog-eared box stashed in the back, probably given to him by his mom. It was sitting forlornly behind a coffee grinder and a lone box of granola. He lifted it out, and for the first time in this grand condo he bypassed the complicated coffeemaker, boiled water, and made himself some Sleepytime Tea. As he sat on a stool at the granite breakfast bar, the aroma reminded him of home. They should use this scent for air freshener or something, so that people could have that homey smell all the time. He breathed in deeply and thought about his life, about his mom, about Tiffany. And he thought about Jayda.

WHEN HE FLEW BACK TO Baltimore from Boston three days later, he knew it was too late in the evening to call Jayda, even though he wanted to. Besides, both her phone message and her reply to his e-mail said she wanted to talk to him in person. He briefly considered going over to her apartment, but he resisted the urge. He couldn't be sure of the reception he'd get. Hell, he couldn't even be sure she'd be there or that she'd be alone. So, he did the next best thing and drove straight out to Ellicott city to see his mother and Tiffany. He'd missed them while he'd been away, and he longed to spend some time at home. For some reason, his condo no longer merited that designation. When he got there Tiffany was asleep, but he tiptoed into her room to leave the present he'd purchased for her. Quietly, he tucked the complete DVD set of *Boston Legal* next to her in bed and she stirred. Her eyelashes lifted, and the instant she saw him her sleepy face brightened with happiness.

"You're home. That's good," she said with a huge smile. Her puppylike enthusiasm reminded him that this was what life was all about—being close to the people you love.

He nudged a lock of hair behind her ear. "I'm home," he agreed.

She caught sight of the DVD box and turned onto her back to hold it up so she could see what it was. "Yes!" she exclaimed.

"I thought about a doll but knew you'd like this better."

"Dolls are stupid," she said.

"And now you need to get back to sleep."

"Big day tomorrow," she said as she turned to her side once again, DVDs cuddled under her chin.

He'd see Jayda tomorrow, and that made it a big day.

He still didn't know what she'd wanted with him, back when she left that cryptic message on his answering machine. Curiosity had been eating away at his patience ever since. It would also be a big day because they were giving opening arguments to the jury. He looked forward to getting Tiffany's case under way. The sooner they began, the sooner she'd be acquitted and able to resume her life. As always, when he thought about what would happen to her after the trial, he wondered who would look after her. Who would make sure she brushed her teeth? Who would listen to her wax eloquent about the latest episode of *Law & Order?* The possibility that no one would do these things brought a dull ache to his chest that he didn't fully understand.

He pushed aside the vague sense of unease and got ready for sleep himself. Climbing into the narrow bed, he had his notes with him and now he reviewed his points for the jury one last time. When he turned out the light, he tried to recite his opening argument from memory, but another thought kept getting in the way—Jayda would be with him in the courtroom in the morning. Falling asleep took hours. But his dreams made the wait worthwhile.

She was there, bright and early, waiting for Simon at the defense table. "I know you tried to return my call before you left for Boston. Sorry we didn't catch up with each other," she said in a rush. "I need to tell you about something I learned about the case the other day."

Tiffany and Simon's mother were making a restroom stop, so there was no one else to focus on. Jayda just stood there, shiny and clean and as pretty as always. And she smelled great. Not a heavy perfume, but something light and delicate. He fought off the urge to inhale deeply.

"Okay," he said as he set his briefcase on the table and turned to face her. His hope that she'd called for personal reasons evaporated.

"I figured there was nothing you could do about this until you got back from your trip, so I knew it could wait. But it's good news. One of the other foster mothers from the neighborhood told the police she thinks she saw a man watching Hester Amity's house a few days before Derek Baldridge died. She isn't sure, but she thought maybe he wanted to see one of the kids. The cops don't have the manpower to follow up, but I thought we should check it out. Maybe this guy is the one who hurt Derek."

He looked at Jayda, noting the hope in her eyes. What normal social worker could retain that kind of optimism? None he knew of. He hated to see her eagerness trampled, but he had to respond honestly. He owed her that much respect.

"Jayda," he said softly. "The woman 'thinks' she saw a man—she isn't sure? She speculates he was there to see a kid. Which kid? Did she see the man with Derek? Can she give us any information so we can find this guy?" He watched the light fade from her expression and he wished he didn't always have to be so blunt. But it was part of his job—there wasn't always time to be kind.

In a more somber tone, Jayda said, "I thought you could talk to her, see if you could find out anything useful. If there's any chance of determining who really caused Derek's death, we could save Tiffany." Her features had taken on a stubborn expression.

"We'll save Tiffany," he said, trying to match her determination. "And I'll talk to the woman, if you want me to. But don't get your hopes up about this being our big break. It's not like *Perry Mason.* Cases such as this one take a long time, requiring a staggering amount of circumstantial evidence. The prosecution has to prove that Tiffany had malice, intent and means. We only have to introduce reasonable doubt into the minds of the jurors. We do that by presenting lots of possible alternatives, but there's hardly ever a smoking gun."

She nodded, looking down at her feet. Her disappointment was obvious, and Simon had the sudden urge to comfort her with a hug. Where had that come from? Maybe from all the hugs Tiffany had given him so far. She'd taught him that hugging was a powerful way to share happiness and gratitude, a method of giving comfort and showing affection. Who would have guessed he could learn something like that at his age—and from an orphaned child on trial for murder? He still found himself resisting the lesson; still tried to keep himself from feeling too much. He'd figured out long ago that losing parents at a young age could make a person shut down emotionally. While he knew he ought to work on that, learn to open up more fully to people and feelings, he'd never had much success. And keeping his sentiments in check had worked for him so far. But Tiffany was beginning to wear him down, and it scared the hell out of him.

Of course he didn't hug Jayda, and instead he focused on setting out his notes neatly. He knew his opening argument by heart, but he always kept notes handy just in case his mind went blank. Tiffany and his mother came into the courtroom then, and Jayda's smile returned as soon as she saw them. The little girl readily took her place in the chair next to Simon's.

"I want to apologize for how I acted about you going to Boston," she said, looking him directly in the eyes.

"I understand where some of that was coming from,"

he said to her. "Apology accepted." She'd thrown a full-blown tantrum when he'd told her about his trip. She'd even shattered a glass on his mother's tile kitchen floor. But Simon had decided that Tiffany needed something from him other than punishment in that moment. He'd found an inner strength that kept him from wanting to shake some sense into her. Instead, he'd scooped her into a bear hug and promised he'd be back. Over and over, he'd promised—until it became a chant. He'd hated leaving his mother to sweep up the glass while he sat in the kitchen chair with Tiffany, but he'd known the child needed him more than his mother did.

Eventually, Tiffany had calmed herself enough to whisper into his ear, "Do you *promise?*" He'd assured her again, and then she'd slipped out of his arms and gone up to her room without looking back. He remembered from his own childhood being afraid to look adults in the eye at times, thinking that they were lying to him, and he wondered if that was what Tiffany feared, too. Maybe that was why they understood each other.

"I forgot to ask you how things went on your trip," Tiffany said. Their drive to court had been filled with chat about the early episodes of *L.A. Law.*

He smiled. "Very well, thank you. My client was happy, and that's the main thing." He'd become used to talking to Tiffany as if she were an adult much of the time. Certainly, she was too smart for the simple conversation he used to think appropriate for an eleven-year old-girl.

She put her hand gently onto his shoulder for just a moment. "I'm a happy client, too. What will you focus on in your statement today?" she asked. He should have known she'd want to know about his strategy.

"Well, I'm going to focus on you," he admitted.

Her eyebrows lifted. "How do you want me to look?"

He smiled down at her. "I want you to be yourself."

She thought about that a moment. "Okay," she said. "I can do that."

"Of course you can," he said, and he ruffled her hair. She laughed and the sound went right to his heart. While he might be confused about his feelings regarding Jayda, he had fewer and fewer doubts about Tiffany these days. The girl was smart and that kept her from giving in too frequently to that angry, rebellious part of her nature that he'd been learning to deal with. And despite his years of training, he'd somehow come to believe in her innocence. Nothing seemed more important to him than winning this case.

For all his lack of experience, the prosecuting attorney, Robert McGuire, launched into a brutal opening argument that caused the jurors to eye Tiffany with real apprehension. Simon glanced to his left to see how Tiffany and Jayda were dealing with this verbal attack. Jayda held Tiffany's hand to support the young girl. Tiffany's face had gone pale, her lips were compressed and her eyes large and luminous as she stared at McGuire. Hoping to draw her attention away from the prosecutor's version of how Derek had been killed, Simon pulled his notepad onto his knees and drew a little dog. He tilted the crude drawing in her direction, hoping for a smile, but he didn't get one. She looked up at him with a softness in her eyes, however, as if she understood what he'd been attempting to do. Then she slipped her free hand into his, her small palm pressed tight against his much larger one. His heart filled with the need to protect this child, an aching imperative to keep her safe from harm. So powerful was this feeling that he nearly withdrew his hand, nearly gave in to the self-preservation instinct that urged him to remain detached.

But Jayda's steady gaze drew his attention. When he met her stare, he could see the approval in her eyes. That gave him the confidence to leave his hand in Tiffany's clasp, even though what he really wanted to do was punch the lights out of the prosecutor so the kid didn't have to listen to his accusations. Simon took heart in knowing the proof he'd promised the jury was not likely to be forthcoming. The government's case would be stitched together with circumstantial evidence, just as Simon's would have to be. But McGuire had made a certain impression and Simon was glad the defense always delivered after the prosecution. He didn't want these jurors to sit through a trial on the heels of the prejudice the prosecution had created. He'd have his chance to persuade them they wanted Tiffany to be innocent.

When the time came he gave Tiffany's hand a squeeze, then stood and faced the jury of eight women and four men, plus two male alternates. He smiled at all of them, as he had when he'd met each one during the voir dire process. He moved toward the jury box as he spoke.

"Ladies and gentlemen, Tiffany is a little girl. Nothing more, nothing less." He let that sink in for half a beat as he angled his body to induce the jurors to look toward the defense table. "She's been a victim of the tragedy surrounding this case, too. And no one can deny that a terrible tragedy has taken place. Derek Baldridge is gone, but Tiffany didn't cause that to happen. There is no evidence to suggest that she did and every indication that she couldn't have." He walked calmly over to the defense table and stood behind Tiffany, emphasizing her tiny stature in comparison to his size. "She's far too small to have been able to inflict the damage necessary to cause a sturdy boy to die. All you have to do is look at her to see that."

He approached the jury again, holding the gaze of each person who made eye contact. He talked to them about how adults may sometimes lose their temper with children and hit them or shake them until they are damaged inside. He wanted to create possibilities in the minds of the jurors about the many grown-ups who might have had access to Derek. He explained how the evidence would show them that a child can live a long time before succumbing to what's come to be known as shaken baby syndrome. The evidence would show that the children were not well supervised in Hester Amity's care and that someone might have shaken Derek days before his actual death. He wanted them to consider all the other things that could have happened to Derek, things that had nothing to do with Tiffany.

Simon knew the descriptions of these alternatives would be hard for Tiffany to listen to, and he wished he could protect her from them. But presenting other likely scenarios for Derek's death was his best hope for winning Tiffany's freedom. So he went on doggedly, painting a dark picture of foster care, pointing out that a child of Tiffany's age should not have been burdened with the responsibility of watching Derek, weaving the implication there was something amiss in the home where the two children lived. Then he circled back to the main point of his opening argument.

"Experts will tell you during this trial that it would take martial arts training or a great deal of force to kill a human being without a weapon. Tiffany hasn't had the money to get into any tae kwon do classes. And a pint-size girl isn't going to be able to produce sufficient force to do it otherwise. Physics simply won't allow for that. The prosecution would have you believe Tiffany was so angry at little Derek that she momentarily had the necessary strength." He looked over his shoulder at Tiffany, taking in her size and encouraging the jurors to do the same.

"Perhaps the prosecution will suspend Newton's second law of motion so that force will no longer be the product of acceleration and mass. Because there's not much mass when it comes to Tiffany. In fact, the evidence will show you that Tiffany and Derek were pretty close to each other in terms of weight."

He moved to the railing that separated him from the jurors and gripped it firmly, showing through the strength of his hands how critical his words were. "They were also close in terms of friendship. Derek and Tiffany played together every day for months prior to his untimely death. They were pals, despite the age difference. Tiffany is grieving the death of her friend. She's the only one who is, by the way, because Derek's parents can't be found. She was the closest thing to family the boy ever had—the two bonded in their mutual aloneness. Because Tiffany has no mom or dad, either. All she had was Derek. Her playmate, her buddy. And now he's gone."

He returned to the defense table and was gratified to see that Tiffany's eyes glistened with unshed tears. The jury wouldn't be able to ignore how bravely she struggled with her emotions. "Tiffany had no malice aforethought, which is a necessary element for the charge being pursued by the prosecution. This little girl wouldn't consider hurting anyone, least of all her friend. She certainly had no intent to inflict harm likely to result in death. But—and this is the most important point—she doesn't have the size or strength to do so. I have every confidence that you'll weigh the evidence judiciously and then give Tiffany the freedom she deserves. The first thing she wants to do is say a prayer over her young friend's grave."

Without another word, he sat down beside his client. As if on cue, a single tear slipped down her cheek. There was a moment of silence that seemed to stretch across the room. Then the judge blinked and cleared his throat as if he himself had been lost in the story Simon had woven.

"Are you ready to call your first witness?" Judge Becker asked the prosecutor.

"I am," McGuire said.

"Proceed," intoned the judge.

AT THE END OF TWO GRUELING days of listening to the government's witnesses, all saying things that were intended to implicate Tiffany in a murder, Jayda was ready to shriek with frustration. Part of her job as Tiffany's social worker was to help her cope with the bad things she was hearing. But Tiffany had shut down. All she was willing to talk about was how great things were at home, how nice Barbara was to her and how fatherly Simon seemed. She could wax eloquent about movies the family had seen together and books they'd read aloud, but she refused to speak of the prosecutor's case against her. It had to hurt. She was a smart kid and she certainly understood everything that was being said, seeing how it all would come together to paint a picture of her as Derek's killer. But she wouldn't say a word about it.

Jayda was worried. She was also jealous. Simon and Barbara and Tiffany got to spend all that quality time with each other while Jayda went home to an empty apartment. She passed her evenings thinking about her life and wondering why there seemed to be something missing. And her thoughts would inevitably find their way back to Simon, whom she'd been avoiding.

She'd been avoiding him because she was susceptible to his wiles, just as Marla had foreseen. Each day she watched him in court, vehemently defending Tiffany against the patchwork of evidence the prosecution delivered, her admiration for Simon went up another notch—along with her susceptibility.

"Since we finished early today, you and I could go out and talk to that woman who thinks she saw a man hanging around the neighborhood," Simon said to her.

"Sure. I have some things to talk to you about, anyway."

"Can you drive? I have to let my mom take the Honda to get Tiffany home. The ELMO ankle bracelet people aren't going to be understanding if she's late."

She thought of him folding his bulk into her Mini Cooper. Unlike the first time they'd ridden together in his Mustang, now she was amused instead of anxious. "Yes, I can drive," she agreed.

He gave a smile, a real one instead of the version he doled out to clients, and her heart skittered in a way that was completely inappropriate to the professional relationship they were supposed to be maintaining.

"Great," he said. "Let me get the ladies on their way home and I'll meet you at the door."

"What if I go get my car out of the garage and meet you at the curb?" She couldn't believe she was actually looking forward to having him squeeze into her tiny car beside her. It was all she could do to keep her amusement hidden.

"Deal."

In fifteen minutes, she pulled to the curb in front of him.

He continued to scan the street, as if some other car would be arriving at any moment. So she beeped. He looked down, his eyebrows shot up, and the most delightful dumbfounded expression came to his handsome face. She laughed out loud and motioned for him to hop in.

"I see I should have asked more questions before suggesting this plan."

"Too late," she said as she waited for him to slide the passenger seat all the way back and fit his large frame into the space. The car had plenty of headroom, but it probably wasn't meant to hold a guy well over six feet tall. "Fortunately for you, it's not a long ride."

He grunted and buckled up. "It's actually roomier inside than it looks from the outside."

As she pulled back into traffic she became aware of his nearness, but for a completely different reason than the first time they'd driven together. She could smell him—not a strong or overpowering scent, but a clean, masculine fragrance that raised her senses to full alert. As the memory of their shared kiss came drifting into her mind for the thousandth time, she could feel heat rising to her cheeks. Hoping he wouldn't notice her blushing, she launched into the issue she needed to address regarding Tiffany.

"Tiffany is beginning to think of you and your mother as her family."

"I know," he said simply.

"That's not good, Simon."

"Why not? She deserves to have a family, for once in her life."

"But you and your mother can't be that family."

"Why not?" he said again, stubbornly.

"Because…" She didn't really have an answer. "You just can't be."

"I can, if I want to be. She and I have a connection. We understand each other. We're better people because of each other. So why couldn't I adopt her?"

She glanced at him. He was serious—absolutely serious. He had no idea that an unmarried male would never qualify as the adoptive father of an eleven-year-old girl. "Shit," she said under her breath. But he heard her, anyway.

CHAPTER EIGHT

SIMON DIDN'T WANT TO HEAR what Jayda was saying to him as they drove together to Tiffany's old neighborhood. She made no sense. "Are you telling me that the rest of the world assumes that any bachelor who wants to be a father may be a pedophile, without any evidence whatsoever?" The very idea made him furious.

She sighed. "No, that's not what I said."

"But it's what you're implying. You said that Social Services would never let me, an unmarried heterosexual male, adopt Tiffany. But that policy is so wrong. She has no other prospects of finding a family—a kid with her record and temperament and now with a murder rap to her name, no matter how the case turns out. So the system would rather have her in an orphanage or bouncing from one foster home to another than allow her a real home with me. Besides, statistics show that having a woman in the home is no guarantee a kid won't be abused."

"Believe me, I know," she said softly, and her tone made Simon wonder again if there wasn't something in her own background she hadn't yet shared.

"Sometimes it's the women doing the abuse," he added.

She sighed. "That's true. But, Simon, be serious. Are you going to move in with your mother and raise Tiffany as your daughter?"

He hesitated. Until now, he'd been more or less arguing the point without really considering all that adoption would entail. "Honestly, I need to give it more thought. But it sounds right to me, now that I'm talking about it aloud. She's a great kid and she deserves a home. As soon as you said she was thinking of us as her family, I thought, 'Yeah, that's how it should be.'"

In his heart, he knew it would be an intense and difficult thing to see through. But he also believed that taking Tiffany into his life as his daughter would be good for her—and for him. He'd already learned so much from her about resilience and determination and hope. Every day, when she'd hugged him at the end of their time in court, he'd open a little more to her. Even when her temper got out of control, he felt he understood where she was coming from and knew he could handle it. This ability to accept someone just as she was and to welcome her gift of love had been missing from his life for as long as he could remember. Only his mother had been able to slip past the defenses he'd built around his heart during his adult life. Until Tiffany.

"The more you tell me I can't do it, the more I want to," he said.

"That's certainly no reason to make the attempt to adopt her. You'll just get her hopes up, and it'll be so painful when it doesn't work out. You wouldn't do that to Tiffany just to prove a point, would you?"

"I hope you think more of me than that. I don't want to just prove a point. I *want* to be Tiffany's dad." He stopped and thought about those words. Did he really want that, or was he simply reacting to the sadness of Tiffany's life and what she'd been through? Was he latching on to this as his next challenge just because Jayda said he wouldn't be allowed to do it? Was he trying to find meaning for his own life through Tiffany?

Jayda pulled the car to the curb and turned off the engine when they reached their destination. She sat staring ahead a moment, then reached over the console and put her hand on his. "Please think about this some more. Try to find that dispassionate attorney inside you and let him help you. I know you want to do what's best for Tiffany, but this isn't the way to accomplish that. Just win the case for her. That'll be enough."

"And what happens to her if we win?" He paused, and then dared to voice his worst fears. "More to the point, what happens if we lose?"

Jayda remained silent, not judging his rare lack of confidence. not answering the unanswerable questions. After a moment she got out and led the way to the house where their potential witness lived. She knocked on the door and a dog began to bark furiously. A scuffle could be heard inside, as someone told the animal to shut up. Finally, a harried-looking brunette responded. Children's toys were strewn across the floor behind her.

"Mrs. Karowski, I'm Jayda Kavanagh. We talked on the phone the other day. You had some information about the three-year-old boy who was killed on this street. I brought along one of the lawyers on the case, Simon Montgomery."

The woman eyed him as if he was a juicy steak she wanted to taste. She smiled and some of the years disappeared from her face. He revised his estimation of her age from forty to thirty-five or so. Needing her cooperation, he smiled back.

"Come on in," Mrs. Karowski said, stepping aside. "Don't mind the dog. He'll get over himself in a minute."

But the large animal insisted on sniffing crotches. Simon chuckled as both he and Jayda did a dog-snuffle dance until finally the dog padded away, and, with a huge sigh, threw itself onto a worn and lumpy bed in the corner. They took the seats they'd been directed to, and it crossed Simon's mind that Tiffany would probably like having a pet.

"You told me you thought you saw a man near the Amity house a day or so prior to the boy's death. Someone you didn't recognize."

"That's right," she said. She turned to Simon. "Can I get you two something to drink on this hot day? I have lemonade, if you like."

At the exact same moment, Jayda said, "No, thanks," and Simon responded, "Yes, please."

He smiled at their host while also giving Jayda's shoulder a quick squeeze. "We'd both love some lemonade, if you have some made. Thank you."

Mrs. Karowski disappeared into the kitchen of her little row house.

To Jayda, Simon whispered, "Let's ease into our questions slowly. I'd like to get a feel for how she'd be on the witness stand."

She nodded. When the drinks were served, in mismatched glasses on a 1950s-vintage tray, Jayda sipped away at hers and let Simon take the lead with their questions.

"Would you recognize the man again if you saw a picture of him?" Simon asked.

"I might," Mrs. Karowski said. "He was looking for a woman, and I think the kids were somehow a connection between him and her. I'm not sure. You got pictures to show me?" She sidled a bit closer to Simon, as if to look at photos he might produce from a pocket.

"No pictures today, but we'll work on getting some

based on the description you gave the police. Did you get the impression that he was related to any of the kids in the neighborhood?" Jayda asked.

"Might've been," she agreed. After thinking about that for a moment, she added, "He could have been one of them's father. But he wasn't looking to come back into his kid's life. He just wanted to know where some woman had gone off to."

Simon stayed there with Jayda for another twenty minutes, gathering as much information as Mrs. Karowski could give—a vague description, a possible time frame, a muddled recounting of what the man had said when he'd knocked on her door looking for kids in a foster home. Mrs. Karowski hadn't given the roaming man any information, but someone else from the neighborhood might have. Could this man be Derek's killer? Sure. The hard part would be planting that possibility in the minds of the jurors and then backing it up.

As they returned to the car, Simon asked, "Would you drive me to my mother's house? I know it's out of your way but…"

She held up a silencing hand and said, "I'd be happy to. Maybe that will give me a chance to talk to Tiffany about what she thinks of the trial. As I told you before, so far she's refused to discuss it with me. Maybe if you're there…"

Once they were on their way again, sitting close enough so that he could tell she'd used a lavender-scented shampoo that morning, he marshaled his courage and risked an invitation. "Stay for dinner. There's always more than enough when my mother is cooking."

Jayda hesitated, shifting in her seat behind the steering wheel. "Let's see how things go after we arrive."

He shrugged, pretending it didn't matter one way or the

other, but inside he felt like a rebuffed high schooler. Hiding his disappointment, he reverted to light conversation until they got to his mother's house. But when they arrived, things were not as they'd expected.

Tiffany was throwing up in the bathroom, and his mother was rubbing her back, a cup of stomach-soothing ginger tea in her free hand, waiting for a moment when Tiffany might be able to sip it.

"She has a fever, too," his mother said. "She didn't feel well on the ride home, and then she just went downhill from there. She hasn't eaten a thing since lunch."

"Do you think it's food poisoning? Should we take her to the hospital?" Simon asked.

"I don't think so. If it had been the food, she would have been sick long before this. I think she caught something that's got to come out of her one way or the other. The fever might knock it out, so let's just wait and see."

"Can I do anything to help?" Jayda asked.

"Simon isn't much of a cook, I'm afraid. So if you can fix us something for dinner, the three adults need to eat, even if Tiffany can't. I'd like to stay with her and make sure things don't get any worse." His mother attempted a weary smile. "I'm hoping she just needs some tender loving care."

"I can whip something together," Jayda said.

Simon piped up then. "I'll be down to help in a minute. I'm not completely useless in the kitchen." Just the other day he'd managed to boil water for that cup of tea. If Jayda needed hot water, he would heat it for her. Beyond that, he feared he might be out of his league. All he knew was that he couldn't bear to see Tiffany so ill, and neither could he cope with the sense of helplessness that swamped him as he brushed her hair off her flushed face, then helped her rinse out her mouth and get back into bed.

BY MIDNIGHT, JAYDA WAS sitting with Tiffany, Barbara and Simon in the emergency room of the local general hospital. The three adults had had soup and sandwiches for dinner, but Tiffany hadn't been able to eat anything or even manage tea or water. And her fever had gone up, despite a dose of Advil. Finally, the on-call doctor at Simon's boyhood pediatrics office urged them to take her to the ER. Once there, they were told to take seats along with all the other people waiting. The place was packed with men, women and children, coughing, wheezing, bleeding, moaning.

Simon had carried Tiffany into the hospital from the car. He'd seemed strong and capable with her small, listless body in his arms. Now she sat quietly on his lap. Leaning against his broad shoulders, she looked small and weak and miserable. As they waited, Jayda noticed Simon sometimes put his cheek on the girl's forehead. She figured that he was trying to check for a rise in her fever without worrying her more.

"She's really hot," he murmured to Jayda, after they'd been waiting about a half hour. "Isn't that dangerous?"

"I think they'll take her temperature soon," she answered. She didn't want him to panic, despite her own concern. Patience would be their ally at a time like this.

"Should I be insisting that someone look at Tiffany, Mom? She's so hot." Simon sounded exactly like any other worried father. Watching him care for this sick child, Jayda could see that he'd make a great dad someday.

Barbara put her hand on her son's shoulder. "We already told them her temperature was over a hundred and three when we got here. You'll have to be patient—that's all we can do. I sat in this very emergency room with you a few times and I can assure you there's nothing you can do to make things go faster."

Simon seemed to fume, but he stroked Tiffany's hair in a comforting paternal gesture.

Jayda's cell phone rang. She reached to turn the thing off, but then noticed the caller was Marla. She couldn't imagine why Marla would be calling her so late at night, unless something else had gone wrong. "Hello?"

"Tiffany's ELMO has gone off," Marla said. "According to her device, she's not in the house and no one is answering the phone there. Has she run away? Is her foster mother out looking for her? Has anyone called you?"

"Slow down, Marla," Jayda urged. "I'm with Tiffany now. We had to bring her to the emergency room. She's had a really high fever since she got home from the trial today and a local pediatrician told us to bring her to the hospital."

"Oh." And in that single syllable, Marla conveyed an awful lot of meaning. She seemed to say, 'Okay, crisis over, but you're there with Tiffany at the ER and that's a problem, since I specifically told you not to become too involved, and you must be if you're there with her at this hour.' This was followed by a deep sigh. Then she said, "I'll straighten things out for her with the home-detention people. But before I do that, I want to know why you're with that family in the middle of the night. If you were like this with all your kids, you'd be a wreck in no time."

Jayda gave Simon and Barbara an apologetic look and walked a few yards away to have it out with Marla. "I'm here for moral support. Tiffany got sick while I was at her house checking on her."

"Jayda, you're too involved with that child and that family. I have a sinking feeling you're too involved with that attorney, in particular."

Silently, Jayda thought, "You don't know the half of it," but aloud, she replied, "I'm doing my job as guardian ad litem and honoring my promises to help this foster mother who took on a kid charged with murder."

Marla let out a skeptical sigh. "I know there's more to it than that. I can hear it in your voice. You're hooked on the lawyer, aren't you?"

"Are you my boss or my mother?" Jayda regretted the words as soon as they were out of her mouth. She knew she shouldn't talk to her superior that way. Rubbing her forehead, she wished she could retract her remark. "Sorry," she muttered.

"I'm not your mother. But I see you slipping into this situation with Tiffany and her attorney, and I want to shake some sense into you. Look what happened to me. Nothing good comes of a relationship with a client."

"Please don't replace me with someone else. That would convict Tiffany before the case even goes to the jury."

Marla sighed into the phone. "You're on extremely thin ice, Jayda. I can't make any promises right now. I'll have to review the situation and do what's right for Tiffany—and for you as a member of my staff."

Jayda could find no words.

Marla added, "Go home now and get some sleep, so you'll have something to give your other cases tomorrow. I'll square the monitor issue."

"Thank you," Jayda managed to say. Her job might be in jeopardy, but Marla was there to help with the ELMO problem in the middle of the night, so gratitude seemed appropriate. Jayda closed her phone and wished she could let herself fall apart. Pressure seemed to be coming from all sides, including her own insides, where desire warred with fear. And Simon Montgomery, the tough ambitious lawyer who didn't seem to care that adopting a kid would change his life completely... This man tugged on her heart and libido in equal measure. But she couldn't let herself cry or scream or do any of the other things that might relieve some of the strain. Her presence here wouldn't be worth much if she did. So she gave herself a moment to regroup and then headed back to Simon and Tiffany and Barbara.

As Tiffany slept against Simon's shoulder, Barbara and her son stared inquiringly at Jayda. She waved her hand toward Tiffany's ankle. "The ELMO went off. We forgot to call the monitoring company, but my boss is going to take care of it."

"What else?" Simon asked.

Jayda didn't understand how he could know that something else was wrong, but she was too tired to think of a way to dismiss his question. "She wanted to know why I'm here with you. She's worried I'm getting too close."

"Are you?" he asked with a glint in his eye.

"She thinks I'm getting too close to Tiffany," she clarified.

He gave her a nod and looked down at the child asleep in his arms. "She's the kind of kid who gets into your heart." Tiffany stirred and gave a little moan. Concern flooded Simon's face and he shifted the girl into a more comfortable position.

Jayda wondered what would happen if Marla could see her now or look into her thoughts. Because watching him take such gentle care of Tiffany made her ache with tenderness for the man. She wondered if this taste of the downside of parenting would persuade him to give up on trying to adopt Tiffany, but she suspected the ER visit wouldn't dissuade him. He was stronger than that. And far more caring than she'd have thought when they'd first met.

A woman called for Tiffany to be brought to an examination room. All three adults got up, Simon carrying Tiffany, but then Jayda hesitated. She wasn't Tiffany's caregiver, only her social worker.

"I'll stay here. If you need anything, just come and tell me," she offered.

Barbara and Simon trooped through an automatic door with Tiffany and Jayda stood for another moment, feeling bereft and wondering if Marla might not be correct about the dangers of bonding with a client.

But just when she'd seated herself again, prepared to wait it out with the Montgomerys in the hope of being of use as the night wore on, Simon came back to the waiting area looking like a storm cloud. He was empty-handed and obviously furious.

"They sent me out," he growled. His voice was ominously low. Jayda could feel the fury emanating from him as he approached her. "I'm nothing but her lawyer, not a relative or caregiver of any kind, at least in their eyes. My mother has to go it alone. They wouldn't let me stay, even to support my mom. Patient confidentiality, they said."

"I'm sorry," Jayda said, although she knew her sympathy wouldn't help. "Let's go over here for a moment." She led him to an alcove where they could have a little privacy. The lights outside were nearly as bright as daylight. An air conditioner hummed softly above their heads. "Your mother will be fine, and so will Tiffany," she told him.

"But I should be in there with them," he snapped. "I do almost as much of the care-giving as my mother does these days." He paused and glared at the parking lot.

"When I left, Tiffany begged me not to go. She reached out for me and started to cry."

Jayda ached for him. "She sees you as a parent." Left unsaid in this difficult moment was the concern she'd already raised. Tiffany was too attached to him and she had unrealistic expectations concerning his role in her life, wanted more from him than he would be able to give.

Simon remained silent, staring out into the night. Jayda could feel him withdrawing, putting up walls, trying to go it alone—as was his nature, she'd come to realize. But then he opened up, just a little.

"I'm going to talk to Tiffany—make sure she agrees—then file the documents to adopt her. I don't care how long it takes or how hard everyone makes it for me. We have a bond, the two of us. I plan to make that bond official."

Jayda sighed and stared at her feet. Clearly, this hospital incident hadn't dissuaded him from wanting to become a parent. In fact, it'd had the opposite effect. All at once, she understood that this hospital experience had changed *her* mind rather than his. If she couldn't talk him out of it and if Simon applied for the adoption, she would have to do everything in her power to help him. Despite her belief that he wouldn't be approved, supporting his attempt would be the right thing to do. Tiffany deserved a father like Simon.

"You're a good man, Simon," she said. "There aren't many like you."

He looked at her as if this response stunned him. Then he gave her a sloppy half smile, and his eyes went soft. "That's good to hear from you," he said. Reaching out, he pulled her to him, hugging her close without holding her too tightly.

Her first reaction was one of gladness that he'd reached out to her physically. And she realized she could relax in his embrace—she didn't feel threatened in the least. He rested his chin on the top of her head and simply held her. She liked that. A lot. There were no expectations here, no sense that this was the prelude to something more intimate. They just leaned against each other, sharing strength. Jayda could hear Simon's heartbeat as she pressed an ear against his chest. It sounded strong and reliable. She thought perhaps she could get used to listening to it.

For the first time in her adult life, she began to realize it might be nice to have another person upon whom she could rely. Someone who would equally rely on her. Now she began to see why women longed to find a man like Simon to love them. For once, she had a sense of that same longing.

But Simon was the wrong man. Tiffany's lawyer was the last person Jayda should be yearning for. She'd worked hard to shake herself loose from her past, and being with Simon reminded her of it too frequently. While she could stand with him for now and help him through this frightening, frustrating night, she would have to dismiss the fantasies about there ever being anything more between them. Those were the rules of her life, the ones that allowed her to pretend she was normal.

SIMON MANAGED TO PERSUADE the judge to suspend the trial for a week while Tiffany recovered from the stomach flu that had taken her small body by storm. She'd spent a day in the hospital, and then she'd been sent home with instructions to remain in bed, drinking lots of fluids to rehydrate. It had seemed like a miracle that Simon's mother hadn't succumbed to the illness, as well. He'd discovered that Jayda was like him and almost never got sick.

But it hadn't been an idle week for any of the adults. Though Jayda had come out to the house to visit several times, she'd also had to go to work and try to find the time to track down more information on the mysterious man who'd been in Tiffany's neighborhood just before Derek's death. Simon had put in some time on his other cases.

He'd also talked to Tiffany about making the two of them into a family.

"What would you think of me putting in the papers to adopt you?" he'd asked her one afternoon. He'd just finished reading aloud to her as she snuggled in her bed, still recovering.

Tiffany grinned widely. Yet her gaze held a hint of wariness—as if she couldn't quite accept what he'd said. "I…I…" she stammered, at a loss for words for the first time since he'd met her.

"I can't promise Social Services will approve—I'm not exactly ideal father material. But I'd like to try. If you want me to."

The shine that came to her eyes spoke volumes about how she felt. "What if I'm convicted?" she asked.

He shifted to sit on the edge of her bed and captured her gaze. "I'm going to do everything in my power to ensure that doesn't happen. And no matter what, I'd like your permission to make you my daughter."

A tear slipped from one of her luminous brown eyes. "I think you'd make the best dad ever for a kid like me," she whispered and she sat up to wrap her small arms around his neck, administering one of her world-famous hugs. "I would try hard to be a good daughter," she added softly.

Was she afraid fate would snatch this chance away if she spoke of it too loudly? As he hugged her back, he found himself hoping she'd learn that fate wouldn't be that cruel—to either of them.

Then there'd been the talk he'd had with the partners

at his law firm, who'd expressed concern about the time he was spending on Tiffany's case, at the expense of his paying clients.

Glen Boyden had set the tone for that meeting, taking some of the wind out of Renauld Canter's sails. "How are things going, Simon? Keeping up with your caseload?"

"Yes," Simon answered, even though he knew a few things had slipped through the cracks as he focused on Tiffany's trial. "Craig Dremmel seems pleased." This was to remind the partners that he was the one who had brought that hugely wealthy client to the firm.

"If everything is under control, Mr. Montgomery, why have I been receiving complaints about you not showing up for meetings or returning calls?" Canter glared at him. "Your secretary can't answer legal questions, and you're never in your office anymore. Nor are you reachable by phone."

He gave his nemesis a cold stare. "I've been in court." But it was true he'd missed some critical meetings recently, to his secretary's horror. Denise had been stunned when he'd asked her to reschedule clients on the day Tiffany had been in the hospital. He hadn't even considered leaving Tiffany and his mother there alone. And he'd been allowed to remain in the hospital room with her, once she'd been admitted.

Canter's voice rose a few notes. "On the pro bono case, wasting valuable attorney time on a client who won't be paying a dime."

"That's right. And I believe it was your case to begin with. One of your two pro bono cases for the year. But you weren't available and you passed it over to me. Was I misinformed about your wish for me to take this on as a favor to you?"

Glen piped up. He'd been a lawyer for forty years, and now that he ran the place he'd lost his taste for pissing contests among the members of the firm. "I asked Simon here just to see how things were going." He turned to Simon. "I'm sure you'd let us know if you had any scheduling issues or problems with your workload."

"Everything is going fine," he lied. But things were not fine. Now that he'd decided to adopt Tiffany, he realized some practical changes would be necessary. He would need a different place to live, for one thing. If he had a home more suitable for a family, that might stand in his favor with Social Services. Living with his mother wasn't the answer. He had to demonstrate that he could deal with Tiffany alone, father to daughter. How would he do that if he continued to log his usual hours at work? He couldn't. His dreams of making partner were in direct conflict with the consuming need to keep Tiffany safe, to provide her the home she deserved.

It was all Simon could do to leave the office suite without giving Renauld Canter the evil eye or the universal gesture for "up yours." But instead he left composedly, head high. He tried not to think about the hours he'd be spending on Tiffany's case in the days ahead, how many paying clients he'd have to reschedule, how difficult it was going to be for Denise to cover for him with the partners. His days might very well be numbered with this law firm unless he could figure out how to be in two places at once for the next few weeks.

Regardless, he needed to make an appointment with a real-estate agent to arrange selling his condo and buying a family-oriented place. With the equity from his current home in the heart of the city, he'd be able to pay cash for a house in the suburbs. Maybe he'd even have some funds left to put aside, in case things completely went south at work. He'd need a nest egg to start up his own firm, if it came to that.

Would it? Could he so easily give up his dreams of becoming a partner and living an affluent, high-powered life? He took a cab to his condo and went straight to the parking garage, getting into his Mustang and allowing the roar of the engine to soothe his nerves. Then he set out for a drive, leaving behind all the other things he should have been doing in favor of accelerating onto the highway, feeling the power of the magnificent machine. The experience provided no answers, but he felt better for having done it.

"YOU TWO HAVE BEEN WORKING too hard," Barbara said to Jayda as dinner simmered on the stove. Simon stood in the door frame listening, and Jayda was profoundly aware of his presence just behind her. The man seemed to exude some kind of electric current that made everything inside her shimmer with interest.

"You've been working hard, too, taking care of Tiffany," she replied.

"But you've both been trying to hold down jobs and you've also been coming here night after night to spell me. And, anyway, Tiffany is much better."

"Yes, I am," Tiffany said from the kitchen table, where she drank hot tea and nibbled toast. "And I don't ever want to be that sick again."

The adults nodded their heads in agreement.

"So now that Tiffany is better and we've had a few restful nights, I want the two of you to go out and have some fun. Don't think about work—don't think about anything serious. Go to dinner, go to a movie. Anything! Just go out and have a good time. Unwind."

Simon straightened up as Jayda turned to see his reaction to this command. For a man who always seemed to know exactly what to do and say, he didn't appear to be all that sure of himself. He just stared at her, waiting.

"Simon has other friends I'm sure he'd rather go out with," she suggested, even as she hoped he'd insist that wasn't the case. All the while in the back of her mind, the part of her that always followed the rules kept shouting, "Don't go, don't go, don't go!"

"Not really," he said. "But if you don't want to, I'd understand."

Say it would be best to keep things professional, she told herself firmly. Say you just can't do it. "Honestly, going out for an evening sounds really nice." No, no, no! She chided herself for being so weak. Marla would have a fit if she found out Jayda had gone on a date with Simon.

"Well, that's settled, then," Barbara said. "Be gone, the two of you."

Simon smiled. He was still wearing his suit from his day at work and Jayda felt extremely underdressed by comparison.

"I'll have to go home first and change into something else," she said.

"You look great the way you are," Simon and Tiffany said together. From the corner of her eye, Jayda saw Barbara nudge Tiffany to silence.

"Still, I don't get to dress up much for dinners out, so I'd rather change."

In a voice that seemed full of barely repressed sensual promise, Simon said, "Let's go to your place, then. You can drive, so I can leave my mom's car here for her. Okay?"

"Okay," she said. There was no hint in her voice that her heart pounded furiously as they set off.

CHAPTER NINE

SIMON WAITED IN THE LIVING room while she changed. He paced the floor, remembering when he'd been in Jayda's apartment the first time—remembering their kiss. He knew he shouldn't think about that. Knew he ought to hold to his promise to forget it had ever happened. But he couldn't do it. And when Jayda walked out of a back room, dressed for the evening, he swallowed hard and stared.

"Too much?" she asked.

"No," he managed to say. "No, you look great. Perfect."

She wore a simple black dress with short sleeves and a neckline that scooped delicately below her throat. The hem hovered just above her knee. No extra skin on display, and yet the style and fit suited her figure so well, his heart began to race.

"Should we go?" she asked with a guileless smile. She seemed to have no appreciation of what she was doing to him.

"Yes, let's go." If they were on their way, maybe he'd be able to think about something other than what he wanted to do with the body waiting for his touch beneath that little black dress.

They went to Luigi's, a place Jayda chose, in Baltimore's Little Italy. Simon had never been to this tiny hole-in-the-wall with its checkered tablecloths. It wasn't the kind of restaurant he was used to, but the food was excellent. And the company was even better. Simon couldn't help but notice the differences between this meal and the last one he'd had in the company of a woman. His dinner with Megan had been charged with negativity. With Jayda, he talked about ways to help children in need, about favorite breeds of dogs, about Tiffany, about his mother. It was good for him to be reminded that he was capable of having a good time that didn't involve cutting anyone down.

Over dessert he asked about her family.

"My father's dead," she said with forced nonchalance.

There was a story behind that, but he sensed she might not readily talk about it. "I'm sorry."

She shrugged. "I was little. I don't even remember him."

Gently, he asked, "And your mother?"

Her gaze slanted off for a moment, then slid back to her plate. "I don't really talk to her very often. We never got along that well. She's busy with a whole new life in northern Maryland."

He thought about how hard it must be for a caring woman such as Jayda to be estranged from her mother. "When was the last time the two of you talked?"

"Hmm, a long time. But she called me on my birthday and left a message on my answering machine. That was nice, I guess." She shrugged again, and gave a small, wistful smile.

He ate a few bites of the chocolate confection he'd ordered, sipped his coffee and waited. If she was going to talk to him about her past, he had to leave some space for her to do so. What surprised him was realizing how much he wanted her to confide in him.

"I didn't have the greatest childhood, though nowhere

near as bad as some of the kids' I deal with in my work," she volunteered. "My father was gone and my mother distracted. I never had much luck getting her to listen to my problems. Now that I'm older, I can see she had so much on her own plate, she didn't have anything left to deal with me. But kids need help with issues sometimes, right?"

"Yes. Kids need help," he agreed. "They need guidance and love. Parents have to pay attention, and if they don't, things can go badly." The lawyer in him wanted to ask straight out if something had gone badly for her. But he resisted, sensing she shouldn't be rushed.

She smiled and waved a hand dismissively. "Well, I turned out okay in the end, I guess. Can we talk about something more cheerful?"

They did. And Simon marveled at the way she made him laugh, considering the dismal condition of his legal career and the lousy odds on adopting Tiffany despite everything he was willing to give up to prove his worthiness. The waiter brought the check and Jayda reached for it.

"You're not going to insist we split the bill, are you?" he asked, picking up the tab. "Because I'm still employed at one of the most prestigious law firms in the tristate area. I can handle the cost of a meal." And besides, he might not be able to treat someone else to dinner for much longer. Funds were likely to become tight if he maintained his current course. Renauld Canter would make sure the firm's senior partner saw the wisdom of cutting Simon loose. "Besides, you cooked for me at your house and I want to reciprocate."

A blush crept into her cheeks and he knew she must be recalling that night in her apartment. His gaze dipped to her mouth as he thought of that kiss, too.

"Thank you," she said, and then took a sip of ice water.

He made himself look away, but he couldn't stop thinking about whether he'd be able to kiss her again before the night ended. "So I'm not ready to go home yet," he said. "I know a club near here—there's a dance floor and decent music. Come with me." He almost reached across the table to take her fingers in his own, as if this were a real date and he could persuade her with his touch. But instead, he waited to see what she would say.

As if she couldn't quite make her voice work, she nodded. When they stood up to weave their way between the closely placed tables, he had the urge to rest his hand on the small of her back, as if to guide her. He would have done that with Megan, and the contact would have begun their dance toward ending the evening in bed together. But this was Jayda, and he had no right to expect anything from her. He kept his hands to himself.

Yet all the way to the club, he kept thinking about getting her to slow dance with him and how good it would feel to hold her. Somewhere in the back of his mind he knew he was playing with fire, that he shouldn't be trying to indulge his unanticipated desires regarding this particular woman. But he couldn't seem to stop himself.

SHE HADN'T WANTED TO TALK about her childhood, though she supposed it would have helped to confide in someone. The fact that Simon hadn't pressed her to tell her story said a lot for his sensitivity. Who would have guessed that a go-get-'em guy like Simon could also be patient and considerate? Then again, no one would have expected him to want to adopt an eleven-year-old murder suspect, either.

"I put in the paperwork a few days ago," he said when she asked him about the adoption. "I know it'll be an uphill battle, but I'm hoping the powers that be will see that I'm her best chance for a normal life."

She nodded and sipped her drink. The musicians had been on a break when they'd arrived, but now they came back onto the stage. She turned to watch and applauded with the other patrons, but her attention remained fixed on the man seated next to her at the little cocktail table.

"Do you like to dance?" he asked as he leaned close to be heard over the first chords from the stage. Her heart gave a little flutter and all she could do was smile and nod.

He stood up and put out his hand. She placed her palm against his and got to her feet. "But we'll lose our table," she said, and then immediately regretted the words. They revealed too much about her tendency to cling to safe and familiar paths.

Without hesitation, he took off his suit jacket and placed it over the back of her chair. "Usually the clientele here will respect a sign that a seat is taken," he assured her. "Otherwise, no one would get up to dance and what fun would that be?"

Indeed. No fun at all. Simon led her to the dance floor. But instead of letting her go so they could move independently to the beat of the music, he drew her closer, nearly flush against his lean torso. Looking down, he cocked an eyebrow inquiringly. And she didn't pull away—even though she knew it would be safer to keep some distance between them.

He was a natural dancer and capable of making her body move with his, a first-rate dirty dancer. The titillation, the danger, the sheer sexuality of the movements made her a little light-headed. And hot. If he'd offered to take her home to bed right then, she would have accepted on the spot. But instead he led her back to their table and ordered her another wine spritzer. She fought back disappointment even as a voice inside her whispered that it would be emotional suicide to involve herself with the likes of Simon—no matter what her libido wanted. She sipped her drink, wondering how she was going to extricate herself from the situation. Clearly, she ought to find a way to go home alone without offending him.

And then suddenly a half dozen people walked up to their table, surrounding them.

"Simon Montgomery! Where have you been these past few weeks?" said one woman as she leaned in and placed a red lipstick smooch on his cheek.

"He's been driving his career into the toilet with his pro bono case," one of the men replied. "What are you doing with that loser, Simon? You know better than to let your other cases slip." The man's voice carried a note of censure, but there also seemed to be an expectation that Simon would respond with something sly and witty, as if the great young defense attorney must have something planned, something that would propel his career forward despite appearances to the contrary.

Jayda sat completely still, watching Simon. She hadn't realized until this moment that he'd jeopardized his career for Tiffany's case. Why would he do such a thing?

"I'm just fine, folks. You should know better than to worry about me." He didn't look at the newcomers as he spoke—instead, he looked into Jayda's eyes. His smile had a tautness to it, and Jayda couldn't help but feel that there might be something to his friends' concern. In the next moment, however, she realized his tension might stem from something else.

"Come dance with me, Simon," urged one of the

women. She wriggled closer to him, apparently confident he wouldn't decline.

"Not this time," he said with a chill smile. "I'm with someone." To Jayda he said, "These are some of my professional colleagues."

The eyes of his friends turned to look at her, as if they'd only just realized she was there. And it dawned on Jayda that they'd been behaving as if she didn't matter. She wasn't one of them and perhaps that made her unworthy of notice in their eyes. No wonder Simon had gone rigid—his friends had no manners.

"Who are you?" one of them asked.

To his credit Simon didn't respond for her, although she could tell he was tempted to do so. "I'm Jayda Kavanagh," she said. There were too many of them to make handshakes feasible, so she kept her fingers wrapped around her glass. "I'm working with Simon on that pro bono case."

As if they comprised a single organism, the group pulled back slightly in unison. Did they realize how insulting they'd been so far? As one, they returned to ignoring her presence and spoke only to Simon.

"Canter is gunning for you, Simon. You need to show Boyden you're not slacking."

"Are you planning something? Do you have some strategy going that'll blow everyone away?"

"Did you hear about Greg? He screwed up royally. What a loser."

"C'mon, Simon, dance with me. This is my favorite song."

And quietly, one of the females said to another, "Is he really with her?"

Simon let out a little sigh. "Let's go," he said as he stood up and reclaimed the jacket he'd slung across the back of the chair.

Though this would be a good way to get herself out of any more dangerous fantasies about Simon and where the evening might be heading, Jayda didn't really want to go. She wished his friends would go instead. But she could see that wasn't going to happen. So she got up, too.

"Nice meeting you," she said to the lawyers, even though it hadn't really been all that nice. Interesting, however, to see what Simon's friends were like. Very interesting.

"Simon, you're not leaving, are you? We just got here." This said as if the fun couldn't possibly have started until they'd arrived, so why would anyone leave now that they'd made their appearance? Jayda almost laughed at the arrogance.

"You're gonna get yourself fired, Simon. Canter will jump at any excuse to bring you down," one of his friends said ominously as he held Simon's sleeve to make him listen.

"You should worry about your own career, Jason, and leave mine to me." It sounded like a warning, and Jason immediately stepped back.

Jayda followed Simon out of the club, glad for his wide shoulders, which cleared a path for her through the crowd.

"They're friends," he said, the minute they were buckled into the seats of her Mini Cooper. "I know them from work and sometimes we hang out together. Or we used to, when I had time. I'm sorry if they seemed rude. They're not used to seeing me with someone like you."

"Someone like me?" What, exactly, did *that* mean? She just sat there, waiting to hear what else he would say.

"You're very different from them," he said. "I'm sure you could see that. You're a lot nicer, for one thing. You're a much better person than any of the rest of us."

And just like that, with those few words, the charge of excitement returned. Only now, the intensity seemed to have been magnified a thousand times. She wanted Simon to touch her, kiss her, transform her into the passionate woman she knew she could be. Right here, right now. Her heart rate and breathing raced as she leaned toward him seductively.

His warm hand lifted to her cheek, brushed back her hair, caressed her throat. She felt the quiver of desire running through him as he touched her. But then he drew back, and on a shuddering breath, he said, "Drive home, Jayda."

Her hand shook ever so slightly as she put the key into the ignition and her eyes stung. How could she have misread the signals from him so completely?

As the car began to move, Simon added, "When we get there, you can decide whether you should invite me up to your apartment. If not, I'll take a cab home. But I'll warn you now, if you invite me in, I'm not leaving for a while."

Relief—she hadn't misunderstood at all. Then panic. He'd put the burden of deciding the outcome of this tantalizing evening squarely on her shoulders. She knew what she wanted to do, knew what she should do, and she wished he would take the responsibility of deciding away from her by sweeping her off her feet. And yet she realized that if he behaved that way, she'd likely find herself freezing up until she couldn't respond to him. She didn't want that to happen again. Not with Simon. So she gripped the steering wheel firmly and drove the car, wondering all the while what she would decide once they arrived at her apartment.

SIMON GOT AS FAR AS THE doorway of Jayda's apartment before it sank in that she'd invited him up. When she fumbled with her keys, he lifted them from her fingers, swept her into his arms and kissed her the way he'd been wanting to. Sensuously. Deeply. Somehow, he also got the right key into the lock. The door opened and they nearly fell inside. She kicked the door shut as she lifted her mouth to his again. Paradise.

She tasted like wine spritzer and Simon wanted to kiss her all night long. At the same time, he had to have more. While part of him tried to recall the location of the bedroom, his body urged her toward the nearest wall so he could press his torso against hers and intensify the excitement for both of them. He liked the sounds she made, the little moans. He wanted to find out if her heart beat as rapidly as his, so he slid kisses along her throat, searching for the tender pulse point he knew was there.

"Wait," she murmured. But at least she sounded aroused when that completely undesirable word emerged.

"Why?" he asked, continuing to tease her earlobe with his tongue.

"Because, I…I…" She pushed gently against his shoulders, and after a moment he had sense enough to give way.

"We shouldn't be doing this, is that it?" He'd warned her not to invite him in if she wasn't sure of what she wanted from him. And it seemed clear that her arousal matched his own. "I used to think we should keep a professional distance, too. But now I just want you." He waited, hoping.

She gave a shuddering sigh, music to his ears. "Bedroom, that way," she said, pointing. "Just give me a minute to…" And then she disappeared into the bathroom.

Triumphantly, he went to wait for her.

CHAPTER TEN

JAYDA LOOKED AT HERSELF in the bathroom mirror and saw the panic lurking just beneath the surface. How unbearably frustrating to want something so much and yet feel choked by it, too.

"But you're not being choked," she told herself firmly. "Simon would never hurt you."

She wasn't sure she entirely believed that. He could hurt her so easily. He might not even mean to do it, but the pain would be there all the same. If he understood how vulnerable she was right now, he might take extra care. But she couldn't confess her issues to him. Not now. Maybe never. Her mother's voice was still too clear in her memory, deriding her for making too much of what had happened to her. Jayda knew she shouldn't listen, knew that confiding in Simon was the right thing to do. But she couldn't make herself do it. Not yet. Maybe someday.

"He wants you. You want him. Maybe that'll be enough. So get in there and get through this," she thought. It wasn't as if she hadn't been to bed with a man before. She and Brian had enjoyed a healthy sex life until he'd begun to focus on his career. He'd left her for a transfer to Chicago and he hadn't even seemed too broken up about it. But they'd had a reasonable amount of sex while the relationship had lasted.

Still, sex with Simon would be something altogether different, she felt sure. Someone like Simon wasn't likely to let her retain control, the way Brian had. And that scared her to death. Her theory was that if she could let Simon do his thing sexually—get it over with, so to speak—then her fears might abate. Exposure to your phobias could sometimes be a cure. And no one fit her phobia better—Simon was dominant, masculine, physically intimidating. Inexplicably, those were the characteristics that had attracted her to him. She wondered if he might be the only man who could help her overcome her past.

Besides, if they could get through this one night together, there might be opportunities in the future to adjust their lovemaking to better meet her secret desires.

"Okay, then. Get your game face on. Once we get over this first hurdle, things will be easier." She stripped off her dress before she could change her mind and headed to her bedroom wearing only her sexy bra and panties, just in case this turned out to be the night she'd both dreaded and longed for. It was gratifying to hear him draw in an appreciative breath, when he saw her standing in the doorway.

Though she quaked with anxiety, she also felt a surge of desire as she admired Simon's physique as he stretched across her bed. He'd kept on his pants, but the jacket, shirt and tie were gone, leaving a wealth of hard, naked muscle for her to enjoy. Shoes and socks had also disappeared and he seemed eager to do her bidding. She wished she could keep him exactly as he was, prone and pliable. But he wouldn't stay that way for long. Minutes from now, he'd be over her, dominating her, pressing her down and taking command. She shuddered.

"You're cold," he said. "Come let me warm you up." His smile was inviting, sensual.

So she plunged ahead with her plan. She'd get through it. She might even like it, if she could just keep her mind in the present.

She went to him, and the sensation of his warm hand skimming across her back and thighs felt good. He let her straddle him and that was good, too. When he arched his back and pressed his erection against her, that felt so wonderful she simply gave herself over to the sensation. She rocked her hips tentatively, and felt an unpremeditated moan slip from her lips.

"Yes," he whispered, and his hands on her body didn't seem to be holding her too tightly. He just guided her gently, easing her motion into a rhythm they could both enjoy. After a moment, he slid his palms along her rib cage, tightened those sexy abs to lift himself so he could reach behind her, unhook her bra and strip the confining thing away from her breasts.

"Yes," he said again, and he gazed upon her with admiration.

Her hands pressed to his shoulders, Jayda eased him back against the bed again. He went willingly, then smiled when she took his hands in hers and placed them against her chest, inviting him to touch. He was more than happy to accommodate. And as he stroked and teased her breasts and urged her body into full-blown arousal, she began to think that this might be a more fulfilling experience than she'd had any reason to hope for. If he would just stay where he was, let her do what needed doing, keep his testosterone from taking over…

"I need to kiss you," he said, and then in one fluid motion he had her beneath him on the bed.

His body covered hers and he took charge. And although she'd wanted that kiss, desired his hands on her skin, needed to feel him inside her, the magic evaporated for her. She told herself it would be over soon and that she should just endure it. And she even participated in speeding things along. Unfortunately for her plan, Simon wasn't a stupid man. Nor was he an insensitive one.

"Tell me what you like," he asked more than once.

"I like this," she said. A half truth. "I want you." And that part was true, even if the dynamics were all wrong at the moment.

"I need to please you," he insisted.

She couldn't understand how he could possibly know she wasn't deep in the throes of pleasure, despite her performance. In desperation, she told him the truth. "Just do it," she murmured, and she wrapped her legs around him so he'd be sure she meant it.

"Not unless you're with me," he said, stubborn man. Then he shifted his body over hers, slipping down, clearly intent on using his mouth to bring her to climax.

"Don't!" she called out, her resignation and despair came out with that word. She couldn't help it.

Simon stopped moving instantly and they remained motionless for what seemed an eternity. Completely frustrated, she managed to squirm out from under him and then bolted from the bed. "I'm sorry," she said. "I can't. I just can't."

His stunned expression pained her. "I'm sorry," she said again as she turned away and pulled a T-shirt over her head. "I'm *so* sorry. I thought I could go through with it, but I can't." Tears burned her eyes, and she struggled to blink them back.

"But obviously you want to," he protested with utter bewilderment in his eyes. "You can't fake those physical reactions. You just weren't making any progress. If you'd only tell me what you like..."

"I can't." Oh, this was so complicated. And still she couldn't bring herself to explain. She was nowhere near ready to risk confession. "It's not you," she tried. "It goes way back. I thought I was better—I thought I could do this." Whether she liked it or not, tears were now streaming from her eyes and down her cheeks. She swiped at them impatiently. She shouldn't be feeling sorry for herself when she was the one who'd wronged *him.*

Simon looked at her for a long moment while the muscles in his jaw flexed and his entire body seemed to tremble with frustration. She deserved every ounce of his displeasure. But after a moment, a measure of real softness came into his eyes.

"Tell me," he whispered. "Tell me what happened to you." He sat at the edge of the bed, but he didn't encroach on her space. Did he sense how close to shattering she'd been?

"I'm so sorry. I shouldn't have used you this way. I shouldn't have tried to…to…" She had no way to complete that sentence, so she resorted to covering her face with her hands. But that gesture didn't hide the shame she felt.

"Hush, Jayda," he said softly. "Don't do this to yourself."

Then he was there right in front of her, easing his arms around her, holding her tenderly, whispering soothing nonsense. She wept against his shoulder, soaking the shirt he'd slipped back on. She mourned the innocent childhood that had been stolen from her by the unwanted actions of her mother's brother, regretted wasting time on relationships with such weak men and silently castigated herself for her ill-conceived scheme to deal with her past by bedding Simon. She'd used him, and she knew it and he knew it. How could she have made such a mess of things?

"I wish you'd talk to me," he said, drawing in a breath and releasing it slowly. "But if you're not ready, I won't push you. At the same time, I'm not going to leave you alone when you're this upset. Let's just sit together in the living room. Would that be okay with you?"

She managed to nod. The last thing she wanted was for him to leave. She would never be able to face him again if he did. And if he stayed awhile, maybe she could bring herself to explain. She owed him that, didn't she?

He made her tea, brewing something soothing from a box that had been in the back of her cupboard since she'd moved in six years ago. When he saw that she was shaking, he wrapped a blanket around her. Switching on her TV, he found a chick flick on the movie channel. He settled in beside her and didn't ask a single question.

After awhile, she realized he'd slipped his arm around her shoulders. She found herself leaning on him, comfortingly cradled against his side. Oh, to be held this way—and after what she'd done to him. She felt forgiven, even though she hadn't yet found the courage to tell him why his hopes for a night of lovemaking had been dashed so abruptly. Now, if only she could find a way to forgive herself.

By the end of the movie, drowsiness had set in and her eyelids began to close. She felt his body relax, too, and she wondered if he'd be kind enough to stay the night with her, sleeping alongside her in this blissfully peaceful state they'd unexpectedly reached.

He clicked off the TV but continued to hold her close. In a hushed voice, he said, "I've never had an experience like this before and I don't know what I should do or say. I'm not especially known for my patience. But somehow I can't help feeling you're worth the wait." He paused, then even more softly he added, "Just tell me if there's hope. I need to know I have some chance with you."

The vulnerability in his words shifted something inside her. "I want there to be hope for us, Simon," she murmured. "But I have to figure out a few things, and I can't expect you to wait until I've done that."

"Maybe we could go slowly and just see what happens," He kissed her forehead. "Will you let me stay the night, just holding you?"

She nodded and deepened her hug. Maybe she didn't deserve him, but she'd cling to the chance he had just offered. Loving him as she did, she had no other choice.

SIMON AWOKE GRADUALLY, but he knew he'd have an aching shoulder even before his eyes were open. He'd slept in an awkward position with Jayda nestled beside him all night long. It had been worth the kink in his muscles because she'd said there was hope for them—or at least she wanted there to be hope. That would have to be enough for now. It bothered Simon that she wouldn't tell him exactly what had happened in her past, but he had to believe she would confide in him eventually. For the first time in his life, he would practice patience. He wondered if he'd be able to manage it, and the thought of failing weighed heavily on his mind.

Jayda's expression in sleep was relaxed, youthful and carefree. In complete contrast to her tension of the night before. Simon wished she could be like this with him all the time. He tried not to move, didn't want to waste this peaceful moment, but then she woke abruptly and sat up. He was cold without her nestled against him. "Good morning," he said.

She turned and her eyes reflected surprise, then almost

a smile, then anxiety returning as memories of the night came back to her. "I'm so sorry," she said, and looked away, embarrassed.

"Don't be. I spent the night with a beautiful woman who promised me there's a chance for us. What more could a man ask for?" He pulled himself up from the depths of the comfy sofa. Giving his muscles a tentative flex, he headed for the kitchen. He had a burning need for coffee.

She followed Simon in search of caffeine and they worked together in silence. She pointed to where the ground coffee was kept, and Simon got the automatic pot going. She set out two mugs, and he found cream in the fridge. As the coffee brewed, Simon watched Jayda lean against the countertop facing the sink, deep in thought. He passed a gentle hand over her shoulder, wanting to ease her tension.

"You asked, 'What more could a man ask for?'" she said softly. "And I'm thinking a man could ask for a night of lovemaking, when a woman has given him a clear invitation. I feel terrible about that. And you're being far nicer about the situation than most men would be."

"I'm not most men." Inside, however, he had to concede she was right. He'd been severely disappointed when he'd realized things weren't going to go as he'd expected. But then he'd seen the shame in her eyes and that had changed everything.

Did he love her? Was he in love with her? Had he really changed into a man who found contentment in sleeping on a couch doing nothing more than hugging, a man he barely recognized, because he loved her?

"No, clearly you're not most men," she said, and she gave him a weary smile. "Thank you for staying."

"Thank you for letting me."

She poured steaming coffee for the two of them. "What will you tell your mother and Tiffany? I suppose you can say you stayed at your condo."

"I'll think of something." His mother would be well aware he'd spent the night with Jayda and she'd giddily make assumptions, then begin planning her son's future as a married man. But that wouldn't be the worst of it. He didn't want his mom to tell Jayda she knew he'd been with her because his own place had been put up for sale and was already partly packed. He'd been staying at his mother's house, trying to learn how to be a parent to Tiffany and working on the endless paperwork required in order to file for adoption.

It hadn't been as difficult as he'd expected to list the condo. And his agent was asking for a healthy price. An extremely good thing, because clearly his relationship with Boyden and Whitby, LLC, wasn't going to last much longer. He only hoped the senior partners would see through their commitment to Tiffany's case. He'd need the resources of a large firm to win such a complex case.

"I'll take a cab back to my mother's house," he said.

"I can drive you. Let me just take a quick shower."

"No, that's okay." He didn't want his mother and Jayda together just yet.

She sighed. "You know this is going to be complicated, seeing each other all the time, pretending nothing is going on between us and remembering this confusing night."

He looked at her, wondering what she was really thinking. "I guess I'm okay with 'complicated.'"

"I don't want to hurt your chances of adopting Tiffany."

"Does that mean you'll approve of me going forward with the adoption?"

"I never said I didn't approve. What I said was that it would be nearly impossible for you to be approved by

Social Services. And I can't be your caseworker for the adoption process. I'll have to disqualify myself."

"But if the adoption caseworker asked your opinion as to my worthiness, what would you say?"

Another small smile from her made him feel like Jell-O inside. "I'd say you'd be a wonderful father and a great provider, except I won't be asked because I'll have to admit I'm biased."

"Will our interest in each other cause you trouble at work?" The last thing he wanted to do was jeopardize her career. Bad enough that his own was taking a sudden nosedive.

"I'll be okay." She looked at her feet. "You said we'd take it slowly, right? I…I hope you meant it."

He moved toward her and gently lifted her chin so that she'd look into his eyes. "I meant it. And thank you for your support regarding Tiffany—even if you won't actually be asked for an opinion. That means a lot to me." Then he kissed her cheek, lingered there and kissed her lips softly, waiting to see what she would do. Slowly, she slipped her arms around his neck and kissed him back.

He wanted her—preferably, naked on a bed beneath him. But he'd promised to be patient. So he stepped back and took a calming breath. "I better get going," he said, half hoping she'd ask him to stay.

She nodded and stepped aside, so he could walk to the door. "I'll call you later," he promised as he headed out. He'd never felt so awkward leaving a woman's apartment. He'd never felt so unfulfilled. He'd never felt such longing.

BARBARA AND TIFFANY WERE standing in the kitchen when Simon arrived at his mother's home.

"Smile!" his mother shouted the instant he came

through the door. A flash went off and seared his brain. It was way too early in the morning for this kind of thing.

"She's not with me," he said, guessing that his mom wanted a picture of the two of them after their first night together. This was the woman he'd grown up with and he knew how her mind worked, strange as it was.

"Oh," she said. "Is she still out in the car?"

"She didn't bring me home."

"How did you get here, then?" Tiffany asked.

Simon looked at the girl and wondered what his mother might have told her or suggested. What would a kid as young as Tiffany have worked out about the two of them spending the night together? He rubbed his temples, wishing he didn't have to deal with either of these females right now. "I took a taxi."

"A taxi!" This exclamation came from both of them at once.

"Aren't you supposed to be saving your money so you can open your own law practice? You must have paid a fortune, getting here from Baltimore in a cab." His mother could still make him feel like a ten-year-old.

He sat down heavily in one of her kitchen chairs and gazed at the cereal box that was still standing on the table from breakfast. "It wasn't that expensive and I'm not that broke." *Yet.*

"Well, why did you come home alone?" Tiffany asked. "You were gone all night. Weren't you with Jayda?"

"Nothing happened," he said, eyeing the girl to gauge how much she might be assuming.

"Ah," said his mother knowingly. "She turned you down. That must be a first."

"Mom! For cryin' out loud. I don't think we should be talking about this right now."

"Oh, it's okay. I know all about this kind of stuff," Tiffany said. "I'm eleven, not two. And I've lived in foster homes most of my life. We grow up fast. Barbara and I figured you had to have stayed with Jayda, because you didn't come home. So, did you stay at your empty apartment or something?"

He stared at her a moment. "You're still eleven. And could we just pretend you're not asking me about my sex life and that you're the sweet, innocent kid I wish you could still be—*and* that you and my mother haven't been making wedding plans all morning."

"No chance," she said as she sipped her orange juice and smiled.

He blew out an exasperated sigh. "We talked. All night. Then we fell asleep on the couch. End of story."

"She turned you down," his mother said. "It's about time someone did. Good for that oversize ego of yours."

"She didn't turn me down. In fact, she invited me up. But..." He had no idea how he could end that sentence without revealing too much, so he trailed off. There was no way to save face here. And he couldn't imagine why he should try to in front of his mother and his prospective daughter. "Okay." He held up his hands in surrender. "She turned me down. It's complicated."

"Too bad. She'd be a great mom." Tiffany stared at her juice glass glumly.

"You're not giving up on her, are you?" his mother asked.

"Of course not. Just slowing down a little." He turned to Tiffany again. "I told you before I'll do everything I can to adopt you. But getting Jayda to marry me to improve our chances just wouldn't be right. That's not a reason to get married. I explained all that when I asked you if you'd want to be my daughter."

Tiffany thought for a moment. "There are a lot of reasons for you and Jayda to get married besides my adoption," she said. "For one thing, you're in love with her."

Simon's training as a trial lawyer was all that kept his face from showing the astonishment he felt. "What makes you say that, Tif?" he managed to ask. Was it really so obvious? He'd only just begun to realize his feelings for Jayda himself. How could this young girl already know?

"I can just tell," she said.

"So can I," added his mother.

He considered this. Then looked at the two females, one after the other. "And can you tell how she feels about me?"

"Nope. I don't know her as well as I know you," his mom said.

"I think she wants to like you, but she's afraid," said Tiffany.

He stared at her, then asked, "How did you get to be so insightful?"

"I read a lot," she said, as if this explained everything.

"Well, stop it. You're starting to be frightening." But he smiled at her to let her know he didn't really mean it, even though part of him thought she was possibly the scariest person to ever come into his life. "And both of you need to back off about me and Jayda. No more snapping photographs, no more throwing us together, no more matchmaking."

The younger one looked at the older one and a silent communication seemed to pass between them. Then they responded at the same time, using the same words, as if they'd rehearsed. "No promises," they said.

He stood up abruptly and had to catch his chair before it toppled backward. "Okay, that was just too weird. I'm outta here." He fled to the room he'd been staying in—the one that had been his haven as a boy, the one where he felt safe and vulnerable at the same time.

Pacing about his childhood refuge, he considered what he should do next. He'd already embarked on all the paperwork for Tiffany. He'd made it clear to Jayda how he felt about her. He'd put his expensive condo on the market, in preparation for the inevitable end to his career at the law firm. Now what? There had been few times in his life when he'd had to sit back and wait for things to happen. Always, there'd been something else he could do to manipulate the situation, something he could make happen so he'd get what he wanted that much sooner. Now there was nothing he could do. He simply had to wait and let things take their course.

After another hour he decided to dress and go to the office, even though it was a Saturday. He could work on Craig Dremmel's case, even though the proceeds from his work would go into Boyden and Whitby's coffers. At least it would be something productive he could do, and it would be unlikely he'd have to contend with Renauld Canter, who'd be playing golf on such a lovely summer day.

Besides which, Simon felt the need to get behind the wheel of his Mustang. He'd leave the windows open and let the wind blow away some of his tension. That would be more helpful than continuing to pace in his childhood bedroom. And, anyway, he wasn't sure he'd be able to hang on to the Mustang much longer, given its lack of child-safety features and the money he could rake in on resale. He'd take his pleasure from it while he still could.

CHAPTER ELEVEN

GOOD NEWS AWAITED SIMON when he arrived at the office. Denise, the person he'd miss the most when he left the law firm, had put a message on his desk from the day before. "New report from the private pathologist you hired. Derek's death from shaken baby syndrome. Will testify Tiffany too small to be responsible."

Simon smiled, and without thinking dialed Jayda's cell phone number at once. "Good news," he said as if nothing weighed heavily between them. "Denise tells me our pathologist will testify that Tiffany is too small to have killed Derek."

"Will that be enough to counter the prosecutor's evidence?"

Robert McGuire would be putting Tiffany's former foster mother on the stand when the trial resumed. She'd no doubt tell the jury about the incriminating things Tiffany had said when she'd been found with the lifeless Derek. "Not sure," he replied. "But it's a break I wasn't certain we'd get. It could at least create some reasonable doubt."

"And that could be enough, right?"

"We can hope." And those words reminded him of the question he'd asked her the night before. She'd reassured him there was hope for the two of them. But now, in the cold light of day, Simon wasn't so sure. So much was stacked against them—including Jayda's unwillingness to confide. A long silence became uncomfortable and then both began to talk at once to fill the void.

"I'll let you know…" he began.

"I was going to call…" she started to say. They both went silent again.

"You first," he offered.

"I wanted to let you know Marla discovered a lead in Derek's file and passed it on to me this morning. His social worker noted that Derek's mother sometimes stopped by to see him unannounced, even though those visits were supposed to be supervised. After some digging I found out she last lived in Harrisburg, Pennsylvania.

"The police are taking their time working out jurisdiction issues. They think Derek's killer is already on trial, and they aren't spending any time following up this new lead. So I'm going to go there to see what I can find out."

"I should go with you," he said.

"No." Her response was instant, as if she'd anticipated his offer and was ready to turn it down immediately. "I may have to stay there a few days just to find her, and you'll need to be at trial with Tiffany."

"You should be here with us," he reminded her. He could tell his voice had gone cold, an indication of his disappointment about her absence, but he couldn't help himself. Irritation seemed to be his response to the new experience of not getting what he wanted when he wanted it. Childish, but true.

"There's no rule that says I have to be there every day, as long as Tiffany understands what's going on with the case. And let's face it—sometimes she understands things better than I do." Simon nodded at this, even though Jayda wouldn't be able to tell over the phone that he'd just agreed with her.

"You're sure this lead is worth it?" he asked, worrying now that the jury would make too much of Jayda's absence.

"If I can find Derek's mother and get her to admit she saw her son within days of his death, wouldn't that be worth a lot?"

"Yes," he agreed. "That would be the end of Tiffany's case. Between that kind of evidence and the pathologist's testimony, McGuire would be forced to agree that a more likely killer was Derek's own mother. It would have taken an adult to shake Derek hard enough to cause his death."

"Then I'm going," Jayda said.

"Okay." Simon hesitated. "Call me and let me know what happens." To his ears, this sounded lame, but he had nothing else to offer.

"I will. And when I get back, we'll talk. I should tell you about some things," she promised.

That went a long way toward lightening Simon's mood. "I'd like that," he said.

SHE WOULD NEVER WANT TO BE an investigator of any kind. This sort of work was tedious and thankless. She'd gone from one lead to another in her search of Derek's mother, but so far they'd all resulted in nothing but another lead. If she'd had to do this for a living, she'd have gone nuts long ago. Now she'd been sent to a boardinghouse, of sorts. For a few dollars or a hit of crack, a person could stay with other drug addicts in a crumbling warehouse-style building that had been divided into a warren of alcoves and minuscule rooms. This was no place for her to be knocking on doors alone, but she refused to go back to Baltimore without something they could use. Besides, even the worst of Harrisburg didn't compare to the awful Baltimore neighborhoods in which she found some of the kids she worked with.

"I'm looking for Patricia Baldridge," she said to the first person she encountered. "Have you seen her?" For the hundredth time, Jayda wished she had a good photograph of the boy's mother. If she'd been a real detective, she probably would have thought of that before she'd driven all this way. As it was, all she had was a blurry picture sent by Simon's secretary to her cell phone. She held that up to the inebriated person to whom she spoke.

The grizzled man peered for a time at the tiny photo. "Nope. Haven't seen her today."

Jayda's heart leaped with excitement. He'd said "today." Did that mean he'd seen her recently? She had to be careful. She didn't want to scare the man with too much enthusiasm. Keeping her voice calm, she used the story she'd been giving out for days. "Well, do you know where she is? Because she's got some money coming to her from a recent death in the family and my boss won't let me off the hook until I find her or prove she's dead, too."

"How much money?" the oldster asked.

"Not very much, but enough so that the lawyer I work for is determined to find her."

He thought for a moment, seemed to be rummaging through a messy pile within his mind. "She might be in her room upstairs, for all I know."

"Is there a room number or something?"

"How much money, did you say?"

"I can't tell you that. Confidential. But I've got ten dollars for you if you help me find her."

"Show it to me."

Jayda dug into her pocket for the cash she'd put there for just such a contingency. She waved the ten in front of him. Without another word, the guy turned and headed up a set of rickety stairs.

They found Patricia sprawled across a mattress on the floor of a room without a door, high or merely asleep, Jayda couldn't tell. In fact, Jayda could barely tell whether this was actually the person she was looking for. In the tiny cell phone photo, the woman had been smirking for a mug shot. This woman looked worn out and half dead.

"You're sure this is Patricia Baldridge?" Her guide nodded and held out his hand. Jayda passed him the cash and watched as he ambled away.

Kneeling beside the mattress, Jayda nudged the inert body. "Patricia, wake up."

The body rolled to one side. She groaned, then squinted her eyes open ever so slightly. "What?" It was a disinterested statement rather than a real question.

"I need to talk to you about your son."

Her eyes opened all the way then, wide and brown and bloodshot. In another second, they blazed with anger. "He's dead."

Jayda sat back on her heels, surprised by the bitterness of those two short words. She and Marla had assumed that this absent mother hadn't known of her son's fate. "I know and I'm sorry," she said. "Everyone says he was a good kid."

"Yeah." The woman's eyes softened and shifted away, as if she could lose herself in memories of happier times.

"Listen, can I buy you some coffee—maybe a meal? My car's outside and there's a diner a few miles from here."

"Why?" Patricia asked, her expression full of irritation again.

"I'd like to talk to you about your son. Maybe the two of us can figure out who killed him. You'd like his killer to be caught, wouldn't you?" Jayda took a risk saying this. It required a leap of faith to assume that Derek's killer wasn't the woman in front of her, or at least that she didn't realize she could in some way be to blame. If she understood that she might well be a suspect in Derek's death, she'd never talk to anyone. But the tenderness that had filled the woman's eyes when her son's name had been mentioned made Jayda want to believe there was someone else involved.

Patricia blinked as she slowly processed the issue. "That girl did it. Everyone said. That little girl pushed him down and he hit his head."

"He didn't hit his head—the coroner doesn't think she could have done it. She's too small to have done so much damage, so an adult had to be involved. One of the neighbors told us there was a man in the neighborhood, looking for where the foster kids lived. I'm hoping you'll be able to tell me who that man might have been, if you think about it."

Patricia sat up on the filthy makeshift bed. It had obviously been some time since she'd had a shower or changed her clothes. There were telltale bruises on the inside of her arm running along her veins. But for the moment, she was coherent. If only she'd talk.

"Where's that diner you mentioned? I could use some coffee and maybe a slice of pie."

Jayda stood. "I'll take you there and then I'll take you wherever you want to go afterward."

Patricia took in her small, shabby space. "Anywhere but here," she said.

JAYDA DRAGGED HERSELF INTO her apartment late Friday after helping Patricia get settled into a Baltimore rehab center. There was no guarantee she'd stay long enough to get herself clean, even though she'd gone there willingly. But it was all Jayda could come up with on short notice. Fortunately, there had just been a cancellation and a friend let her snag the opening for Derek's mother.

With the last of her energy seeping from her body, Jayda thumbed Simon's number into her cell phone and hit Send. When he answered, she could hear a little girl's laughter in the background. The sound made her smile, but weariness made her tone sharp when she asked, "Why isn't Tiffany in bed by now?"

"We're almost finished the game. She keeps sending me back to the beginning, so it's gone on longer than we expected." He paused, then added, "Besides, it's only ten o'clock. It's not like she has to get up for school in the morning."

Jayda rubbed her temples with the tips of her fingers. "I'm sorry—I didn't mean to question your parenting. I just wanted to let you know I'm back in town. I didn't get much from Derek's mom, but she's in a rehab center here, so maybe you can talk to her and get something else out of her."

"That's good. Very good. I'll need to hear all the details from you first, about what she's said so far and how she reacted to you. Can you come by the house tomorrow?"

Jayda's stomach tightened at the thought of seeing him again. "Yes, I can come tomorrow."

"Come early. We'll do something for breakfast together."

"Okay." She especially welcomed the thought of that family setting after being entwined in Patricia Baldridge's hopelessness the past few days. More than that, she wanted to see Simon—she wanted to confess her fears to him and explain their origins. She longed to start again with him, despite Marla's discouragement. And to hell with protecting herself from terrible memories and hiding from possibilities because of what had happened to her so long ago.

"Great. Tiffany will be excited to see you." He paused and then added in a softer voice, "So will I."

"I missed all of you, too," Jayda replied cautiously, knowing it lacked the intimacy of his words. She could almost feel his disappointment over the phone. But she simply wasn't ready to acknowledge what was in her heart. Not yet. Frustration went hand in hand with that uncertainty, because she wasn't sure what she was waiting for, either.

She spent the rest of the night tossing and turning, even though she was exhausted. Marla thought she was getting too close to Simon and Tiffany. Simon might be denied permission to adopt Tiffany and anything they had between them could be destroyed by the disappointment, leaving her heartbroken.

Maybe it would be better to wait. But if she waited, she could lose him completely as he focused more and more on settling himself into family life. Plus there was the nagging concern that Simon might be confusing true love with the desire to improve his chances of winning Tiffany's adoption. She knew he'd never string her along intentionally, not even for Tiffany's sake. But what if he was confusing his feelings?

It became a long, long night of troubling doubts and impossible hopes. Yet when she awoke, she felt ready to face the three people living in the Montgomery home. She even looked forward to it. While she still dreaded telling Simon about her past, she knew that would be the first step in moving things forward between them. She would find a way. After all these years, she had to stop fighting so hard to protect herself from pain. All that accomplished was walling her off from joy.

She drove out to the suburbs gripping the steering wheel and reviewing the issue of how she would tell Simon about her uncle. There would be happiness at breakfast with the people she was going to see, and she didn't want to ruin that. She'd wait until she and Simon were alone. Later in the day, perhaps. Maybe tomorrow. *Never* sounded even better, though she knew that wasn't really an option.

Driving up to the house, Jayda noted the Honda was missing from its usual parking spot. Perhaps Simon had decided to leave before she arrived.

As she walked up to the door, however, she could hear a masculine voice speaking loudly. So Simon was still here. But what was he shouting about? She drew closer and her blood seemed to freeze in her veins as she heard Tiffany scream.

Running now, crashing through the front door, hearing a struggle upstairs and acting on instinct.

"Stop it, it's going to hurt!" cried Tiffany. "Don't!"

"Be still, Tif. You have to cooperate," Simon ordered.

Jayda's heart hammered as she flew up the stairs and adrenaline coursed through her veins. She wasn't even aware of racing down the hall. She only knew that she would save this girl, the one who was crying out for help, the one just like the girl she had been.

Jayda heard Tiffany's cries and the memory of pleading with her uncle joined with Tiffany's voice until they were inseparable. The bedroom she entered took on the scent and color of the bedroom she'd had all those years ago.

At that moment, Jayda became an avenging angel rushing onto the scene, barely registering that the man held the girl only by one of her feet. He looked up at Jayda with a deer-in-the-headlights expression of complete astonishment.

"Let go of her!" Jayda shouted as she reached for Simon, clutched his T-shirt and pulled for all she was worth. He didn't resist, as she'd expected him to, but rose from the bed too fast and stumbled away. Something clattered to the floor as he shifted to keep himself from falling. In the red haze of her anger, she saw her uncle's face. Her fury felt exactly the same, too.

"How *could* you? How could you touch a little girl?" Jayda shouted at Simon. "I won't let you hurt her. I won't let you near her." And she stood there trembling with fury. A glance over her shoulder told her that the child was huddled against her pillows, curled almost into a fetal position except for the one foot sticking straight out. The one the man had been holding.

"Stop it, Jayda," she heard Simon say calmly but firmly. "You don't understand."

"Get out!" she shrieked. "Get out of her bedroom this instant!" She approached him, very nearly growling. Then she lashed out with both fists, beating against his chest.

He didn't budge, but his eyes widened in horrified surprise. He held her wrists to stop the attack. But he couldn't quell the mayhem inside Jayda. She twisted away and yelled once more for him to get out.

"Stop it!" came a high-pitched voice from the bed. "Stop fighting!"

Simon glanced over Jayda's shoulder at Tiffany, then put his hands up in surrender and backed toward the door. "Get hold of yourself," he said.

"Don't go!" the girl called. "Simon, come back."

"Don't leave me!" cried Tiffany as Simon backed out of the room and into the hall.

He stood there looking in. "Stop this right now, Jayda. You're scaring her," he said, gesturing toward the bed.

Jayda spared Tiffany a glance and saw the terrified expression on her face. "*You're* the one who scared her. I got here just in time. Don't worry, honey," she said without taking her eyes off Simon. "I won't let him hurt you."

"Will you listen? He was just trying to *help,*" Tiffany shouted.

Slowly Jayda turned, horrified that a victim would take the predator's side. But as she came about, her mind began to register certain facts.

There were tweezers on the floor that had clattered to the hardwood when she'd first accosted Simon. A needle rested on the bedside table, along with a box of Band-Aids and antibacterial cream. An open sewing box was there as well, the source of the needle, most likely. And an open bottle of rubbing alcohol and some cotton swabs rested nearby.

"Oh, God," she said as the awful truth sank in. After all her years in counseling, after all the work to let go and move on, after all the pains she'd taken to identify herself as so much more than someone who had been sexually abused by a relative, she still hadn't been able to perceive reality and instead she'd replaced Tiffany with her youthful self. Had she been taking on the role of protector that she'd wished so hard her mother had accepted?

"What's going on here?" said Barbara from the hallway. Jayda looked to see the older woman standing with a bag from Krispy Kreme in one hand and a set of car keys dangling from her fingers. "I could hear the yelling from the street, for heaven's sake."

"We've had a terrible misunderstanding," Simon said stiffly. "But I think we all see things more clearly now." He stepped into the bedroom, slipped past Jayda eyeing her warily, and sat down next to Tiffany. "We have a serious splinter to get out of Tiffany's foot. Maybe you could give me a hand, Mom."

Barbara stepped around Jayda, too, her expression puzzled. Jayda felt paralyzed by the horrific depths of her mistake. "Oh, God," she said again.

"I'll take care of Tiffany's splinter," Barbara offered. Nodding toward Jayda, she added, "You go take care of her."

Jayda could only see Simon in a blur, because her eyes were filled with tears. She felt his hand on her upper arm as he turned her toward the door and led her away. She had no volition of her own anymore. All her energy had been spent on her unforgivable mistake.

CHAPTER TWELVE

SIMON DREW JAYDA ALONG gently until she wouldn't move anymore. She came to a standstill in the hallway, then slumped to one side and slid down the wall until she was sitting on the floor with her knees up and her chin down. Simon dropped to the floor and sat next to her. Staying silent was hard to do.

He wanted to demand an explanation, make her see how hurtful her assumption had been and hear a heartfelt apology. But he knew Jayda's behavior had to be related to the things she hadn't told him about her childhood. Railing at her wouldn't help. So he waited.

It didn't take long before she curled up even tighter, with her forehead on her knees and her arms wrapped around her legs, as closed off and protective of herself as she could be. In the other room, they could hear Tiffany sobbing that it was going to hurt as Barbara implored her to hold still.

"There, see? You survived and the splinter is out," the older woman said a moment later. "Now, let me clean and bandage it. Then we'll dive into the doughnuts."

"Okay," agreed Tiffany in a tremulous voice. She sounded so much younger than her usual self, and Simon's heart ached a little. He wanted to be there with her, hugging her and letting her know that it was okay to be a kid sometimes, even if it made the removal of a splinter more difficult. He'd have to remember to tell her that after he'd done whatever he could for Jayda.

Tiffany and Barbara emerged from the bedroom and headed for the stairs. "Sorry, Simon," Tiffany said as she passed. "I didn't mean to cause trouble." She gave a darting glance toward Jayda.

"It's okay. You're no trouble," he said, and his throat went tight as he registered her expression of remorse. "I would have made a much bigger fuss," he joked, and Tiffany cracked a tentative smile. But then her expression became worried when her gaze drifted back to Jayda.

The social worker lifted her head from her knees and tried to give Tiffany a reassuring look before the child disappeared down the stairs. After another moment, when they were alone and could hear Barbara and Tiffany moving around in the kitchen, Jayda began to talk.

"I'm so sorry," she said. "I can hardly believe I said those things to you, that I thought..." She seemed unable to go on.

"Can you tell me why you leaped to that conclusion?" He had to force himself to say the words that would have come easily enough in court, in reference to someone else. "Why you thought that I was molesting Tiffany." He fought off a shudder.

"You've probably already guessed," she said.

"You were the victim of a sexual predator when you were a kid," he offered, trying to make it easier.

"Right." She sighed. "My mother had a brother, Wayne, who liked underage girls way too much. Or at least he liked me too much. But honestly, that wasn't the worst of it. It was the fact that my mother always dismissed my complaints that messed me up so completely. We lived in a crowded house with some relatives, and my bedroom was in the basement. It was a tiny room, but I had it all to myself. That was wonderful, having a place of my own, until my uncle realized how easy it would be to visit me there."

She stared into space, and Simon understood she didn't want to make eye contact. He didn't speak, just hoped she would be able to get the story out. Surely she would feel a little better once she did.

"I told my mother," Jayda said, with an edge of anger in her voice. "But she just asked if he'd put himself inside me, if he'd raped me. And when I said no, she told me to stop whining. Can you believe that? I was a little older than Tiffany is, so I knew what rape meant. But I also knew that having a grown man touch my body and wanting me to sit on his lap was wrong. I knew he shouldn't be telling me the petting could be our little secret, that no one had to know, and that if I let him feel my private places he'd keep on lending my mother money and buying me nice things." Tears filled her eyes.

"I didn't want *things,*" she said. "I just wanted to be a kid, to be left alone. But most of all I wanted my mother to take care of me, protect me."

Simon wanted to put his arm around her. His own parental instincts had been kicking in overtime as he worked toward adopting Tiffany, and this story of a young girl left to fend for herself was heartbreaking. He longed to do something to show he cared and to comfort the child still suffering inside of this woman. But he held back, certain his touch would be unwelcome at this moment and hoping that listening would be enough.

"Mom had a drinking problem. I see that now. But when I was younger I didn't focus on the possibility she had her own demons to deal with. I just knew she'd let me down. I was trapped there, and so Wayne did what he wanted. At least until I was about fifteen, and I threatened to slit his throat if he ever came near me again. I'd gotten my hands on a big, sharp knife to help me make my point."

Simon couldn't keep himself from saying, "Good for you." He actually wished Wayne had pressed his luck and the knife had done some damage. His comment won a weak smile from Jayda. He took this as permission to ask, "Where is Wayne now?" He wanted to kill the bastard with his bare hands.

"Dead. I went to his funeral just to make sure it was really true. That was the last time I saw my mother."

"How long ago?"

"Seven years."

A long time, he thought. But with a mother like hers, maybe Jayda was better off this way. "What did you say to each other when you were at the funeral together?" What he really wanted to know was whether Jayda had gotten any closure from that meeting.

"I didn't say anything. She looked at me so accusingly, as if I'd killed her brother. Maybe I did, in a way. He was drunk and he drove into a tree. I used to think maybe he felt guilty about me and that made him an alcoholic. But now I can see he was a mess his entire life. Alcoholism seemed to run in the family. How the hell could a crazy, child-molesting drunk be so damned successful in your profession? How could he get away with it over the years?"

Simon reacted as if she'd slapped him. "Wait. Go back a second. Are you saying this monster was an attorney?"

She nodded and more tears fell from her eyes, sliding down her cheeks and onto her knees. "He made partner in his firm before he died."

"Shit," he whispered. The two of us never had a chance,

he thought silently. Jayda was never going to choose him—if his profession reminded her of her predatory uncle. And as hard as he tried to keep his focus on this wounded woman sitting beside him, tried to remember that Jayda was baring her soul and deserved his undivided sympathy, he couldn't ignore the sensation of his heart being crushed.

"So now you know my dark secret. I hope you can begin to understand those childhood experiences shaded what I saw, what I *thought* I saw in Tiffany's room this morning." She sounded more in control of herself now, more like the social worker he knew.

He managed to make his words come out evenly, devoid of any hint of the emotions churning inside. "Yes, I can understand that. Still, I'm sorry that you would ever associate me with someone like Wayne." That was where the pain in his heart must be coming from, he decided. How could she have ever mistaken him for a child molester? The concept was beyond him.

"I didn't really see you," she explained. "I didn't even see Tiffany today. I heard her crying and pleading with you, and it sounded exactly like what used to go on inside my head with Wayne. I would get slapped if I cried out loud, but that didn't stop me from screaming in my mind. And Tiffany became me and you became Wayne, and it all just got muddled inside me. I'm so sorry. You must be so hurt."

He nodded, acknowledging the apology, but unable to trust his voice.

She looked away, off into the distance again. "I thought I'd worked my way past this. I've seen therapists, practiced letting go, worked on myself so hard. Obviously, I still have issues."

"Don't give up on yourself," he said. What he really

wanted to say was, "Don't give up on us," which shocked him. That was something he wouldn't dare say aloud, even if he understood it. Her response might increase that horrific heart-crushing sensation he was trying so hard to ignore.

"I won't. If I did, I'd be giving in to him and letting him control me, even from his grave. As long as I breathe, I'll work on shaking loose from those awful memories. I think this experience today may be the kick I've needed to get me moving again toward healing myself."

"I'm not going anywhere, Jayda. I'm here if you need someone to talk to," he said.

She stared at him for a few moments, but her eyes were unreadable. "You're crazier than I am," she said, but a glimmer of humor lit her watery eyes. "And you don't know what you'd be getting into. I don't even know what will happen next."

"None of us really does," he said, thinking of how he could never have predicted a month ago that he would be sitting here with a woman such as Jayda, on the verge of abandoning his career in favor of adopting a child. Life took crazy turns sometimes.

Another sad smile from Jayda. "I have to go now," she said as she got to her feet. "I have some things to think over."

"You came to tell me about your trip to Pennsylvania."

"I'll send you an e-mail. Right now, I need to be…not with other people. Maybe for a long time."

"You'll be in court on Monday, right? It would confuse the jury if you didn't come back," he said, grasping for one more straw.

She seemed to think about this and remained silent for a long moment. At last, she said, "Yes, I'll be there. You shouldn't have to work with me, but I don't want to do anything to jeopardize Tiffany's case." And with that promise, she left.

He stood in the hallway, his fists clenched at his sides, and listened to her footsteps go all the way down the stairs and across to the front entrance. He heard the rasp of the door, as it opened, and the thud of it being closed again. She was gone.

JAYDA DROVE TO HER APARTMENT on automatic. Exhaustion was overtaking her rapidly, but there remained a seething undercurrent of anger—only now the rage was directed toward herself. She'd made an unforgivable mistake. It could never be undone. *No backsies,* as the kids said. She'd have to live with the consequences, just one more side effect of her screwed-up childhood. Resentment toward a dead man welled up in her heart, right alongside the sadness regarding Simon.

Her eyes filled again with hot, stinging tears. She wiped them away, then picked up her empty suitcase and carried it into the closet to put it away on the shelf. Something to do.

But fate wasn't done with Jayda for the day, because as she shoved the suitcase onto the shelf it dislodged a shoe box, which came tumbling down. The contents scattered. Not shoes. Photographs. She wanted to leave them where they were. Instead she knelt and began to gather them together, refusing to look as she replaced them in the box. But as she began to place the cover back on the cardboard container, her gaze fell on one photo that protruded from the others just enough to show the image she most wanted to avoid.

She sat down hard on the floor. The box came to rest

between her legs, and her mother's smiling face looked up at her from the snapshots. Taken when her mother had been a few years younger than Jayda was now, the photo made Margaret Kavanagh seem so confident and bold. Her eyes blazed with intelligence, her hair was glossy, her skin fresh and unweathered. This was not the woman Jayda remembered from her childhood. This was a stranger. And yet she knew it was her mother—it said so on the back of the picture.

The woman Jayda had known during her childhood had been weighed down, with world-weary eyes and a lined face. She'd had a smoker's cough that had worried Jayda as a child. Margaret Kavanagh hadn't been among the worst of all mothers. But the betrayal she'd perpetrated when Jayda had spoken up about her uncle, the refusal to offer protection… That had left deep, jagged wounds that had never really healed. Something had to change. Jayda sighed heavily, weary and heartsick and perplexed.

Her cell phone beeped and she pulled it out of her pocket automatically to find a text message there. "Please let me know you got home safely," it said. She saw that it had come from Simon. As she thumbed in a reply, she wondered at a man who could be so thoughtful about her welfare after she'd just insulted him beyond imagining. "Yes, got home. Plan to stay here and think," she typed.

She didn't have much time to do that, however. In the next instant, the phone rang. Her heart skittered as she looked at the caller ID, both hoping and dreading that it would be Simon. But the name that lit up in the tiny window was Marla's. Unusual for her to call on a Saturday, so Jayda answered.

"Hi, Jayda," Marla began cheerfully. "Did you find anything out about Derek's mother?"

Jayda had told Marla about the reason for her trip and

her boss had given her the go-ahead to leave the area in the middle of the work week to pursue Patricia Baldridge. "I persuaded Ms. Baldridge to return to Baltimore with me and I have her in rehab." She named the facility.

"Not one of our best centers, but they took her on short notice and at least she's cooperating with you. Please tell me she didn't kill her own son."

"No, I don't think she did. Her guilt seems to be only about leaving him in foster care. But I think she might know something about the man who was hanging around the neighborhood in the days before Derek's death. She wouldn't tell me much, but I think she'll have something to say eventually."

"That's good news," Marla said. "Well worth the trip."

Jayda hesitated only a moment, then something inside her made her say, "I need another favor from you. And a few more days away. I…I have to go talk to my mother."

Marla let out a sigh. "Wow. I've been wondering if this day would ever come."

"Bad timing, I know. But I think I have to do this now."

"Yes. That's how these things work. No waiting for a convenient moment. Just, bam! And you have to deal with it or you may never get another chance. So go. But…"

"I promise I won't be gone long. And I have lots of vacation time I haven't used."

"I know that—I was just wondering about Tiffany's case. Court reconvenes on Monday, right? Does that lawyer know you won't be there?"

"That's actually the favor I need from you."

"Oh, so asking for time off with no advance warning wasn't the favor?" But there was amusement in her voice.

"I hate to ask this of you, but can you tell Simon I had to go take care of something for a few days?"

"Why don't you call him yourself?"

"Complicated."

"I see." And Jayda knew that she *did* see. Marla added, "Was he what prompted this sudden need to talk to your mother?"

"It wasn't his fault. I really screwed up, Marla." And then she told her boss about wrongly accusing Simon.

"WHY CAN'T SHE BE IN COURT today?" Simon barked at Marla when she called him early Monday morning. He was just pulling into the parking lot at the courthouse. He'd been nurturing a tiny spark of hope that he and Jayda could find a way to go forward.

"She's taking care of something important," Marla said. "She'll be gone a few days."

"She could have told me that."

"She didn't want to. She asked me to do it instead."

He could hear the frost in the woman's voice. "Why?"

"She said it was complicated. Have you made things complicated in any way?"

Now he understood Marla's coolness toward him, but that didn't stop anger from beginning to take the place of his heartache. "Not on purpose," he hedged. "And where is she—what does she need to take care of? What about Tiffany's trial? Doesn't she care about that? Letting me know at the last minute is so…"

"Frankly, Mr. Montgomery," she interrupted, "I could have told you sooner. She talked to me Saturday afternoon. But I was worried that you'd want to know where she is, that you might start calling her or maybe even try to go after her. But she needs some time to herself. Waiting until the last minute to tell you was my idea, to ensure she got that uninterrupted time."

Seething now, Simon did what he could to control his voice. No good would come from growling at Jayda's boss. "I'm afraid you don't know me very well. If Jayda says she needs time alone, I'll give it to her."

"Well, I'm relieved to hear it. She's an excellent caseworker and I want her to continue doing what she does so well."

Finally, Simon understood that this woman was just looking out for Jayda. How could he fault her for that? Jayda needed someone on her side. If it couldn't be him, then it might as well be Marla. "I would never want to take Jayda away from her work. She's the best I've ever seen at dealing with her kids."

Marla was silent a moment. "I know you've applied to adopt Tiffany. I admire your willingness to take on that responsibility. But I also know you're a man who will do anything to get the result you want. That's how you've become such a famous Baltimore attorney."

His first thought was to deny that he was famous. His second was to deny he'd do anything to get what he wanted. But he said nothing. They would have been lies, after all. He diverted his adversary with the truth instead. "I'll do anything it takes to adopt Tiffany," he said.

"I know," she said softly. "That's what I'm worried about. A man like you could probably persuade Jayda to do whatever you needed to enhance your chances for adoption."

"She's stronger than you give her credit for. And I have no intention of taking advantage of Jayda. I..." He trailed off, realizing that Marla thought he might attempt to persuade Jayda to marry him, whether they loved each other or not, just so his adoption would go through. It struck him that the idea of marrying Jayda was not unwelcome, despite everything.

"Well, that's good to hear. But I don't know you. All I know is the man the media has written about over the years. I hope you won't lead her on."

"Isn't that really for Jayda to decide for herself?"

"Touché." She paused, then added, "I'm just trying to give her some time to deal with her past. If you're a man of your word, you'll do the same."

He sighed, his anger simmering to dull irritation. He hated having no control, and he certainly had no control over this situation. Nor could he control his growing confusion about his feelings for Jayda. Did he love her?

He had to clear the tightness from his throat before he asked, "When will she be back?"

"I don't know. She told me she'd need a few days off. She told me to be sure to tell you that Derek's mother is in rehab in Baltimore. She said you'd want to talk to her, see if you can get her to tell you more about the man who'd been hanging around the kids' foster home."

She gave him the address and a number to contact at the center.

"Thanks," he said. "I'll talk to Mrs. Baldridge. And if you talk to Jayda…"

"I'll tell her the case is going well and that she found Tiffany the best lawyer in the State of Maryland."

A reluctant smile crept over his face. He hadn't known what he wanted Marla to tell Jayda, anyway. "Gotta go to court," he said, and then closed his phone.

CHAPTER THIRTEEN

JAYDA RESOLUTELY WALKED UP to the front door, fighting her instincts to turn and run in the other direction. Her hand felt like lead as she lifted it to knock on the door. Three hard raps and then an interminable wait that probably only lasted a few seconds. She'd lost all sense of time from the moment she'd parked her car in front of her mother's apartment building in Hagerstown. This isolated upstate Maryland town didn't seem like a place her mother would want to live, but it was where she'd settled after her brother's death. So Jayda had driven the two hours north and stayed in a local motel overnight. Now minutes seemed longer than they should be, but then she'd lost track of a few and found herself wondering how she could have gotten from her car to the door so quickly.

Should she knock again or go back to her car and try phoning? She'd decided to make this trip without giving her mother any warning. But now she saw the flaw in her plan. There was no way to know when her mother would be at home without…

A sound from the other side of the door caught her attention.

"Who is it?" came a woman's voice.

"Mom. It's me. Jayda." The words came out flat, dead.

Just the way she felt inside. Except that her heart was beating too fast and her guts burned. She wasn't dead.

"Jayda?" Then the sound of a metal chain, the click of a dead bolt, the scrape of the latch. The door swung inward. And there stood her mother.

The two of them froze, staring at each other, not speaking. Time started acting up again, making the moment seem endless. Some calm, clinical portion of Jayda's brain registered the fact that her mother seemed shorter than when they'd last been together. She didn't stand as straight. She'd lost weight. There were dark circles under her eyes, but the gaze holding Jayda's eyes so avidly appeared steady and sober for once.

"Hi, Mom," Jayda managed to say. But then tears came and overflowed unexpectedly. Her nose began to run. She raised her wrist to stem the tide and wondered if there was any way she could have gotten off to a worse start. She tried to speak again, wanted to ask for a few moments to talk, but her throat was closed.

"Well, don't just stand there," her mother said. "Someone could see you carrying on!" And she ushered Jayda inside, peering down the hallway as if to make sure no one had glimpsed the weeping crazy lady at her door. As the door eased shut on its hinge, Margaret Kavanagh looked at her daughter. "The bathroom is down the hall to the left. Go pull yourself together."

Hanging her head in mortification, Jayda did as she was told.

She went into the bathroom and closed the door, then looked at her tear-streaked face in the mirror. She barely recognized herself. Disgusted with herself for falling apart, she called upon all that inner strength she'd been building up over the years and then dashed cold water on her burning cheeks and eyes. When she straightened up and reached for a hand towel, she almost laughed. The towel was pink with a ribbon along the border. It was exactly the same type of towel her mother had used in the bathroom when Jayda was a child. Glancing around the tiny space, she saw that everything looked astonishingly familiar in this room that she'd never been before. There was a pink lampshade and a pink rug, pink toilet seat and pink curtains. All of it, exactly as she remembered from a different place and time. Laughter bubbled up inside her, but she knew she must not give in to it or risk sounding somewhat deranged. Covering her mouth with her hand in an effort to keep her raw emotions contained, she focused on breathing—in and out, in and out. After a moment, she regained some self-control. And the moment of mirth over her mother's bathroom decor helped her put this visit into perspective.

She gazed once more into the mirror and saw determination in her eyes. Certainty of her own worth shone from within. Her mother could only hurt her if she allowed that to happen, she reminded herself. Time to put that theory to the ultimate test.

Jayda found her mother in her living room. The old furniture was the same, although a little worse for wear. Margaret sat on the recliner, but she'd remained bolt upright on the edge of the seat. Clearly she would be unable to relax until she could account for her daughter's unexpected visit.

"I've come to talk about a couple of things from my childhood," Jayda began.

"Psh," Margaret said, with an exaggerated look of disgust. "No one can go back and fix their childhood. Everybody's childhood stinks, anyway. Why would yours have been happier than anyone else's?"

A bit stunned, Jayda had to think about that. Why, indeed? She spent her working days surrounded by kids with issues at least as bad and often far worse than hers had been. And yet she knew she shouldn't, couldn't give in to what her mother was suggesting—that Jayda had deserved no better than what she'd gotten.

"The thing is, lots of people have had lovely childhoods with only the problems that are natural to growing up. I didn't get one of those." She used a professional tone, trying hard to remove the blame from her mind and her voice as she said what she'd come to say.

Her mother looked at her blankly but said nothing. This was an encouraging sign.

"I didn't come here to try to fix things that went wrong back then. I know that's not possible. But I need to say a couple of things out loud that I couldn't ever say to you before."

"Why?" Wariness had crept into her mother's voice and she seemed to shrink into herself.

"Because I want to move forward with my life and I seem to be stuck on old issues. There's a chance that if I can get things off my chest, I may be able to put the past behind me."

Her mother looked skeptical. "Must have something to do with a man you want to start something with," she said. "But a worthy endeavor, I suppose."

Even though she knew better than to harbor hopes regarding Simon, Jayda had to admit that this visit had something to do with him. Her mother's insight was impressive. And it struck Jayda then that her mother had used words like *endeavor* all through the years they'd lived together. She was clearly intelligent and articulate, when she wanted to be. What had gone wrong in this woman's life to make her so miserable? For the first time ever, Jayda wished she knew.

"What I'm asking for is also pretty selfish. If I were a better person, I might have come here just to find out how you're doing after all these years."

Margaret waved her hand in front of her face, as if swatting away a pesky fly. "People are never altruistic, unless they have lots and lots of money. Do you have lots and lots of money?" she asked slyly. A hint of humor glinted from Margaret's eyes.

"No," Jayda answered, tempted to smile again. Had she acquired her own intelligence and love of words, her eagerness to learn from this woman? Probably. It struck her that she'd never once considered the good her mother had done her during her formative years. Yet now she remembered gifts of books and the freedom she'd been given to read into the wee hours of the night. She recalled visits to libraries and museums and historical sites. That had been before Wayne had come onto the scene to help his younger sister financially. His presence in their lives had wiped all those other things from the memory slate. Another thing he'd taken from her. From them.

She sighed and decided to cut straight to the most important reason for her visit. "I guess the main thing I want to say to you is that Wayne was an awful person who did terrible things to me. He was bad and he hurt me inside, even if he didn't actually harm me physically. He touched me sexually, and he tortured me with his threats and his blame. And none of that happened because of anything I did or didn't do."

She took a breath, her heart beating hard, and pressed on. "I wish you'd protected me from him," she said softly. "I wish you'd listened to me and accepted that he was hurting me in a fundamental way—and I wish you'd done something about it. I'm really angry and resentful that you didn't. I want to forgive you, but I don't know how."

That was the main point, really. She needed to forgive this woman for what had happened and move beyond the past. Forgetting that she couldn't expect all that much from her mother, she asked, "Is there a reason why you didn't do anything about him touching me? Or did you really believe that his behavior with me wasn't a bad thing?"

Margaret stared for a long moment. Then she shook her head slowly, as if she was denying something. Jayda waited with her pulse pounding.

When her mother didn't say a word, she understood she wouldn't be getting a response to her questions and she fought down her resentment. "The answers don't really matter, Mom. Now that I'm an adult I can understand that bad things sometimes happen to good kids, and that their parents aren't always going to protect them. It is what it is." She let out her pent-up breath and imagined her anger and hurt disappearing. Maybe someday it really would. Standing up for herself, speaking of her anger and her desire to forgive felt surprisingly good.

Her mother blinked a few times. Then slapped her thighs and stood, saying, "I need a drink. You want one, too?"

This sounded like Jayda's cue to get out of there fast, in the hope of retaining what she'd gained from the experience without poisoning it all by watching her mother get drunk. She stood. "No thanks, I'll just go. And thank you for listening to me. It was kind of you to give me a few minutes of your time."

Margaret's hands went to her hips. Jayda was struck

again by how small she was, how much she'd aged. "For God's sake, Jayda, have a drink with your mother. We might not see each other again for a long, long time."

"It's a bit early for alcohol," Jayda answered, sounding absurdly prim and proper even to her own ears. Lots of people had a drink with lunch.

"As judgmental as you ever were, I see. From the time you could talk, you were judging me." Margaret moved toward the side of the room where bottles and glasses sat on a fifties-style trolley. She poured herself something amber as Jayda stood frozen in the center of a throw rug.

Was that true, what she'd just said? Had Jayda judged her mother? Probably. That's what kids do, after all.

Margaret took a gulp from her glass. "Wayne was a bastard, certainly. We're in complete agreement there, even if he was my brother. But he was the one who got the good education, made it all the way through college and law school while our parents supported him. So my brother was a wealthy bastard and your father left us with nothing. Do you know what that's like, Jayda, my girl? Do you have the first idea what it's like to have a baby to care for and have a dead husband, dead parents, no education, no job and no money at all? We shared that house with my equally undereducated sister and your cousins because I couldn't afford a place of our own. And don't start telling me how welfare would have solved my problems. You've never been on welfare—you have no idea what it's like."

This was true. Jayda had only secondhand experience with welfare. But she'd seen what some mothers had to go through to make ends meet, the grinding poverty those checks did little to repair, the endless lines and the reams of paperwork necessary to get anything at all from the state or county. You could only make a limited amount of money at a job before your benefits were cut off, but daycare often cost as much as an entry-level job paid. The cheaper babysitters the state recommended were awful, even dangerous. Better to stay home and raise the kid yourself and collect those welfare checks, barely enough to survive on. And heaven help you if there were problems, because months could go by without a precious check. No check, no rent money. No water. No lights. No food. No hope.

She'd seen it happen too many times to the families of kids she'd tried to help. Is this what her mother had faced?

"Wayne was better than the streets, I figured. If you don't agree with that decision, then you don't. But it was the choice I had to make and I made it. I didn't like it, not for one minute. But I can see you turned out okay in the end. You're educated, successful, pretty, healthy.... Without Wayne, you'd probably have died young." She took another swig of her drink and sighed. "Because health insurance costs money and there was that time when you had that horrible lung infection and no one at the clinics knew what to do about it. Maybe you were too young to remember, but Wayne gave me the money for a specialist. And as long as I kept him happy, he kept helping. So sue me. I'm a bad mother. But you're alive to complain, at least."

Jayda nodded. She'd heard this sort of horror story before. She knew it was all too likely that this had happened exactly as her mother described it. An impossible choice and one that left a daughter scarred forever. But that same daughter had also been fed and clothed and had a roof over her head. Was there something else her mother could have done? Who could say? How could anyone tell Margaret she should have done something else?

She watched her mother drain her glass. If she stayed

any longer, she'd have to watch as alcohol made the woman's words clumsier and more hurtful. She didn't believe she could endure that, given her fragile emotional state.

"I have to go now," she said as she edged toward the door.

Margaret poured another drink, then put her glass down on the trolley, ice clinking. "Will you come back sometime?"

It surprised Jayda that her mother would ask that question. "Do you want me to?" A deep longing trembled in her heart and at the same time she inwardly recoiled.

"Sure. If you feel like it. I could make you banana bread." This was one of the few things Margaret had found time to make from scratch during her daughter's youth. She'd used overripe bananas that had cost only a few pennies.

"Okay." Jayda hated banana bread and she associated it with Wayne's unctuous presence, but she wasn't about to decline the peace offering. "I'd like to come see you again sometime," she said more decisively, despite her inner turmoil. "It doesn't have to be a long visit and we don't have to talk about the past, if you don't want to."

"Are you going to call first?" Margaret said, gulping her drink. "Because just dropping in like this is a little too much excitement for a woman my age."

Jayda smiled. "I promise I'll call first." She reached for her purse and withdrew her phone. "What's your number?"

SIMON DIDN'T HIT HIS STRIDE as quickly as usual when hammering through cross-examination. He suspected this was because of Jayda's absence from the defense table. He missed her. But in the end, his instincts took over and he found the balance he needed to create doubt in the minds of the jurors.

"Dr. Westin, you testified earlier that Derek died of blunt-force trauma. Isn't it equally possible that he suffered from shaken baby syndrome?"

"He was hardly a baby," the witness said.

"I have a study here from the *Boston Medical Journal* that explains that shaken baby syndrome can be found in toddlers as well as infants. So you agree that this is possible." He said it like a statement rather than a question.

"Objection," called Bob McGuire from the prosecution's table. "The witness hasn't yet given his opinion on this syndrome."

Judge Becker turned his impassive gaze to the witness. "What is your opinion regarding shaken baby syndrome and the death of the victim under discussion?"

"Well, as I said, the trauma to the brain was extensive, and my best assessment is that blunt force from a blow caused the damage."

"But could there have been other causes?" Simon persisted.

"Of course," Westin said with exasperation. "He could have fallen on his head or something heavy could have fallen on him. But that's not..."

"Thank you, Doctor," Simon interrupted. "Are you familiar with any of these medical texts?" He picked up a stack of books and articles from the defense table, wincing at the sight of Tiffany sitting there alone. Barbara was right behind her on the opposite side of the rail, but Tiffany looked so small and almost frail without Jayda right there to support her. He brought the reference books to the witness box and presented them to the doctor. "Can you read the titles for the jury?"

"Indications of Child Abuse. The Abused Child. Shaken Baby: Symptoms and treatments."

"Objection, Your Honor," called out the prosecutor. "This has nothing to do with the testimony this witness gave on direct."

"To the contrary, Your Honor," Simon rebutted. "The government presented this witness as an expert regarding cause of death. I intend to ensure the jury knows the full extent—and limitations—of Dr. Westin's expertise."

The judge waved his hand loosely. "Go ahead."

"Please read the rest of the titles, Doctor," Simon urged. Westin read the remaining titles, all medical texts related in one way or another to child abuse. When he finished, Simon asked again if he was familiar with them.

"I don't have time to read every book or article related to my field." Westin shifted in his seat and a sheen of sweat began to glisten on his forehead.

"Of course not," Simon said cordially. "But you're here today to establish cause of death in a child under four years old. Surely you considered the possibility of child abuse and specifically shaken baby syndrome. You have professional knowledge of how it can culminate in death quite some time after the shaking incident and that it takes adult strength to cause that kind of damage. You're aware that…"

"He's putting words in the doctor's mouth," objected McGuire.

"I'll rephrase," offered Simon before the judge had a chance to rule on this latest objection. While he knew he would be allowed a great deal of leeway on cross-examination, he was also satisfied that he'd shown the jury what he'd wanted them to see. Time to move on to the most important thing he wanted to accomplish with this medical expert. "Dr. Westin, have you ever heard of Dr. Samuel Greenbaum?"

Westin blinked a few times, then said, "Of course. He's retired now, but he was the state's medical examiner for years."

"And if he had a different opinion about what caused Derek's brain injuries and death?"

"Well..." Westin clearly wished he didn't have to respond. But after a moment, he admitted, "Dr. Greenbaum is a well-respected expert. I feel sure he'll agree..."

"Thank you, Dr. Westin," Simon interjected. "That's all I have." He moved toward his seat next to Tiffany.

"Redirect?" asked Judge Becker.

Bob McGuire stood, but didn't move from behind his table. "Dr. Westin, please clarify for the jury... What caused Derek Baldridge's death?"

"Blunt-force trauma, which caused a hemorrhage in the brain."

"Thank you," McGuire said, and returned to his seat.

Simon was still standing. He turned when Judge Becker asked if he had any re-cross questions. "Could Derek have been the victim of shaken baby syndrome?" he asked Westin.

"Well, I... That is..."

"It's a yes or no question, and one that Dr. Greenbaum had no trouble answering after he'd seen the autopsy test results."

This seemed to deflate Westin, and the man quietly said, "Yes, there could have been an element of shaken baby syndrome involved."

"Thank you," Simon said, then he sat down beside his client, drawing the jurors' attention to her slight and almost fragile physique once more. Thank goodness they hadn't seen her playing Nerf football with him in the family room the night before with her robust tumbling and tackling and fearless leaps over furniture to make catches. Nor had they witnessed her temper, for which he'd need to set up some anger-management classes. He needed the jury to see her as the innocent young child she appeared to be today.

Judge Becker excused Dr. Westin from the witness chair, then turned to McGuire. "Was that your last witness?"

"Yes, Your Honor. The prosecution rests."

"Very well. We'll adjourn for the day and Mr. Montgomery can begin with defense witnesses in the morning." He banged his gavel, rose from his seat and disappeared through a door behind the bench before the bailiff had the chance to herd the jury from the room.

Tiffany bestowed her usual hug and thanked Simon for his efforts on her behalf. He'd become used to this ritual and even expected it. But now for the first time, as he received the girl's love and patted her shoulder in return, he realized there was another benefit to Tiffany's embraces beyond the good they did for his soul. A straggling juror noticed them together and her expression turned soft, as if she was moved by the bond between them. Even in his most ambitious days, Simon wouldn't have thought of using Tiffany's hugs to sway the jury. But the fact that one of them had seen the moment by chance filled him with lawyerly satisfaction. He didn't care what it took to convince the jury that Tiffany was incapable of killing someone, as long as he got her acquitted.

"That seemed to go well, but I wish Jayda hadn't missed it," his mother said as she joined them near the defense table.

"She had something important to take care of," he said. He hadn't had time to explain his phone conversation with Marla to his mother, and he wasn't sure he wanted to.

"More important than me." Other kids would have said it like a question, disbelieving. Tiffany said it as a statement, as if it was accepted fact.

Simon put his hand on her small shoulder. "There's nothing and no one more important than you, Tif. Don't ever forget that." He could only hope Jayda would return soon and confirm that.

As he drove Tiffany and his mother out to the suburbs they both slept away some of their exhaustion, leaving him with time to think. Underlying his mental review of what he would do and say in court the following day, there was a burning desire to see Jayda, to touch her, to reassure himself that all was not lost. Her absence was distracting him.

Reluctantly, he admitted Marla had been right not to tell him where she'd gone, because he might not have been able to keep himself from trying to find her. He wanted desperately to prove that Jayda had nothing to fear from him, that he was nothing like her uncle. The longing, the need, the helplessness—these were foreign and frightening. But then, without conscious effort, that mind of his tripped over the beginnings of a plan, a way to help Jayda see she could trust him. His heavy heart lightened. And he smiled.

CHAPTER FOURTEEN

"SIMON," GLEN BOYDEN BEGAN, leaning back in the leather chair behind his huge mahogany desk. "I've treated you like a son, and for the most part you've been everything I could have hoped for."

Simon sensed the "but" that was about to be delivered, but he said nothing.

"You're slipping and I need to know why." The older man looked at him intently through his wire-rimmed glasses.

Simon hesitated, not relishing the reaction this man inevitably would have to his particular situation. But he owed Boyden an explanation. "I'm in the process of adopting a child," he said without preamble. "But before we can live happily ever after, I have to get her acquitted of murder charges—I need to stay focused on that. I realize I'm not giving the firm what's expected of me."

Boyden stared, momentarily stunned into speechlessness. "Are you talking about the girl you're defending pro bono? You've got to be kidding. You're not a family man, Simon. At least not yet. And not without the right woman at your side."

It was painful for Simon to realize this was everyone's impression of him. No one who'd heard about his plans had believed him at first. After his secretary, Denise, had taken a call from the adoption caseworker about him, she'd gone so far as to make an appointment for him with his doctor, but he'd assured her he was quite healthy and certain of what he wanted for his future. And a completely different future it was turning out to be, compared to the one he'd previously envisioned.

"Apparently, I am," he said to his boss. Taking mercy on the man, Simon leaned forward and offered the concession he'd worked out when he'd first realized he'd have to part ways with Boyden and Whitby, LLC. "I'd hoped it wouldn't come to this. Being unemployed won't look so great on the adoption application, but I can see it's time to go. I'll accept half my contractual severance pay if you'll continue to support Tiffany Thompson's case straight through any appeals she may require."

"You're quitting? But you've been our biggest rainmaker." Boyden seemed to have forgotten that he'd been about to fire him. Which Simon knew from the secretarial gossip he'd become privy to through Denise. No one was better informed about the plans of the partners than the all-powerful secretaries.

"I think it's time I struck out on my own. Renauld and I don't get along well, and I can't see the two of us making a go of working together after you retire. Time for me to make my own way in the world. But I need your assurance that Tiffany will continue to have the support of the firm until her case is concluded."

"We can't very well abandon a pro bono case, especially not one as visible to the media as hers," he admitted. Simon had been counting on this. "I assume you have a contract to that effect already drawn up."

"Of course," Simon agreed. He rose from his chair and leaned across Boyden's desk to shake the man's hand.

"Thank you for the education I've gotten here. I hope we'll work together again someday."

Boyden clasped his hand in both of his and his eyes misted over. "I think you're making a terrible mistake, Simon," he said. "But I wish you the best."

Simon left Boyden's office, endured Renaud's self-satisfied smirk from across the secretarial area without comment and went to his own office to begin packing. Denise followed him in and closed the door.

"You're really leaving?" she asked, her dismay evident.

"Looks that way. I'm not the rainmaker anymore. Not sure I want to be, now that I have other responsibilities." Or at least he hoped he'd have other responsibilities. He knew his bid to adopt Tiffany would be an uphill battle, but he had to go on believing he'd succeed.

"Take me with you," Denise said.

He looked at her, stunned. "You're kidding, right? I couldn't pay you anything close to what you're making here."

"But you're the best boss I've ever had. Exacting and pompous at times, but I've always liked you, anyway. And that woman you've become involved with—Jayda? She's changed you for the better. You're a kinder cut-throat-lawyer now." She smiled. He stared at her, wondering about her belief that he was involved with Jayda, that it was Jayda who had changed him. Could she be right? He'd been asking himself about his feelings for Jayda for some time, and he couldn't seem to nail down the answer.

She added, "I'd rather work for you and be happy than stay here. Besides, you'll be wildly successful on your own and end up paying me exactly what I'm worth to you soon enough."

He laughed. "You mean your weight in gold every day of the year?"

"More or less," she said sweetly.

Rounding his desk and approaching her, Simon did something he never would have seen himself doing before Jayda and Tiffany had come along. He hugged his long-suffering secretary. She hugged him back, too, patting him maternally on the shoulder.

"I'd be honored to have you come work for me, Denise. But let's not give your notice here until I've got myself established. Too many start-up costs in the first few months, and I don't want you to suffer."

"I like that plan," she said, and with a nod she headed out again. Before she disappeared, however, she turned and said, "By the way…"

"Uh-huh?" Simon was only half paying attention. He'd already began stowing his personal possessions in boxes and he couldn't quite figure out why he didn't feel worse about his time at the firm coming to this abrupt end.

"Craig Dremmel is planning on sticking with you when you leave here."

Simon looked up, startled. Dremmel was one of the most lucrative clients he'd brought to the firm. "I can't take him with me, Denise. He's the firm's client, not mine." But wouldn't it be nice if he could, he thought.

"Well, he's already in the process of severing ties with the firm. He heard from Renauld Canter about your imminent departure, and he told me he made his decision on the spot. But mum's the word. He doesn't want to tip his hand too soon."

"Why?" Simon asked. "Why would Craig Dremmel do that?" The high-powered land developer would do far better being defended by a large firm with all the clout it could bring to the legal system, and Dremmel knew that. It made no sense for him to take a chance on Simon's smaller as-yet-to-be-established law firm.

"You just don't see yourself the way others do, Simon. People believe in you and they trust you. It's true you're a hard-nosed attorney who'll do almost anything to win, but you're also a good person who wants the best for his clients, and those are the traits people want in their lawyer. Dremmel didn't get to be as wealthy as he is without noticing such things about other people."

Bemused, Simon could only say, "huh," to let her know he'd heard the words. It would be awhile longer before he'd completely understand them and be happy about this unexpected good fortune.

JAYDA ENTERED THE COURTROOM on Wednesday as nervous as a kid on the first day of school. She expected a cool reception from the Montgomerys and Tiffany after the scene she'd made the last time they'd seen one another, and she feared they might even snub her completely. She wouldn't blame them. But the thought made her stomach hurt, anyway.

"Jayda!" Tiffany cried the instant she saw her. The girl flew through the short swinging gate in the rail and launched herself into Jayda's arms. "I missed you," she said as she held on tight.

"I missed you, too," Jayda said, meaning it more than she'd ever be able to express. During her drive home from her mother's place, she had tried to come to terms with the fact that Tiffany would be gone from her life soon. The trial would end and either the child would go to prison or she'd be released into an orphanage or foster care. Or maybe somehow Simon would surprise everyone and persuade Social Services to let him adopt her. No matter what happened, however, Jayda wouldn't be seeing Tiffany on a daily basis anymore. She found herself burying her nose in the crook between Tif's shoulder and neck and breathing in the little-girl scent of her. She would miss this child so much. And the same went for Simon and his mother.

"We're so glad you're back," Barbara said from beside her. Jayda lifted her face to look at the woman. Tiffany released her from the hug, but kept a hand firmly clasped in one of Jayda's hands.

"I'm glad to be back. I'm sorry I wasn't here the past two days." She had no idea how she should explain her absence to these people, who really didn't need to be burdened with her childhood story.

"Simon said you had to take care of something important," Tiffany said. "Did you do that?"

Jayda scooched down so she could look Tiffany in the eyes. "It was very important, and I did do what I needed to do, but the only reason I wasn't here with you was because I was sure you were in good hands with Simon and Barbara. How did things go?"

"Simon was great!" Tiffany said. "He tore down Mr. McGuire's medical witness and then he presented that nice Dr. Greenbaum, who said Derek's injuries indicated trauma from shaking that took place days before he actually died. That's what we hoped he'd say, right?"

"Right," Jayda said as she straightened up, then she looked to Simon's mother for confirmation.

"Things seem to be going as well as Simon could hope with the trial," she said. But Jayda could tell that something else was weighing on her mind in regard to her son.

"I'm sorry I wasn't here," she said again.

Barbara waved a dismissive hand. “You can’t be in two places at once. I decided maybe you were trying to figure out some things related to Saturday morning at my house.”

Leave it to Barbara to be so direct. No proverbial six-hundred-pound gorillas would be left unmentioned by this woman. Jayda liked that about her. “Yes, that’s what I was doing,” she admitted. “I apologize for how I behaved that day.”

Barbara moved in for a quick hug of her own, saying, “We understand and we still love you.”

Instantly tears threatened and Jayda struggled to blink them back. Barbara was already returning to her seat in the spectator’s area by the time Jayda regained self-control. Tiffany, too, made her way toward the defense table. Standing there, Jayda let Barbara’s words envelop her. This was hard to do after years of dismissing the possibility that anyone could care about such a damaged human being. But after spending much of the previous day with her therapist, Jayda knew she had to let the kindness of people such as Tiffany and Barbara help her heal. Already, she could feel the old open wound beginning to close. But she had one other person to face.

He came through the door behind the judge’s bench with his serious, focused lawyer’s expression on his handsome face. The determined set of his jaw made him look older, a force to be reckoned with. The prosecutor came out after him and his face was grim. But Jayda gave him only a split second of her attention because Simon was striding toward the table where Tiffany sat. When he focused on the girl, he smiled broadly, warmly, lovingly. The sight of this child transformed him back into the man whose image Jayda had imprinted in her mind—and on her heart.

Tiffany said something to Simon that Jayda couldn’t

hear from where she stood. But Simon sobered and looked in her direction. His gaze met hers. Jayda read more emotions in his eyes than she was able to identify. She'd expected a man such as Simon would tame his feelings and keep them hidden. But he wasn't making any effort to hide the mixture of tenderness and sorrow inside him. Once again she had to blink away the sting of tears, even as she wondered how he could look at her with anything other than anger and resentment after what she'd done.

Somehow, she found the strength to move forward, through the swinging gate and over to her seat at the defense table. Simon stood still, watching her.

"We're glad you're back," he said softly.

All she could do was nod. She felt she'd been forgiven, and she hadn't expected that. Yet she couldn't help noticing that he'd said "we're glad" rather than "I'm glad." Understandable that he'd distance himself with words, even if he couldn't hide his feelings completely. She'd hurt him in such a fundamental way that he was right to protect himself from her as best he could.

Getting back to business, Simon motioned toward the door from which he had just emerged. "I persuaded the judge to let us call Patricia Baldridge as a witness, even though she wasn't on the list we gave the court before trial started. McGuire isn't happy about it. He wants time to talk to her first. I'll be there when he does, but he might still be able to confuse her."

"Did you meet with her?" Jayda managed to ask, grateful for court-related things to address.

He sat down in his usual chair, with Tiffany between them. "Yes, and you were right that her story could help us. My theory is that Patricia's ex-husband managed to get Derek alone, probably out in the yard. God knows the kids weren't well supervised. Unbeknownst to anyone, the father tried to shake the whereabouts of Derek's mother out of the boy. Patricia told me her husband had been violent toward the child before. And she'd heard that he'd been looking for her. But I'm not sure we can trust what she'll say on the witness stand. I'll have to handle her carefully."

Jayda understood that Derek's mother couldn't be counted on for consistency. If she didn't say what they expected her to say, she could do Tiffany more harm than good. Still, she had a story to tell that might make her appearance worth the risk, put doubt into the minds of the jurors, even if no one ever actually proved who killed the three-year-old. It would be up to the police to reopen the case, if Tiffany was acquitted. Maybe they'd eventually find enough evidence to convict Derek's father—if the man could even be found.

"You'll do great," Tiffany told Simon. "Just like you did with Dr. Westin and Dr. Greenbaum." She turned to Jayda. "You should have seen him," she said with enthusiasm. "He was awesome!"

Jayda had to smile—her first smile since returning from Hagerstown. Tiffany's positive attitude in the midst of her trial was something to admire. If she could remain undaunted even now, surely Jayda could face her own demons and find a way to move on with her life. She'd be alone for a while, but there would be other people with whom she might be able to forge relationships.

"Thanks, Tif," Simon said with a smile.

"Will you be putting me up there on the witness stand soon?" Tiffany asked. She'd made it clear that she wanted the chance to speak up for herself, to tell what happened that day in her own words.

At once Simon's expression shuttered and those cool, clear attorney's eyes returned, hiding the man beneath. "It's all about timing and how things play out with the other witnesses," he said. Not lying to the girl, but not revealing the fact that he didn't want to put his youthful client on the witness stand, where she'd have to endure a grueling cross-examination. Simon had confided this to Jayda a week earlier.

"Okay," said Tiffany, oblivious to the possibility she might not get the opportunity she longed for.

Jayda found herself reaching across the gap between their chairs and taking Tiffany's small hand in her own. When the bailiff announced that Judge Becker was about to enter the courtroom they stood together, hand in hand. They kept their clasped palms together through most of the long day, watching as Simon used his impressive skill to coax exactly what he wanted out of each witness and then having to sit silently as Bob McGuire undid at least some of Simon's work through clever cross-examination. By the end of the day, Jayda's stomach hurt and Tiffany appeared to be completely exhausted. Barbara had wilted, too.

"Let's go home," Simon said to Tiffany and his mother after he'd packed his notes into his briefcase.

Jayda watched the three of them prepare to leave and a powerful longing tightened her chest. They looked like a family, and they were going home in the comfort of one another's company. She thought about her silent, empty apartment. Not even a cat waiting to greet her. How had her life come to be so unutterably lonely?

"Come for dinner?" Barbara called over her shoulder. "We'd really like to have you with us when we talk with Tiffany about the day's events."

And that was her job, after all. Jayda knew Barbara had put it in those terms so she could accept the invitation comfortably. Simon's face remained unreadable. Tiffany, however, made her weary way back to where Jayda stood. She slipped her hand into Jayda's once more and drew her along to where the other two adults waited.

"We need you," Tiffany said softly as they went. And Jayda couldn't say no.

Avoiding eye contact with Simon and Barbara, she went out of the courtroom and into the parking garage. She followed them in her own car, feeling like a stray puppy trying to worm its way into the hearts of new family members. Pathetic. But she'd stay in their home awhile, anyway.

She'd take what she could get, and at Tiffany's bedtime, she stored up memories of the child's laughter and Simon's fatherly kindness as he tucked her into bed and kissed her on the forehead. Barbara watched from the bedroom doorway beside Jayda and said softly, "He reminds me of his father these days—I've never seen this side of Simon before. We have you to thank for bringing this to us."

Jayda could think of nothing to say in response. "It's time for me to be heading home," she said, and then bade Barbara good-night and slipped out of the house while Simon was still in Tiffany's room. No sense in waiting around for awkward moments between them. She couldn't bear that. So she drove home through the darkness and then the bright lights of Baltimore, and slept fitfully in her silent apartment until it was time to head back to court the next morning.

THURSDAY EVENING. SOCIAL Services representative Frances Smith sat across from Simon in his mother's living room as he squirmed over her questions about becoming an adoptive parent.

"You live here with your mother?" she asked for the second time.

"Just temporarily," he said. "I'm looking for a house of our own." He knew that being a homeowner would show him to be responsible and dedicated to Tiffany's well-being.

But the woman seemed to want to twist things. "So you'd be living alone with an eleven-year-old girl," she said. There was no accusation in her voice, just a flat statement of fact, but Simon knew how those words sounded, strung together in that way. Words were his whole life and he knew, himself, how to shift their meaning with little effort.

"Yes," he admitted. There was no hope of claiming that his bachelor state would be temporary. As much as he wished he could rekindle something with Jayda, the way things were going he might never marry.

"Do you have a girlfriend? A significant other?"

This was where Simon wished he had led a less openly heterosexual life. If he could only claim he batted for the home team, his chances of winning Tiffany's adoption might be stronger. He'd toyed with the idea of enlisting Jayda to pretend they were together romantically to persuade Ms. Smith that he was no threat to Tiffany, but that seemed wrong. And some newly tapped well of morality wouldn't let him ask Jayda to lie for him, anyway, no matter how important the reason.

"No, not right now. I date, of course, but there's no one to distract me from being a good parent," he said. Hey, he could manipulate words to his advantage, too, and felt no compunction about doing so. There was a tape recorder whirring beside them, and he wanted to go on record as claiming that his main focus was Tiffany's well-being.

"Have you always lived with your mother?" she asked.

That took Simon by surprise. "No!" he rushed to say.

"I just sold my condo in Baltimore. I've lived there since landing the position with my law firm."

"Yes, let's talk about the law firm. I hear from Mr. Canter that you're planning to leave and open your own law office."

Damn that bastard Canter. Simon had known Ms. Smith would need to talk to Glen Boyden. But she wouldn't normally have chatted with Canter. The man would have had to manipulate his schedule on purpose to be at the office at just the right time to come across the social worker.

Simon hid his distaste for his colleague. "I've been thinking for some time about starting my own firm so that I'll be able to spend more time at home with Tiffany." Did he sound as nervous as he felt?

"Would you mind sending us your financial records? We need to be sure there won't be income problems, since you're making so many life changes at one time."

"Sure," he said, fighting irritation. "Even after leaving Boyden and Whitby, I'll be more solvent than most of your prospective adopting parents. My penthouse sold for nearly a million dollars." He didn't mention that paying off his mortgage had eaten up a chunk of that. "And if things get tight, I also have a classic car worth nearly another quarter million that I can sell." His brain froze for a moment as he contemplated selling his beloved car. That Mustang was like a beautiful mistress to him and he loved it. Yet he knew he would sacrifice it if he had to for Tiffany.

"Speaking of your car, I understand it doesn't have normal seat belts or air bags," the social worker pointed out.

His heart pounded. He'd have to get a safer car immediately. Because he'd also be going through money to open his own office, the need for another car meant he'd be parting with the Mustang no matter what. That Shelby 500 had defined him for so many years, he wasn't sure he would be the same man without it. But he fought away the ache in his heart and willed himself to appear calm and collected.

"Yes, I know I'll need a more suitable car. I'll get right on that. The only reason I haven't done so already is we've been using my mother's car. And we've been busy with Tiffany's trial."

Ms. Smith leaned back and looked at him with a penetrating gaze. She wasn't a bad person, but clearly she took her job more seriously than some. She wouldn't be giving him the okay on this adoption just because Tiffany was an accused felon and had no other options. "Why would you want to take on the responsibility of becoming the father of an eleven-year-old girl?" she asked. "I mean, you're successful and well respected. Our background check indicated no lack of female friends. So why would you turn that life upside down for this child?"

He returned her gaze, the way he would when trying to see inside a client's mind, steadily holding eye contact. "Because she's a wonderful girl who deserves more than she's gotten so far. Because she and I understand each other, when others don't seem to. Because she's wormed her way into my heart over the course of this trial. Because she's innocent, no matter how the jury decides. Because I know what it's like to need a family, and given that no other parents will step forward to take on someone with Tiffany's history, I figure a father is at least halfway to a family. I'm all she's likely to get."

"And what's in it for you?" she asked evenly.

That was a much harder question. Even though words usually came easily to him, describing what he got out of his relationship with Tiffany would be nearly impossible. But he knew he had to try. "You've observed us together, Ms. Smith. So you know how much alike we are. We even have the same temper, though I hope I've learned to control mine better now that I'm an adult. But more than what we have in common, it's what she's brought to my life that's important." He hesitated, searching for the words to describe exactly what Tiffany meant to him without giving any ammunition to those who worried he might be a predator and the others who figured him for an emotional cripple using a child to make his life meaningful. "She's taught me about reaching out to people, to comfort and be comforted. She's shown me how to open up to loving another human being, no matter how frightening that can be. I didn't expect to understand her so well or to find something unique inside myself that would help me to deal with her upsets. But I do and I can. We share similar pasts. I'd like us to share a future, too."

Frances Smith looked mildly impressed. Simon hoped that was a good sign. He hoped she'd recommend approval of him as Tiffany's adoptive father. But she gave no indication one way or the other. By the time the interview was over, he felt utterly exhausted and frustrated. He wanted more than anything in the world to talk to Jayda or even to just sit beside her watching a movie the way they had that one night they'd spent together in her apartment. But he didn't dare reach out to her yet. He had a plan—a weak plan, to be sure, but it was all he had and he was going to stick with it. That plan called for him to wait until Friday night, when the main portion of the trial was over, and the weekend stretched before them.

THEY WEREN'T GOING TO APPROVE Simon's adoption of Tiffany, and it made Jayda sick inside to realize this. She'd heard talk in the office about Simon. Not one of the other social workers thought the adoption should be approved. Each of them believed Tiffany would be better off in foster care than chancing a life with a man who seemed to be such an unlikely candidate for fatherhood. Jayda wanted to shake them all and explain that Simon was one of the best men she'd ever known, that he would protect Tiffany and would never, ever harm her. But she couldn't do that, and she'd been cautioned on more than one occasion by Marla to remain neutral.

As she listened to Simon query Patricia Baldridge on the witness stand, Jayda couldn't help but worry. What would happen to Tiffany if Simon didn't prevail? What would happen to her if he *did?* Even if she was acquitted, she couldn't live with Barbara indefinitely. Simon's mother was only allowed to take on a preteen because of the desperate circumstances. At seventy years old, the woman's age made her unsuitable for the long-term care of a growing girl. Feeling helpless, Jayda tried to focus on Simon's voice once more. But listening to him did nothing to ease the sorrow in her heart, and she couldn't help wishing that soothing, reassuring voice could be part of her life—along with the man it belonged to—even after the trial ended.

"Mrs. Baldridge, I know this must be hard for you. But if you could tell the jury about your husband, that would help a great deal. We need to understand all the possible circumstances related to your son's death."

Patricia sniffed and then ran her hand beneath her nose. She looked better than when Jayda had first met her, but not by much. Detoxing was not an easy experience, and every agonizing moment of it showed on the woman's face. And then there was the growing pain of her young son's death to contend with, as the effect of the drugs wore off and she gradually came to understand that he was gone forever. "My husband—my ex-husband—is now and ever shall be a son of a bitch."

"And was he trying to find you?" Simon prodded.

"Yes. He'd been trying to find me because he thought I had something of his."

"What did he think you had?"

"A bomb of tragic magic. But I never had it," she said as she eyed the men in uniform who were standing guard inside the courtroom. "I never had it—he just thinks I do. So he was looking for me."

Simon moved closer to the woman to distract her from the crowd. "Can you explain to us what 'tragic magic' is?"

"I told you before, it's cocaine. A whole bomb. Stupid idiot lost it somehow and he thinks I have it. Or he figures I've got the money from selling it. Wrong on both counts."

"So your husband's name is...?"

"Joe Martin Baldridge."

A name for the jury. The name of someone else to blame for Derek's death. Someone other than Tiffany. From this initial triumph, Simon carefully, gently, painstakingly guided the woman to describe the abuse she and Derek had endured at Joe Martin's hands, tell how she'd run off to protect herself and her son. She explained how Derek had ended up in foster care because she hadn't been able to take good enough care of him, how her husband hadn't cared about his son—only about getting his hands on his ex and the drugs he believed she'd stolen from him.

"If your husband had found Derek and if your son wouldn't or couldn't tell him where you were, would Joe be capable of harming Derek?"

"He slapped us both around enough when we were together, so I guess he could have. But Social Services said they wouldn't even let me know where my kid was staying, so I don't see how Joe would have found him."

This was more than Simon had wanted her to say, Jayda knew. But he appeared unfazed by it. Calmly, he asked again, "But if he was desperate and clever enough to find Derek, in the hope of finding you, would he have been capable of hurting your son to try to get at you?"

"Sure. He'd have done anything to find me."

"That's all I need for now, Mrs. Baldridge, thank you." He came back to the defense table and Jayda could see he was on edge. His body seemed to exude tension. They both knew that cross-examination could undo most of the good Simon had just done for Tiffany's case. It was only a matter of how much damage McGuire would do.

On cross, the prosecutor focused first on the woman's own drug abuse. He used the simple tactic of asking where she currently resided. She had no choice but to give the name of the rehab facility—she had no other address.

"How long has it been since you last saw your husband, Joseph Baldridge?"

"His name isn't Joseph, it's just Joe Martin. That's the name his mother gave him."

McGuire smiled congenially at the woman, as if he wanted to be her friend. "My apologies. How long since you last saw Joe?"

"A year. Maybe more."

"Then how would you know he was trying to find you after all that time?"

"Because I know Joe and he wouldn't give up. Plus, on the streets, nothing is secret. I heard it from people I know, that he was looking for me. Looking real hard."

"But for all you know, he could be dead. Drug dealers don't have long life spans."

"Did I ever say he was a drug dealer?" Patricia retorted.

"You said you took his crack cocaine and that's why he was after you."

"I said he *thought* I took his crack. I never said I actually took it." She glanced at the bailiff again as if she half expected the handcuffs to come out.

"Did you take it?" McGuire asked. "Remember, you're under oath."

The witness hesitated, looked at Simon, who appeared impassive even though Jayda could tell he was wound tight and hyperfocused. Patricia's gaze shifted to the guards and then to the judge.

Becker interjected, "Just answer the attorney's question, Mrs. Baldridge. Perjury is also a crime."

"All right," she said. "I did take it. But it's gone, long gone. And I'm clean now at the rehab."

"That's all I need from this witness, Your Honor," McGuire said. Indeed, he had taunted her into revealing that she was a drug user and that she was willing to lie under oath. As a defense witness, Patricia Baldridge was almost as bad as having none at all.

Simon stood respectfully. "No redirect, Your Honor." He sat back down, and they waited while Patricia Baldridge was led out of the courtroom again.

"Further witnesses?" asked the judge.

"Yes, Your Honor. Tiffany Thompson would like to take the stand in her own defense."

CHAPTER FIFTEEN

JAYDA KNEW SIMON FELT he had no choice about having Tiffany testify. He couldn't leave the jury with the lasting memory of Patricia's muddled testimony. And if he tried to rest his case now, Tiffany might never forgive him. As much as Jayda didn't like subjecting the girl to the prosecution's cross-examination, she'd agreed with Simon about letting her have her say on the witness stand.

She looked tiny and meek in the witness chair—her toes didn't even touch the floor. No one could have looked less like a murderer than Tiffany. And she told her story calmly at first, reviewing with Simon the events that had led up to Derek's final moments. When it came time to explain what happened just prior to Derek's death and after her foster mother came home, Tiffany seemed frightened and vulnerable. Jayda banked on Tiffany's vulnerable state negating some of the damage her foster mother had done as a prosecution witness.

Though Simon had done a solid job of discrediting the foster mother, Hester Amity—who'd left two young foster children alone, against both the law and fostering regulations in Maryland—he hadn't shaken the woman's recollection of what Tiffany had said that day. This was the basis for the prosecution's dogged pursuit of Tiffany as an adult murderer, despite her age and the controversy the case had raised in the media.

After Simon finished guiding Tiffany through her story, the prosecutor stepped halfway to where she sat between the judge and the jury and spoke from the center of the room. "When Ms. Hester came in from outside, she saw you with Derek, didn't she?"

"Yes," Tiffany said warily.

"And you spoke the words, 'I didn't mean to do it.' Is that right?"

"I can't remember saying that." She'd already told the jury the same thing moments before.

"But your foster mother says those were your exact words."

Tiffany didn't say anything. Simon had previously explained to her that calling her foster mother a liar might make her seem older and angrier and that it could work against her.

"And you feel guilty about Derek's death?" McGuire asked.

"No, I feel sad that I couldn't do anything to help him." Her voice seemed to be getting stronger and more determined, much like it did other times when she was building up to one of her outbursts of anger. Jayda began to fear that Tiffany would lose her composure. At the very least she would seem older to the jury if she talked in that mature way of hers.

"When someone says, 'I didn't mean to do it,' wouldn't most people assume that person was guilty of something?"

Simon leaped to his feet and called out "Objection! He's asking the child to speculate about what other people would think."

"Sustained," Judge Becker said. "Mr. McGuire, are you almost finished?"

Tiffany looked at the judge and said in a clear voice, "Sometimes people say things because they're scared or because they've gotten used to being blamed for things they didn't do or because things just blurt out for no good reason, right?"

Judge Becker smiled at her. "Sometimes that's right."

Relief washed through Jayda. That exchange couldn't have gone better if they'd scripted it. The judge seemed to be favoring Tiffany and that was bound to affect the jury to her advantage.

But McGuire wasn't done. "Ms. Thompson, you have a history of violent behavior, isn't that right?"

"No, sir," she said with a tiny lift of her chin.

"Your record clearly shows..."

"But you asked me if I have a history of violence and I don't. I know what my record says, but sometimes people exaggerate. Sometimes people make too much out of other people getting angry. I get angry sometimes. Have you ever been in foster care, Mr. McGuire?"

Uh-oh, now she'd been pushed to the point of asking clever questions far beyond her years. And that steely look had come into her eyes that indicated her fury was growing. Simon had worked so hard to paint her as a child, frail, softhearted and incapable of adult forethought and strength and rage. But here she was, standing up for herself in an extremely adult manner and on the precipice of a meltdown. Jayda had to will herself not to groan in dismay.

"I'm not on trial for murder, Ms. Thompson, so I'll ask the questions," McGuire said curtly.

Simon got to his feet again. "Your Honor, this has gone

far enough. Prosecution is attempting to twist this child's words and make her out to be something she clearly is not."

The judge looked at Tiffany, who did her best shrinking-violet imitation, now that Simon had reminded her of how she was supposed to appear. "I agree," said the judge, scowling at the prosecutor. "Any redirect?" he asked Simon.

"No, Your Honor. She's been through enough today," Simon responded, getting in that last little point of sympathy in front of the jury. "The defense rests."

Jayda let out a sigh of pent-up breath she hadn't realized she'd been holding. It was over except for closing arguments, which were to be given on Monday. Then the instructions would go to the jury and Tiffany's fate would be in the hands of these men and women. But at least she knew she'd done her best for the girl. And Simon had been the right choice for this case.

Looking on as Simon accepted his usual hug from Tiffany, who remained in his arms longer than usual, clinging to him for support after the ordeal of testifying, Jayda wished once more for a place in the family these two were attempting to build. But soon, very soon, she wouldn't see either of them again.

SIMON CARRIED TIFFANY INTO the house without waking her up, even when he laid her down on her bed and took off her shoes. Her ankle monitor chafed her delicate skin and he hated that she still had to wear it. Almost over, he told himself. If only he could feel sure he'd be allowed to give her a home after her acquittal. If only he could be sure he'd won that acquittal for her. His closing argument on Monday would need to be nothing short of spectacular. The responsibility weighed heavily on him. Yet he still vibrated with leftover nervous energy. He needed an outlet.

He called Jayda. "She's asleep and Mom's going to bed, too. But I'm still pumped with adrenaline from court today. I need to get out, expend some energy. Come with me?"

"Um," she said. "To do what?"

"It doesn't matter. We could go dancing, or walk around the harbor or see a movie. Please don't leave me trapped here alone tonight."

"You have lots of other friends you can call," she said.

"Not anymore. Funny how quitting the law firm killed off all those superficial relationships based on coattails and ambition."

"You *quit?*"

"Boyden and I mutually agreed to part ways. But he was going to fire me if I hadn't agreed to go. I've been spending too much time on Tiffany's case to suit them."

"What will you do?" The dismay in her voice raised his spirits. She must care at least a little.

"I'll open my own practice. Listen, let's talk about this after I pick you up. I'm selling the Mustang, so this will be one of my last opportunities to take it out for a spin. I can be there in half an hour." He knew he was being pushier than he ought to be with Jayda. But he was feeling desperate to see her and he couldn't stop himself.

"Okay," she said after a brief hesitation.

Step one of his plan to win Jayda was accomplished with that single word from her. He hoped he could coax her to say it over and over again, all through the night.

"HOW ABOUT THAT COMEDY playing at the Charles?" he suggested as he opened the door out on to the street for her.

"In all the years I've lived in this city, I've never been to the Charles theater. Some pretty odd movies play there."

"You'll love it," he said. "This movie isn't all that odd, for once, and the Charles is old and quaint—it's sort of a throwback to old-fashioned cinemas."

"Sounds like fun. We could both use some laughter."

He smiled at her as he opened the car door, once again appreciating her sexy legs as she slid into the low bucket seat. Then he was beside her, enthralled by her scent and nearness and that aura of wholesomeness she always seemed to exude.

"I'm sorry you have to sell your car," she said. And she sounded completely sincere. What other woman on the planet would care that he had to part with his beloved vehicle?

"I'll need the money for start-up costs for my law office. I'd rather sell than build up debt before I even get going. Anyway, I bought her as an investment," he said as he smoothed his palm lovingly over the dashboard. "Time for her to pay off."

"What will you get? A hundred grand?"

"I'm holding out for a quarter million. And I think I'll get it."

She made an appreciative sound, and he noticed that she, too, ran her fingers delicately over the inside of the passenger door. Watching her reverent treatment of the car made his chest tighten and his body heat. He silently reminded himself he needed to be gentle with this woman, had to hold back, let her take the lead, cautiously persuade without ever making her feel pushed. That had seemed easier to do when he hadn't been sitting in such close proximity.

IT WAS GREAT TO HEAR Simon laugh during the movie. Fun, too, to discover that they both found the same sorts of things amusing. At times, they were the only ones chuckling, because the wit in the script was often subtle. The film ended before Jayda was ready to give up on the happy feeling she'd gained while sharing the evening with Simon.

In no time, he'd parked his car near her apartment. They walked to her door in silence, but it was a congenial, comfortable quiet. The atmosphere didn't become awkward until they stood right outside the entrance to her place.

She hesitated only a moment, afraid he'd decline but determined to give it a try. "Do you want to come in for a while?" she asked.

"Yes," he said, and the quickness of his response made her insides flutter with happiness.

"Can I get you some wine, or coffee, or tea?" she offered once they got in her living room.

"Wine would be nice, if you'll join me," he said.

Sure, why not, she thought. A glass of wine might make them both forget what had happened that fateful morning in Tiffany's bedroom when she'd ruined everything. She opened a bottle. When she turned back toward the kitchen doorway, he was there beside her with that hungry look in his eyes. She froze, waiting to see what he would do.

"I want to kiss you," he said in that sensual voice of his.

"Okay," she said.

He moved fractionally closer. "I don't want to frighten you off."

"I'll try not to let you." She leaned a little toward him, encouragingly.

"Then it's all right if I touch you?"

"Yes," she said. And she dared to press her palms against

his chest, slowly passing her hands over the muscles that lay beneath the shirt.

He sucked in a breath, and then bent down to close his mouth over hers. But he didn't touch her with his hands. He let her do all the touching. Though he raised his arms as if he longed to pull her close, he seemed to be resisting. The strain of holding back became more obvious as he continued to kiss her.

She took the initiative and fitted her body against his. Clearly he wanted her—and she wanted him. Did he know how much? Could she show him? Wrapping her arms around his neck, she pressed herself closer, making him groan. But he still restrained himself. She was grateful that he had such self-control, that he gave her all the power, but she wondered how long it would last.

Not long. In another heartbeat, he extracted himself from her arms and turned his back to her, giving a rueful chuckle and breathing hard. "This isn't how I'd planned it," he said.

"You planned how you'd kiss me?"

"Oh, I had a plan, all right. But it wasn't only about kissing."

She stared at him, joy and relief racing through her. He'd truly forgiven her, she realized. Somehow, he'd gotten past what she'd done that terrible morning and he still wanted her. At least for kissing, and maybe for something more. It wasn't a promise to love her forever, but it was certainly a start. And she'd take it.

"I went to visit my mother after I… After the incident with Tiffany's splinter."

Simon leaned back against the kitchen countertop, prepared to listen. "Did that help?"

"I think so. It's what some of my therapists had suggested years ago. I needed to confront her and try to forgive her, they said, before I could move on."

"That's not possible," he said with a scowl. "What she did was unforgivable."

"Maybe not. I told her that as an adult I can see the things my uncle did were not my fault. And I know that bad things sometimes happen to good kids. I told her I wish she'd protected me and that I resent her for not doing that." She paused to assess how she felt about the experience with her mother. "It turns out that sometimes just saying the words out loud can make a difference. That, and a lot of therapy."

"That's where you've been going when you've declined my mother's dinner invitations?"

She nodded. "Seems to be working. I...I don't think I was ever really afraid of you. Just overwhelmed by what you seemed to represent."

He scowled. "I still represent the same kind of man. That isn't going to change, even though I'm not with a high-powered firm any longer."

She couldn't deny that.

"I had this plan," he said. "I figured I'd let you be in complete control of anything and everything physical between us. My assumption was you'd feel more comfortable that way. And honestly, the thought of being at your mercy makes me want you even more."

Her heart began to beat rapidly, and the air around her seemed to grow warmer as she listened to his seductive voice saying such seductive things.

"But I'm not sure I'll be able to hold back. I'm used to taking charge and I might forget I'm not supposed to be doing that. I couldn't even keep on kissing you, standing in your kitchen, without the overpowering urge to sweep you off your feet and carry you into the bedroom."

"That's okay," she said, even though she couldn't be sure that it would be. If he'd swept her up a few minutes ago, would she have reverted to her old self—would she have panicked?

"Well, I'm not so sure it would be okay in the long run. And frankly, it might do me good to relinquish control to you. It would certainly be a new experience." He was smiling wistfully now and he'd moved a little closer to her. When he spoke again, he touched her cheek ever so gently with the tips of his fingers and stood with only inches separating their heated bodies. "So I figure there's only one solution," he whispered.

"What's that?" she murmured as she thought about his mouth and the silky probing of his tongue and the masculine scent of him and the beauty of his muscular body.

"You'll have to take me to your room and tie me to your bed. Then you'll be able to have your wicked way with me, and I'll be completely at your mercy."

Her heart began to race in earnest then, and she sensed he was equally affected by his own daring suggestion. But he said one more thing that clinched the deal.

"Please," he whispered into her ear. She could hear the carnal hunger in his voice and she couldn't deny him.

CHAPTER SIXTEEN

THERE HAD CERTAINLY BEEN other times in Simon's life when he'd had no control over what would happen to him next. But those times had all been years ago and he had no clear memories of them. All that remained imprinted on his psyche was the need to be in command of events around him. He'd gone to law school to acquire the skills he needed to be the one with the greatest competence in most situations. He'd honed those skills until he'd become a force to reckon with. While he'd tried to be careful not to wield his authority thoughtlessly or use his ability to influence people lightly, he realized only now for the first time that giving up the dominant role was going to be enormously difficult.

And yet he wanted to give it all up to Jayda. As she led him by the hand to her bedroom and quietly suggested he make himself comfortable on her bed, as she went to her dresser and pulled out two colorful silk scarves, he knew he wouldn't regret subjugating himself to this woman.

But his heart hammered in terror all the same, even as his body responded with an urgent sexual need. She approached him with the scarves, stood over him for a moment, and he both feared and desired her with equal fervor.

"I don't think I can do it," she whispered. "It doesn't seem right. You shouldn't have to do this for me."

"The longer you hesitate, the more convinced I am that it's necessary," he heard himself saying. Inside, part of his mind told him to leap at the reprieve she offered. He could be gentle with her without the restraints, he told himself. But the part of him that loved her knew that he should follow through.

"But I trust you," she said as she sat down beside him on the bed.

Even fully clothed, her nearness made his blood course hotly through his veins. "I'm not sure I can trust myself," he said with a laugh. "Don't make me rely on my honor tonight. There'll be other times to test my self-control."

She didn't seem to be able to make herself move, so he lifted his arms until they were positioned where they'd need to be for her to secure his wrists to the bed frame. With a shake of her head she did what he'd asked, tying him down, taking away that dominance he'd grown so comfortable with. As she leaned over to finish, a surge of lust poured through him. But there wasn't a thing he could do about it.

"Too many clothes," he rasped.

She smiled at him, and he could see that she was empowered by this daring thing they were doing. She straddled his hips and began to unbutton her blouse. A groan came unbidden from his throat as she revealed herself to him. He wanted to touch her, but he could only look. Soon, only panties and bra remained, but she left them on while she worked on his clothing.

His shoes and socks fell to the floor and she ran her finger along the soles of his feet, sending bolts of sensation over his flesh. Then she undid his shirt, spread the cloth to either side and ran her palms over his chest. His breath came fast and sharp now, and he found himself straining against his bonds, flexing abdominal muscles as she touched him.

As she slowly, methodically, removed the rest of his clothing, Simon realized he could twist his right hand free from its tether if he wanted to. But he didn't. He just let Jayda have her way with him, let her press her body to his and kiss him as deeply and sensuously as she desired. Clearly, she was enjoying her power. Freedom from the constraints of her past did wonderful things to her, transforming her into a confident, wholly sexual woman. And he loved every inch of her, even if only with his eyes and the portions of his flesh she chose to touch.

"You're everything I'd imagined," she said as she raked her gaze along the length of his body. She'd discarded every stitch of her clothing now and he lay nearly as naked, with only his open shirt still on.

"You're going to be the death of me, Jayda. Come closer and feel how fast my heart is beating. Come find out how heated my skin is now. Please make love to me." There was that burning, insistent need in his voice again—a tone he never thought he'd let anyone hear. But with Jayda he didn't care. He trusted her to respect this unfamiliar vulnerability of his.

"Yes," she said as she straddled him once more. "Yes," she sighed as she shifted into an ideal position. "Yes," she moaned as Simon lifted his hips, the only thing he could do under the circumstances, and joined their bodies together in the most intimate physical connection a man and woman can enjoy.

There were no more words after that. Raw pleasure took hold of him, and if Jayda spoke, he could make no sense of it, so focused had he become on the sensations rushing over him. Nearly beyond endurance, he held himself back just long enough for her to find her own way, felt those glorious contractions take hold, listened to the sounds of her ultimate pleasure, and then let himself go, too, into that intoxicating spiral of ecstasy, more profound than he'd ever experienced before.

JAYDA LAY BESIDE Simon in blissful fulfillment, wondering how her life could have gone from utterly hopeless to so full of promise in only a few hours. She smiled and nestled closer against his side, caring not at all about the lingering dampness of their bodies. The exertion had been well worth it. When she felt his hand sweep gently down her arm she even shivered a little, as the sensation of his touch rekindled desire.

Then she remembered that she'd tied him up, that he must be uncomfortable—and that he shouldn't be able to touch her at all. She lifted herself to look at his face and found him grinning a well-satisfied smile at her.

"You're not tied up anymore, I see."

"You're not very good at tying knots. We'll have to work on that." His smile widened.

Her heart expanded as she looked at him and realized what this implied. He'd said he had to be tied up, but clearly he'd been able to keep himself in check without the restraints. So he'd done the whole tying-up deal for her to make her more comfortable, to help her feel safe. Love filled her heart and the emotion seemed to want to spill over from her eyes. Before she could blink them back, two tears landed on Simon's chest, surprising them both.

"Hey, hey," he said as he rubbed her back and touched her cheek to stem the tide. "What's this about?"

"I'm in love with you," she blurted. Then in acute embarrassment, she buried her face into a pillow, wishing she could take the words back. It was too soon to make such a declaration. She'd embarrass him, make him struggle to find words to appease her without leading her on.

"Is that a bad thing? Doesn't sound like a bad thing to me. Certainly not something we should shed tears over, right?" He seemed completely perplexed, and she recognized a man who didn't cope with a woman's tears easily.

"No," she said with a half laugh. He hadn't said he loved her, too, but he hadn't rejected her, either. She wiped away her tears and tried to come to terms with the riot of emotions. "I'm just so overwhelmed. You've been so good to me."

He smiled. "You were just pretty good to me, too, Jayda. And you can be good to me again that way any time you want." Even though he made light of it, she knew he understood what she'd meant.

"I thought I'd ruined everything."

"Did you really believe I'd give up that easily on what I want? I guess you still have some things to learn about me. As far as I'm concerned, we're only just beginning."

She liked the sound of that and decided it was a good sentence to let the night rest upon. She snuggled beside him once more, remembered his other wrist, still tied to the bed, and reached up to undo the knot. When the scarf had been discarded, she turned her back to his front and let him envelop her in his embrace. It felt safe and warm and true.

In the morning, she found out she'd developed an appetite for sex she hadn't known she was capable of. And Simon eagerly did everything she wanted. It was well past noon before hunger for food forced them from the bed.

As she whisked eggs for a late breakfast, Jayda remembered that the hurdles they'd surmounted the night before—and all through the morning, too—were not the only ones they had to overcome. She hadn't had the heart to tell him what she'd heard regarding his adoption of Tiffany. And she couldn't bear to tell him while the glow of their lovemaking still suffused her body. Later, she promised herself. She'd tell him a little later. Maybe after the case went to the jury, so the news wouldn't affect his closing argument. Yes, that made sense. For now, she'd give him all she could of her devotion and store up as many memories as possible. She didn't see how their relationship could survive the loss of the child they'd both grown to love.

"WHAT WILL YOU TELL TIFFANY if the adoption doesn't go through?" his mother asked Simon as they sat alone on the back deck Sunday evening. He had a printout of his closing argument in front of him. He already knew it by heart, but he wanted to be sure he had just the right tone at key points. He didn't want to look back and have any regrets.

"I haven't thought about that. It seems more productive to stay positive and assume things will work out the way they should."

His mother harrumphed. "Jayda feels you're setting the child up for disappointment. And yourself, too. I'm worried about all three of you."

He took in a deep breath and let it out slowly, trying to push back the ache that his mother's words brought to his heart. "I just have to keep going forward, Mom. There's no sense playing 'what if' until we know something definite."

"But Tiffany's heart is set on it."

"I know," he said as that now-familiar ache began to twist inside him.

"If you were married, they'd approve the adoption," she said, out of the blue.

That got his undivided attention. "Mom!"

"Don't tell me it hasn't crossed your mind."

"Of course it has. But what do you want me to do—go to Jayda and ask her to marry me so I can adopt Tiffany? That would be romantic. How could she say no to that?"

"Interesting that you assumed I expected you to ask Jayda," she said slyly.

He scowled at her. "What, you think Megan would make a good mom for Tiffany?"

"Simon, I don't even know who Megan is, but I bet she's one of the many career-oriented women you casually dated while you thought there was nothing more important than your legal career."

He nodded, staring off into the trees along the border of the yard.

"You're in love with Jayda. Why don't you just tell her that and explain that speeding things up a little might save Tiffany's adoption? She'll understand."

"No, she won't. You know she's been through her own childhood traumas. I'm not going to coerce her into marriage. I mean to take things slowly, ease her into the idea, ask her at a time when she can be certain there's no other reason in the entire world that I'd be proposing to her—just the fact that I love her."

Barbara blinked a few times. "Oh, that is so sweet!" she exclaimed. "You're more like your father every day. Did I ever tell you how he proposed to me?"

Simon smiled. "I think you should tell me again, Mom. This time, I'm primed to hear it the way you've always wanted me to."

"THE DEPARTMENT IS GOING TO deny Simon's adoption of Tiffany," Jayda said to Marla. Her tone was one of accusation and outrage.

"We'll find a more suitable placement for Tiffany. You're too involved to see her case clearly anymore. This is exactly what I was afraid of—that lawyer has you all mixed up."

"You spend an awful lot of time telling me how I should keep myself from becoming involved with Simon while you go home to your beautiful child each night." Jayda knew she shouldn't be so blunt with her boss. But she didn't care about her career as much as she cared about Simon and Tiffany. And it was time to speak the truth. "You weren't supposed to get involved with your client, either, but it didn't turn out entirely bad for you, given how devoted you are as a mother."

"Yes, but I had to move to a different county and start my career over."

Jayda shrugged. It made no difference to her whether she helped kids from inner-city Baltimore or kids from some other city. She'd have a positive effect on at least some kids somewhere. That's all that mattered.

"Is there anything I can do to change the outcome of this adoption review?" she asked. "If you could see them together… If that nearsighted Frances Smith would just spend more time with them, see how much alike they are, understand how they're bonded."

Marla stared at her for a long moment. She shook her head slowly back and forth. "It's hopeless. I tried my best, but I haven't succeeded." She sighed. "You've gone and fallen in love with Simon Montgomery, not to mention that little girl."

Jayda stared back defiantly. There was no use denying it.

Her boss leaned forward and put her elbows on her desk. She steepled her fingers together and took Jayda's measure with her probing gaze. "You want to know what you can do to make the adoption go through?"

Jayda's attention went on high alert at those words. "Is there something I could do to help?"

"Yes, Jayda. There certainly is. But you'll have to be brave. More courageous than you've ever been. For someone like you, it'll feel like jumping out of a plane without a parachute. But my bet is you'll do it."

"I'm listening," Jayda said.

AN AUSPICIOUS DAY, MONDAY. It was the day Simon would deliver his closing argument to Tiffany's jury. The decision would be up to them after that. The very idea seemed ludicrous to Simon, for the first time in his legal career. A jury shouldn't be able to decide this child's future. They didn't know her the way he did. Their judgment was clouded by Bob McGuire's arguments and the written record of Tiffany's past. They could as easily convict her as acquit her, and Simon's soul burned with the knowledge of that.

If they lost, he'd appeal, of course. He'd already begun to work out his strategy, just in case. It might be a good thing to remain positive in the face of possible defeat, but it would be irresponsible not to plan for the worst. He didn't share any of this with Tiffany, or with his mother. The only person he'd confided in was Jayda. She, more than anyone, knew how tormented he felt as he reviewed his notes on this critical day. He didn't let it show. His demeanor gave off the same cool confidence he always had in the courtroom. Practice made perfect, even though this was the first time he'd admitted to himself that he wasn't as cool and confident as he wished he could be.

Again, the prosecutor went first, delivering a damning

and eloquent closing that Simon could only hope the jury wouldn't fall for. It helped that he'd have the last word. But when his turn came and the judge called him forward to address the jury, Simon couldn't remember a single syllable of his prepared closing. All he could think of was how much he loved that little girl who was counting on him today. Minutes ticked by as he searched his mind and fought back an upwelling of emotion he didn't want anyone to see. Juries were moved by facts, by reason, by cogent argument. Even in this age of reality TV and voting by phone for one's favorite rising star, jury members tended to take their jobs seriously and did their best to come to conclusions in the interest of society. This was not the time for emotion or theatrics.

And yet his eyes burned for an endless moment and his throat remained tight. He fought for control but found himself losing the battle when he looked back at Tiffany, sitting there waiting for him to save her life. He blinked back the tide and turned his gaze to Jayda.

She gave him what he needed. Her strength, her confidence in him, shone from her eyes, and he borrowed from her the fortitude he didn't seem able to produce on his own. She held his gaze, and the determination in her beautiful brown eyes flowed into him. He knew she would stand by him, no matter what happened today. She'd fight for Tiffany with him for as long as it took.

"Ladies and gentlemen," he said as he approached the railing in front of the jury box. "There's a young girl who needs your help today. She needs you to see her the way everyone close to her sees her—the way I see her." He hadn't planned to say that. It was never a good idea to bring personal opinions or feelings into a closing argument. But he didn't seem able to hold back the truth. Fortunately, he saw sympathy in the eyes of many of the jurors. Parents, he suspected, who understood the powerful love an adult could have for a child. "A more intelligent, caring kid I have yet to meet," he said as he looked behind him toward the object of his speech. "Tiffany could not have killed Derek Baldridge. She didn't have the motive and she didn't have the means. You heard the evidence in this courtroom that she simply didn't have the strength."

Regaining his composure and hitting his stride, he reviewed with the jury all the flaws he'd uncovered in the prosecution's case. He reminded them of the alternative theories for the cause of Derek's death, reiterated for them the opinion of a renowned medical examiner regarding the trauma the boy had suffered and the likely cause. He went over the fact that even Derek's own mother thought there was another likely explanation for Derek's death and that her suspicion of her husband had been corroborated by the testimony from Mrs. Karowski, who'd proven to be a more valuable witness than he'd expected.

A man had been lurking in the neighborhood, unnoticed by Tiffany or the distracted foster mother, Hester Amity. A man with the strength and motivation to shake his child in frustration until the boy's brain was so badly bruised that he would never be able to survive. It would be up to the police to discover evidence about the real killer in this terrible tragedy, he told them. That would come later. Just because they couldn't produce the actual killer right now didn't mean there wasn't reasonable doubt regarding the child on trial.

By the time he got around to asking the jury to acquit Tiffany, his heart took over his better sense once more. He paused, looking at the girl he hoped he could raise into adulthood, and he couldn't say a single word for a time.

He knew this might play well to the jury, but he preferred to engage such tactics with a clear and reasoned purpose and not because he was overcome with raw emotion. What would he do if these people convicted his daughter? What would he be capable of in order to save her from imprisonment while she awaited appeal?

"Don't multiply this tragedy by claiming another child's life. Acquit this girl and let her get on with her life. Let her visit Derek's grave to say goodbye, let her go to school and make friends and struggle through a normal adolescence and grow into a productive member of society. If you set her free, I give you my word I'll make sure she gets every chance she needs to fulfill her destiny."

He thanked them and sat down and nearly succumbed to the certainty that he'd screwed it up. He closed his eyes as pressure built inside his head, and he remembered every flaw in his argument and replayed every tiny misstep. But then, just when he thought his head might explode, he felt a small hand slip into his and realized Tiffany had made contact again, when he needed it most. Not her usual hug—they had to sit through the judge reading the instructions to the jury first. But her hand in his made all the difference. His headache ebbed and he remembered he was supposed to be the strong one. He sat up a little straighter and once again played the part. Catching Jayda's eye once more, he gave her his best imitation of the indefatigable attorney. It was the least he could do. No matter what, he needed to be strong for his family.

CHAPTER SEVENTEEN

ONCE THE CASE WENT to the jury, there was nothing left to do but wait. Barbara took Tiffany back home and that left Simon and Jayda free to return to their offices.

"You want to get some coffee?" Jayda asked him. "You look like you could use something a lot stiffer, but it's kind of early."

He smiled, but it was a weary, worried smile. He glanced at his watch. "I have an appointment in an hour. It'll take me awhile to drive to it. You want to come with me?"

Confused, she said, "To your meeting?"

"It's not a lawyer meeting. But I think it'll help take your mind off the jury. My sense is they'll be out for some time. There was a lot of evidence and testimony to review. If they make a decision, I'll get a call and we'll all meet back at court."

She sensed he needed company. She'd never seen him so edgy. "Okay, let's go."

"I'll pick you up in front of the courthouse in ten minutes," he said.

When he pulled up to the curb, he was driving a used BMW 325i. It was a nice car, even if preowned.

"I'm still pretending I'm a high-powered attorney, so I need to keep up appearances as best I can," he said when she asked him why he'd chosen this model to replace his

Mustang. "I got a good deal. What? You didn't think I was going to buy a minivan, did you?"

She smiled. "I can't see you in a minivan. Ever."

He became thoughtful. "It could happen someday, if I collect more kids." He said it casually, but Jayda couldn't help remembering what Marla had said about helping him win Tiffany's adoption.

They pulled up to a split-level home with a two-car garage in the suburbs of Baltimore. A For Sale sign stood in the center of the front yard, and Under Contract had been added to the lower edge.

"What's this?" she asked.

"I'm meeting the home inspector here today. I put a bid on the house, but I've stipulated it has to be inspected."

She smiled at him. "It's in the suburbs. I thought you liked living in the city."

"Tiffany will do better in Howard County schools away from the city. You want to walk through the house with me and tell me if you think it would make a good place for Tiffany?"

She looked through her car window at the house. What would happen to Simon if he ended up living there alone without an adopted daughter? Could she live with herself if she didn't do everything in her power to make sure that didn't happen?

"Okay," she said softly. "Let's look at it."

The inspector hadn't arrived yet, and they toured the empty house alone since Simon's real-estate agent had let him borrow the key. There were three bedrooms, two bathrooms, a big family room in the basement.

"The kitchen is a little dated," she said.

"But the price reflects that. I'm hoping to remodel it after we move in," he said. He handed her the price sheet.

"I don't know the first thing about real estate," she said, looking at the paper. "But it's an awfully nice house."

He started to speak, rethought his words, then asked, "As a social worker, do you think this place would improve my chances in the adoption? Ms. Smith seemed to take exception to me living with my mother. Of course, she also seemed worried about me living alone with Tiffany." He ran his fingers through his hair, messing it up.

Jayda had never seen him so unsettled. He was usually so strong, so sure of himself. She wished with all her heart she could reassure him. But the words wouldn't come. She recognized she was afraid—terrified of taking the leap that Marla had suggested.

"There's something else I want to ask you," he said before she found sufficient courage to speak.

Again, her heart raced as if it had some sense of where he might be heading.

"If the jury convicts Tiffany, she's going to be sent to prison."

This wasn't the subject she'd expected, but she rallied quickly. "You'll appeal and win her freedom."

He began to pace through the vacant living room, looking like a trapped animal. "She wouldn't survive prison, Jayda. Even if she survived physically, her spirit would be dead in no time. I can't let them put her there."

"Let's just hope that it doesn't turn out that way. You gave the jury lots of reasons to doubt her guilt. That's all they need to let her go."

He stopped and looked directly into her eyes, and she could see the fear that had taken hold of him. "But what if they don't?" he asked.

"We'll both do the best we can for her," she tried. But she could see that her efforts to be positive weren't working.

"I'll need your help," he said as he approached her.

"I'll help any way I can," she said.

He faced her and took her two hands in his. "Will you? Because the thing I'll need from you is huge. But if the worst happens when the jury returns, I'll be desperate, so I'm going to ask this of you, anyway." He took a breath. "I'll need you to get Tiffany out of wherever they'll be holding her."

"I don't understand."

"If the jury convicts, I'll need you to escort her away from whoever is in charge of her, get her to me somehow. I'll take things from there, but I can't get her free without your help."

She blinked at him and her mind reeled. "Are you saying you plan to abduct her?"

"I want to save her. And I can't think of any other way to do that, if she's convicted."

"Simon, think about what you're saying," she reasoned. "Where would you go? What would you do to support yourselves? Do you really think you could hide indefinitely from the authorities? And what about your mom?" *What about me?* she almost asked.

He turned away, frustration in every muscle. "I've got some of it worked out, but I can't tell you the details. It's better if you don't know, so you can deny any involvement."

"So I'm supposed to say I took Tiffany to the bathroom and you kidnapped her from me? Is that the idea?"

"That's a good plan," he said. "Take her to the bathroom. I can get her from you then."

She stared at him, unable to believe that he'd come up with such a desperate plan.

He didn't speak, but paced a little more, then leaned against a wall looking dejected.

She went and stood beside him, shoulder to shoulder. "I know you just want to protect Tiffany. I want that, too."

"I guess there's only so much positive thinking I can muster," he murmured. "I'm all out."

"Well, I'm not. The jury *has* to acquit. It's the only decision that makes sense."

"I'm glad you think so. Unfortunately, the police aren't likely to dig up much evidence that Derek's father shook him to death, even though they've promised to investigate that angle. Even if they come up with something, or find Joe Martin Baldridge, it won't be soon. The jury could easily decide to convict simply because she's the one that got charged and no one else is readily available."

He looked at his feet and took in a deep breath, then let it out. "I know your office isn't going to approve me to adopt Tiffany." He said it in a flat, dead voice.

She couldn't deny it, as much as she wanted to. Her heart broke for him.

"I need a place of my own, anyway, so I put a bid on this house. But I realize it's not going to help change anyone's mind about whether I'd be a suitable father. When were you going to tell me?" he asked without accusation.

"The final decision hasn't been made yet. There's still a chance—"

"Stop it!" he shouted suddenly. "You know what the decision is going to be. Stop wishing for something else. It won't help."

She could think of no words to comfort him. So she stood beside him in silence. And she made a decision. She loved this man, after all. Loved him so hard, it hurt inside. Marla's advice had been sound. And there was no reason to hesitate, other than her own insecurities.

Yet she didn't want to say anything right here, right now. The atmosphere was all wrong. And the inspector could arrive at any moment to interrupt them. Later, she'd do it later. But not much later. They didn't have much time left.

BY THE TIME SIMON GOT TO his mother's house after dropping Jayda at her car, he'd pulled himself together. He regretted asking Jayda to participate in his desperate plan. He'd never get away with it, anyway.

He sat in the BMW after he parked at the curb and took a few moments to practice pretending to be confident about the outcome of Tiffany's trial. There was no sense in weighing others down with his fear and helplessness. Fortunately, he had a great deal of experience on how to make people see what he wanted them to see. He walked through the door into the kitchen with a smile on his face.

His mother took one look at him and said, "What's wrong?" There was stark terror in her eyes.

He held up his hands to defend against her X-ray vision and rushed to assure her. "I haven't heard anything one way or the other. They can't tell me the verdict before Tiffany hears it herself. You know that."

"Then it's the adoption. Something's gone wrong."

He sighed deeply. "Where's Tiffany?" he asked.

"Playing with your old Nintendo. It helps calm her."

Heavily, he sat in a kitchen chair and let his arms hang limply at his side. There was no sense putting on a stoic front if his mother was going to see right through it. "I'm pretty certain they're not going to approve me as her dad," he said, and his voice broke on the last word. At the same moment, his eyes began to sting. He couldn't look at his mother for fear he'd lose all control. Instead he stared out the back window, into the yard he'd played in as a boy. The tire swing was gone now. The tree it used to hang from had grown quite tall.

"Well, then I'll apply to adopt her," his mom said as she sat down across from him. "I may be old, but she doesn't have a whole lot of prospects. They'll come to see that."

He managed to smile for her. "Sure, that might work." But he already knew it wouldn't. There was no way on earth anyone would allow a seventy-year-old woman to take on a preteen of any kind, never mind one with Tiffany's temperament and history.

"Jayda's here!" Tiffany called from the other room.

Simon didn't understand. He'd just left her at her car an hour before. She hadn't mentioned coming out to the house tonight. Did she know something? Had she somehow persuaded Social Services to change their minds?

He scrambled to his feet and rushed toward the door, but Jayda stepped inside before he got to it.

"Hi," she said, and he could hear the nervousness in her voice.

"Why are you here?" he said without preamble. His mother and Tiffany both hovered nearby as if they also sensed that something was about to happen.

She lifted her eyebrows. "I need to discuss something important with you."

"About what?" he asked, wanting her to spit out whatever she'd come to say as quickly as possible.

"Um, I think we should all move to the living room," she said.

"Why?" Impatience ate away at his civility.

"Simon," his mother admonished. "Do what the lady asked you to do."

Feeling like a chastised child, Simon went into the

living room and sat on the sofa. Tiffany and his mom sat on either side of him. They all looked expectantly at Jayda.

"Uh, could you move to the chair?" she asked him.

"Why?"

"Simon Tyler Montgomery!" That from his mother again.

"Fine," he said, and moved to the chair.

"Okay," Jayda said, and now her hands were trembling. "Okay," she repeated, and Simon's patience nearly crossed the breaking point.

But then she did a very strange thing. She got down on one knee in front of him and grasped one of his hands in both of hers. He was so startled, his brain seemed to come to a complete stop and he just watched her.

"Simon." She seemed to be having trouble catching her breath. "I thought this would be best done with your mom and Tiffany as witnesses. But don't let their presence sway you one way or the other."

"Okay," he said, because she paused and seemed to expect him to speak. His bewilderment mounted.

"I know of just one thing we can do to persuade Social Services to approve Tiffany's adoption. But that's not the only reason I'm doing this. Mostly, it's because I believe we'd eventually get around to this point in the long run. And if speeding things up will ensure Tiffany's well-being, then I think that's what we should do." She took in a deep breath. "So, Simon Montgomery, will you marry me?" And she pulled from her pocket a little black jewel box and opened it in front of his stunned eyes.

"You don't have to wear it if you don't want to," she rushed to say. "It was my grandmother's. The best I could do on short notice. I had to go home to get it. But then I came straight here—because we don't really have time to waste. And I would wear it for you, if you want. It just happens to be my size. But, well, I guess you have to say yes first."

She looked up at him with huge, bright eyes, waiting to see what he would say. Her chin trembled ever so slightly, telling him just how much this beautiful drama cost her emotionally. Glancing at his mother and longed-for daughter, he saw they were completely stunned, frozen in their places with matching expressions of wonderment.

He looked back to the woman kneeling before him and smiled broadly, his heart filled with love instead of the dread that had overtaken it before. "I would be honored to be your husband, Jayda," he said. "I love you so much."

She launched herself into his arms, knocking him into the depths of the seat—a recliner that tipped backward so that he lay flat on his back with his new fiancée sprawled across him in an extremely intimate manner. She was kissing him all over his face, and he had to grasp her head to keep her still long enough to plant a real kiss upon her lips.

"Isn't it supposed to be the other way around?" he heard Tiffany whisper to his mother.

"Whatever gets the job done," his mom replied. "Now, let's leave them to a few minutes of privacy," she suggested.

But Jayda was off Simon and on her feet before anyone could vacate the premises. "No!" she said. "We need to get back to the courthouse."

"Is the jury in already? How could you find that out before…"

"No, no, nothing about the jury. But we need to get married now, today. That way, the adoption papers can be changed to reflect both of us as parents and Marla will fasttrack them to signature."

"You should wait until after the verdict," Tiffany said calmly.

Simon had gotten to his feet, too, so that he and Jayda stood side by side. They both looked down at Tiffany, and in unison, they said, "No, we shouldn't."

All of them laughed. Ah, the human spirit, ready to laugh in the face of possible doom. It made no sense but it didn't have to. Still, he had to be at least a little bit practical about rushing to the courthouse.

"We'll go first thing in the morning," he assured them. Pointing to the clock on the mantel, he added, "It's too late to get a marriage license and persuade the clerk to marry us now, anyway."

"Are they really getting married?" Tiffany asked Barbara with excitement in her voice.

"It looks that way."

Tiffany ran to him, and he swooped her up and she wrapped her arms around his neck. "Thank you," she said to him. "I knew you'd make it happen."

"Don't thank me. Jayda was the one who proposed." He set Tiffany down and she went to Jayda, looked up at her with happiness dancing in her eyes.

"That must have been hard for you to do, backward that way. Thank you for wanting me to be your daughter."

"Maybe I should have asked if you'd have me for your mother beforehand. I'm sorry I didn't even think of that," Jayda said.

"That's okay," the girl said. And she hugged Jayda hard.

"Let's go get ready for bed," Barbara suggested to Tiffany, eyeing Simon and Jayda as if they'd both lost their minds, but with a glint of humor, too. She ushered her foster child up the stairs.

Jayda tipped her face up to Simon. "You won't change your mind, will you?"

He leaned down and whispered into her ear so that only she could hear him. "Why don't you stay the night and make certain I don't."

She laughed. "I will."

He smiled back. "I know."

CHAPTER EIGHTEEN

THE JURY CONTINUED TO deliberate while Jayda and Simon applied for their marriage license. It continued to deliberate while they waited the required two days before standing in front of the clerk of the court to exchange vows. Barbara and Tiffany were there beside them. Marla had also come, eager to get copies of the documentation so she could push through the adoption.

The bride wore a pretty blue dress with a demure hem that went to mid-calf. She didn't wear any cosmetics and she didn't need them. Simon thought she was the most beautiful woman he'd ever seen.

He'd confessed to her earlier that he'd already set his heart on marrying her, but he'd worried she'd think he only wanted her to secure the adoption. She'd responded that Tiffany was a good reason to get married and the only excuse his mother would have accepted for not having an elaborate wedding. Their ceremony lasted less than ten minutes.

As Simon kissed his bride with all the tenderness and passion he planned to bring into their long marriage, his phone rang. It was a special ring tone that meant Denise was calling. She'd missed the wedding so she could stand by for news of the jury, and she wouldn't have called him on his wedding day if she didn't have news.

"Yes," he said into the phone.

"The jury is ready to return a verdict," Denise told him.

"We're on our way." He closed his phone and looked at the faces around him, all tense and expectant. "The jury has reached a decision," he said, trying hard not to let them hear the emotion that gripped his insides in a stranglehold.

"Let's go," Jayda said. She seemed calm, sure.

"Congratulations," Marla said. "I'll get copies of the documents and see how much clout I really have in my agency regarding this adoption. Call me as soon as you know something."

They thanked the clerk and filed out. They had to drive to a different building to get to the courtroom they'd been in all through the trial. It seemed an odd drive to be making on the heels of a wedding. Jayda sat silently, stoically, beside Simon as he maneuvered through traffic. Tiffany and his mother were in the backseat, equally quiet. Simon couldn't think of anything to say, either.

As they took their places at the defense table, Jayda took Tiffany's hand in hers. "I went to see my mother last week. It seems like months ago. She and I hadn't seen each other in a long time. While I was walking to her house and right up to the minute she opened her door, time seemed to do strange things. Slowing down and speeding up randomly. This is kind of like that, too." She gently squeezed Tiffany's fingers. "We want this to be over with, but at the same time we're all so scared we don't want the moment to arrive."

Tiffany nodded, her eyes larger than Simon had ever seen them. She looked as terrified as he felt. But then he had to give his attention to the court proceedings as the bailiff called for them to all rise. The judge took his place and the members of the jury filed in.

"Mr. Foreman, has the jury reached a verdict?" Judge Becker asked.

"Yes, Your Honor, it has."

"Will the defendant please rise," the judge said to Tiffany. Simon stood up with her, and without thinking it through, he put his arm across her narrow shoulders. He got as much comfort from the physical contact as he meant to give. But his heart continued to pound violently under his ribs.

"What has the jury decided?" the judge asked.

"Not guilty, Your Honor."

Silence whistled through the room for a moment. Every soul there seemed to have suspended breathing. Then all at once, Simon found himself laughing amid cheers and whistles and general chaos throughout the court. Even the bailiff wore a smile.

Robert McGuire marched to the defense table and put his hand out to Simon. "I did the best I could to get the conviction my boss wanted. But in the end, this feels like the right conclusion."

"Thank you," Simon said, shaking the man's hand. "I hope you can find and prosecute Derek's real killer."

"I'm working on that," said the younger attorney. "I'll ensure the police go after Joe Martin Baldridge. He's a person of interest now, if not an outright suspect." He gave Simon a nod and walked away.

"Is it over?" Tiffany asked in a barely audible voice.

"Yes, it's over," he said to her. "You're free!"

She looked up at him, her expression unreadable. A tear slipped from one eye, and then the other. She sniffed and tried for a smile, but instead she began to sob. All the emotion she'd done so well to contain came pouring out of her. Simon lifted her up into his arms and held her close as if she were five years old instead of eleven. In another moment, Jayda and Barbara joined them, each wrapping their arms around the pair.

He didn't realize he'd been crying, too, until he lifted his face away from Tiffany's hair. He thought about pretending the dampness on his cheeks was from Tiffany, but then he decided against it. His days of pretending to be cool and controlled and in complete command of his world were over.

At least in front of his family.

"WHY CAN'T I BE HOMESCHOOLED?" Tiffany asked again from the backseat of the minivan Jayda had gotten to replace the Mini Cooper.

"We've been over this a hundred times," Jayda said as she stood by the sliding door while her new daughter climbed out onto the sidewalk in front of her school. "Howard County has some of the best public schools in the nation. You'll like it. And you need to be with kids your own age."

"I prefer adults," she said, not for the first time. Yet for all her bravado, she was clearly terrified.

"And the adults in your life prefer you, too," said Simon, who stood beside them. "But you still have to go to school."

"But I could come to your office and you could teach me in between clients," she insisted.

He put his hand gently on her shoulder. "The thing about negotiating, my young apprentice, is that you need to recognize when you've achieved the best deal you're going to get. I agreed you could come help at the office on Saturdays. But you're still going to go to school."

She sighed in defeat. "I had to take one last shot. I figured you might be feeling particularly vulnerable, seeing your first kid go off to school, and maybe you'd relent."

He smiled at her. "Not a chance."

"Okay. Well, I'll see you when school's over." And with that, she marched toward the entrance and only looked back at them one time.

She disappeared into the flow of students entering the school, but Simon and Jayda stayed on the sidewalk an extra moment. "Is being a parent always going to be this hard?" he asked his wife.

"Psh. You're asking me?" She realized she'd spoken in the tone of her own mother, and that freaked her even more than seeing Tiffany off for her first day integrating with suburban kids. "I've never been a parent, either," she added. "Your mom says it could get worse. God help us."

"She also says it's the best job there is. I think we'll be okay."

"You want me to take you home so you can get your own car or should I drop you at your office?"

"Take me to the office. Denise can bring me home later."

"Don't work too late," she said as she got back into the van.

From the passenger seat, Simon reached across and tucked an errant strand of hair behind her ear. "Those days are over, Jayda. You and Tiffany are my life now."

Jayda smiled and pulled away from the curb. "I love you, too," she said.

* * * * *

Ladies, start your engines with a sneak preview of Harlequin's officially licensed NASCAR® romance series.

Life in a famous racing family comes at a price

All his life Larry Grosso has lived in the shadow of his well-known racing family—but it's now time for him to take what he wants. And on top of that list is Crystal Hayes—breathtaking, sweet…and twenty-two years younger. But their age difference is creating animosity within their families, and suddenly their romance is the talk of the entire NASCAR circuit!

Turn the page for a sneak preview of
OVERHEATED
by Barbara Dunlop
On sale July 29 wherever books are sold.

RUFUS, as Crystal Hayes had decided to call the black Lab, slept soundly on the soft seat even as she maneuvered the Softco truck in front of the Dean Grosso garage. Engines fired through the open bay doors, compressors clacked and impact tools whined as the teams tweaked their race cars in preparation for qualifying at the third race in Charlotte.

As always when she visited the garage area, Crystal experienced a vicarious thrill, watching the technicians' meticulous, last-minute preparations. As the daughter of a machinist, she understood the difference a fraction of a degree or a thousandth of an inch could make in the performance of a race car.

She muscled the driver's door shut behind her and waved hello to a couple of familiar crew members in their white-and-pale-blue jump suits. Then she rounded the back of the truck and rolled up the door. Inside, five boxes were marked Cargill Motors.

One of them was big and heavy, and it had slid forward a few feet, probably when she'd braked to make the narrow parking lot entrance. So she pushed up the sleeves of her canary-yellow T-shirt, then stretched forward to reach the box. A couple of catcalls came her way as her faded blue jeans tightened across her rear end. But she knew they were good-natured, and she simply ignored them.

She dragged the box toward her over the gritty metal floor.

"Let me give you a hand with that," a deep, melodious voice rumbled in her ear.

"I can manage," she responded crisply, not wanting to engage with any of the catcallers.

Here in the garage, the last thing she needed was one of the guys treating her as if she was something other than, well, one of the guys.

She'd learned long ago there was something about her that made men toss out pickup lines like parade candy. And she'd been around race crews long enough to know she needed to behave like a buddy, not a potential date.

She piled the smaller boxes on top of the large one.

"It looks heavy," said the voice.

"I'm tough," she assured him as she scooped the pile into her arms.

He didn't move away, so she turned her head to subject him to a *back off* stare. But she found herself staring into a compelling pair of green…no, brown…no, hazel eyes. She did a double take as they seemed to twinkle, multicolored, under the garage lights.

The man insistently held out his hands for the boxes. There was a dignity in his tone and little crinkles around his eyes that hinted at wisdom. There wasn't a single sign of flirtation in his expression, but Crystal was still cautious.

"You know I'm being paid to move this, right?" she asked him.

"That doesn't mean I can't be a gentleman."

Somebody whistled from a workbench. "Go, Professor Larry."

The man named Larry tossed a "Back off" over his shoulder. Then he turned to Crystal. "Sorry about that."

"Are you for real?" she asked, growing uncomfortable with the attention they were drawing. The last thing she needed was some latter-day Sir Galahad defending her honor at the track.

He quirked a dark eyebrow in a question.

"I mean," she elaborated, "you don't need to worry. I've been fending off the wolves since I was seventeen."

"Doesn't make it right," he countered, attempting to lift the boxes from her hands.

She jerked back. "You're not making it any easier."

He frowned.

"You carry this box, and they start thinking of me as a girl."

Professor Larry dipped his gaze to take in the curves of her figure. "Hate to tell you this," he said, a little twinkle coming into those multifaceted eyes.

Something about his look made her shiver inside. It was a ridiculous reaction. Guys had given her the once-over a million times. She'd learned long ago to ignore it.

"Odds are," Larry continued, a teasing drawl in his tone, "they already have."

She turned pointedly away, boxes in hand as she marched across the floor. She could feel him watching her from behind.

* * * * *

Crystal Hayes could do without her looks,
men obsessed with her looks, and guys who think
they're God's gift to the ladies.
Would Larry be the one guy who could blow all
of Crystal's preconceptions away?
Look for OVERHEATED
by Barbara Dunlop.
On sale July 29, 2008.

COMING NEXT MONTH

#1506 MATTHEW'S CHILDREN • C.J. Carmichael
Three Good Men
Rumor at their law firm cites Jane Prentice as the reason for Matthew Gray's divorce. The truth is, however, Jane avoids him—and not because he's a single dad. But when they're assigned to the same case, will they be able to ignore the sparks between them?

#1507 NOT ON HER OWN • Cynthia Reese
Count on a Cop
His uncle lost his best farmland to a crook, and now Brandon Wilkes is losing his heart and his pride to the crook's granddaughter…who refuses to leave the land her grandfather stole from them! How can he possibly be friends with Penelope Langston?

#1508 A PLACE CALLED HOME • Margaret Watson
The McInnes Triplets
It was murder in self-defense, and Zoe McInnes thinks she's put her past behind her. Until the brother of her late husband shows up, and Gideon Tate's own issues make him determined to seek revenge. Not even her sisters can help Zoe out of this mess. Besides, she thinks maybe Gideon is worth all the trouble he's putting her through…and more.

#1509 MORE THAN A MEMORY • Roz Denny Fox
Going Back
Seven years ago Garret Logan was devastated when his fiancée, Colleen, died in a car accident. He's tried to distract himself with work, but he hasn't been able to break free of her memory. Until the day she walks back into his pub with a new name, claiming not to remember him…

#1510 WORTH FIGHTING FOR • Molly O'Keefe
The Mitchells of Riverview Inn
Jonah Closky will do anything for his mom. That's the only reason he's at this inn to meet his estranged father and brothers. Still, there is an upside to being here: Daphne Larson. With the attraction between them, he can't think of a better way to pass the time.

#1511 SAME TIME NEXT SUMMER• Holly Jacobs
Everlasting Love
When tragedy strikes Carolyn Kendal's daughter, it's Carolyn's first love, Stephan Foster, who races to her side. A lifetime of summers spent together has taught them to follow their hearts. But after so much time apart—and the reappearance of her daughter's father—will their hearts lead them to each other?

HSRCNM0708